ALSO BY KIMBERLY MULLINS:

Notebook Mysteries ~ Emma (Book 1)

Notebook Mysteries ~ Decisions and Possibilities (Book 2)

Notebook Mysteries ~ Changes and Challenges (Book 3)

Notebook Mysteries ~ Unexpected Outcomes (Book 4)

Notebook Mysteries ~ Haunted Christmas (a novella)

Notebook Mysteries ~ Suspicions (Book 5)

Notebook Mysteries ~ Parisian Intrigue (Book 6)

Notebook Mysteries ~ A Party to Remember (a novella)

Stand alone novels:

Divided Lives (K.R. Mullins)

1897 A Mark Sutherland Adventure

Notebook Mysteries

Notebook Mysteries

KIMBERLY MULLINS

NOTEBOOK MYSTERIES ~ SUSPICIONS

Notebook Mysteries Series

Mailing address for JKJ books, LLC; 17350 State Highway 249, STE 220 #3515 Houston, Texas 77064

Library of Congress Control Number: 2022922560

ISBN (paperback): 979-8-9871148-2-7

ISBN (hardback): 979-8-9871148-1-0

ISBN (ebook): 979-8-9871148-3-4

This is a work of fiction. It is based on historical events within Chicago during the time period of the 1880s.

Edited by Kaitlyn Johnson, Strictly Textual

Cover Art by Miblart

Claudia, thanks for being my friend.
Jonathan and Joshua, thanks for hearing all of my plot lines and
different directions my books take.

CHAPTER 1

NEW YORK CITY, 1889; JANUARY

Wham!

Something hit Emma on the back of the head, and she pivoted toward the assailant. The old woman stopped her by jumping on her back, pulling her hair, and stabbing at her neck frantically with knitting needles.

Enough is enough! Emma thought as she fell backward on the floor, taking the old woman with her.

Her attacker screamed, trying to get out from under Emma. Emma took the opportunity to flip over and grabbed the woman's hands, holding them above her head.

"Old woman, I have had enough!" she growled at her.

That didn't quell the woman's spirit, and she continued to struggle in Emma's hold. *Who would have thought she'd have so much energy?* Emma thought. The woman was in her sixties!

When she finally appeared to be worn out, Emma wrestled her into a chair. She yanked the knitting needles and yarn from the woman's hands and threw them to the floor. "You stay there or there will be consequences," Emma warned. When she saw the woman's mutinous expression, she continued in an exasperated tone, "Are you going to stay there, or do I have to tie you up?" Her patience was gone.

The old woman kept the same expression but stayed motionless.

"They wanted me to talk to you first because I could keep you calm," Emma muttered. She stepped back and took a moment to pull her long blonde hair back into a ponytail. Once she felt more settled, she got a chair and sat it in front of her suspect. "Okay, let's start again. Your daughter was Mavis Franklin?"

"Yes," the woman answered, hacking a wad of spit her way.

Emma wiped the spit from her face and held out her other hand in warning. "Coreen, stop that."

They stared at each other. The light coming through the windows had started to dim in the small room. Emma didn't want to end the staring contest by turning up the gas lamps, so she stayed where she was.

The tactic worked and the old woman asked in a low voice, "What do you want to know?"

"Your daughter, why didn't you go to her funeral?"

"I was told not to," she answered shortly.

"Who told you not to go?" Emma asked, knowing that was the answer they were after.

When Coreen's response didn't come immediately, Emma followed up with another question. "Was it the person behind the child kidnappings?"

"Yes," Coreen replied, in a clearer voice this time.

"Who is he?"

Instead of answering her question, Coreen asked, "Can I have my knitting back?"

Emma scrunched up her eyes and considered the request. She finally acquiesced, bent down to pick the needles and yarn up, and handed them to her. The sound of the needles filled the quiet room. While Emma waited for her to start talking, she glanced out the window. Something there caught her eyes. *What was that?* Frowning, she started to stand and investigate. At that moment, the woman started talking. Emma sat back in the chair to listen.

"He's my son," Coreen said, not looking up from her task.

Son! "But he…"

"Had his sister killed? Or I should say, half-sister. Though they were so alike. Rotten to the core, the both of them." Coreen's mouth twisted into a semblance of a smile.

"Like their mom," Emma said. She had a file a foot thick on this woman's criminal activities. She had been the head of a criminal organization long before her children came along.

Coreen sent her a shrewd look. "They followed in my footsteps."

Emma let that go. "Why didn't he want you to go to the funeral?"

"He knew the authorities could link me to her and then to him. He'd do anything to prevent that."

Emma nodded and thought about the census records she had reviewed. "You had a son Christopher. He dropped off the census records at the age of 15. We thought he might have died."

"No, that was his way of hiding. He changed his name. Didn't even want to be called Christopher at home. He changed overnight and moved out to start his new identity. He was never seen with us again."

It was time. "What name is he using?" Emma asked, her voice hardening. A name floated through her head. She shook it, thinking it was impossible. *It can't be him.*

"He'll kill me," the other woman stated.

"We can protect you," Emma said, thinking ahead. They could get her an apartment far outside of town.

"Can you? I don't think you can. But I'm old, maybe I've outstayed my time," Coreen said and continued to knit.

Emma had to keep pressing her; they needed answers. She

was their only connection to the child kidnapping case. The people involved had targeted the poor who didn't have the money to advocate for their children. The number of children that had been taken had grown, with new information coming in from all over the country. There was someone behind this, and Emma wanted that name!

"His name!" she prompted loudly.

"John Harden," Coreen stated, not looking up.

Though spoken in a low voice, the sound vibrated through her ears. *John Harden! But he's in prison and has been for a while now.* Memories flooded her mind. John Harden was a known gangster and had been part of her first major case—part of the coverup and murder of her mother. Oddly, at the time, he felt he owed her something by removing the man who had taken over his business. There had been no contact between them since that time.

"Yes, you know the name," the other woman stated and stopped her knitting. She straightened in her chair.

Emma wondered about the airs Coreen was putting on. Her son wasn't famous as much as he was infamous. She continued to watch her.

"Operations have never run so well as when he went into prison," Coreen said proudly.

"Why did he kill Candace?"

"He let her have her way with that business, though he never agreed with it. I think he was relieved when the operation had to be shut down. I think he was also relieved to be rid of her." She looked over and explained, "They never got along."

Emma looked at her, wondering what kind of childhood these two had. She asked, "Did you want them to get along?"

Coreen shrugged, taking up her knitting again. "It was interesting when they fought for attention. I would get nice things from their competition."

Emma just shook her head. *Never a family-only competitors.*

Emma stood and said, "Don't move. I'm going to get someone to take you into custody."

Her head still bowed as she concentrated on her knitting, Coreen replied softly, "Do what you need to, dearie. I'll do what I need to do also."

Emma exited the small room, the needles clicking as she pulled the door closed.

She turned and saw Cole Tilden, the Director of the Chicago branch of the Pinkerton detectives, sitting at a small table. He was dressed in his standard black suit, white shirt, and black tie. He stroked his reddish goatee and considered the cards in front of him. Jeremy Tilden, his son and Pinkerton detective, was sitting across from him. He was dressed in a similar manner to his father but the main difference was his rakish nature. Jeremy's hat was shoved back on his head and his auburn curls fell down his forehead.

"I have some news," Emma commented, waiting for them to turn to her.

They didn't look up. Instead, Cole showed his cards. "Two pairs."

Jeremy laid down his hand and said with a grin, "Flush." He looked over at Emma and asked, "Have some trouble in there?"

"No," she said wryly, "she was perfectly behaved." She grabbed a chair and dragged it up to the small table. "Didn't you hear us?"

"Yes," Jeremy admitted, "but we knew you could handle it." Cole nodded his head in agreement, absently shuffling through the deck.

When he started to deal the cards again, she asked in exasperation, "Would you like to hear what I found out?"

They both turned toward her, giving her their full attention. She gave them the details of the interrogation.

"John Harden! Wow! We lock them up and they get stronger. How's he managing this?" Jeremy asked.

"And how do we investigate someone who's already in prison?" asked Emma.

Cole sat back in his chair. "Someone is carrying out his orders on the outside. We'll go after them."

Jeremy looked contemplative. "Any information we find out about his operations could help us leverage John and find out where the missing kids might be located."

"What leverage?" asked Emma. "Even if we find someone on the outside, how do we use that to push John for information?"

"We'll find something," Jeremy said confidently.

"Hmm." Emma, drummed her fingers on her lips, planning.

"What do we do with Coreen in the meantime?" Jeremy asked, gesturing toward the room where John's mom was located.

"She's expecting him to come after her for talking. She'll need protection," Emma said.

"I noticed an accent. Maybe we send her back to Ireland? That would keep her out of the way," suggested Cole.

"I'm not sure she'd want that," she warned. "She's very stubborn and will have definite ideas on her treatment."

"She'll listen to reason," Cole stated. He stood suddenly and strode determinedly to the door. Jeremy followed closely behind.

"Will she?" Emma muttered to the empty room before following them. She bumped into Jeremy, who had stopped abruptly just inside the door. Cole's voice reached her. "Where did you put her?"

Jeremy moved aside so that she could view the room. "There." She pointed to the empty chair.

"She isn't there," Jeremy said, stating the obvious.

She looked over at him and said sarcastically, "You think?"

They looked around the small room. There were no closets and the windows were nailed shut.

"Where could she have gone? There are no exits other than the one we just entered," observed Cole.

Emma looked around the room and then up at the ceiling. "No, but she could have gone up."

"Spry old lady," commented Jeremy, studying the ceiling. There was an opening she could have gone through.

"You have no idea," Emma said as she rubbed her neck. It was still tender from being stabbed with the knitting needles.

"Do we go after her?" Jeremy asked, looking at his father.

"Probably not; it might be safer for her to disappear on her own. The more people who know where she is, the more likely she is to be found." He looked at Emma. "Do you think she's capable of hiding on her own?"

"Yes, you've seen her file. She used to head up an organization bigger than John's. He must get the instincts from her." She continued to look toward the ceiling. "I think she'll be just fine."

"So, what next?" asked Jeremy. "It looks like we're done here."

"Prison, to see John Harden," replied Cole.

"Where is he located?" Jeremy asked.

"Sing Sing. I kept track," Emma said quietly.

Jeremy walked over, took her hand, and laid his forehead on hers. "Are you up for this?"

She leaned in and commented, "This might be interesting. You know he owes me a favor."

Cole looked over. "A favor? We might use that to our advantage."

Jeremy stepped back and kept her hand in his. "There's no reason for us to stay here. Why don't we head back to the hotel?"

"We need to lock up," Emma reminded him. "Clair is having this building rehabbed for the charity." The charity was started by Emma's team a few years ago to help people make better lives for themselves.

They exited the building, locked up, and headed to their hotel. It was evening and the three of them agreed it was time for dinner. A café was located close to where they were staying and was quiet enough to discuss their plans. Dinner was ordered and their drinks were delivered.

"How do we go about getting in to see John?" Emma asked as she sipped her beer.

Cole had a whiskey in his hand and sat back in his chair. "I'll contact the warden tomorrow. We should be able to get permission to talk to him."

"Will you tell him why we want to see John?" Jeremy asked.

"No, I don't think so. I'll just tell him we want to question him," said Cole.

"Won't he think it's odd, since the man has been locked up since 1881?" commented Jeremy.

"Probably, but he knows not to ask too many questions."

"Agreed," said Emma. "John's mom indicated that he has the run of the place."

"If that's true, why does he stay there?" asked Jeremy.

"Why leave? He has the perfect alibi for any crime committed at his behest," Cole replied.

With their plans in place, the three of them went back to the hotel to gather their bags. They met downstairs to hand over their keys and check out.

"You weren't here long. I still have to charge you for the whole night," the clerk said matter-of-factly from his position behind a desk and windowed wall.

"That's fine," Cole said as he pulled out his wallet. "Our business wrapped up more quickly than we anticipated."

"Where are you headed next?" the clerk asked as he took the money through the opening in the window.

Emma scrunched her eyes at the clerk. "Haven't I seen you somewhere else earlier?" she inquired.

"I don't think so," the man said as he tried to avoid her glance.

She reached through the opening, grabbed his tie, and yanked him toward her, slamming him into the window.

"Let me go!" His scream was muffled by the glass.

"Uh, Emma, what are you doing?" Jeremy asked.

"Jeremy," she said, not taking her eyes off the clerk. "he knows something. He was there this morning when I was questioning Coreen. I saw him on the fire escape outside the window." She paused before tightening her grip. "What do you know!" she demanded of the clerk, keeping her hold on him.

His voice was muffled on the glass.

"Emma," Cole suggested, "I think you need to loosen your hold so he can answer."

She didn't want to let go, but she finally gave him some slack that allowed him to pull his face back from the glass. It freed his hands; he grabbed a pair of scissors and cut the tie she still held. The scissors clanged loudly as he dropped them to the ground, then turned and ran out the back door.

They chased after him. The man was like a rabbit, darting around the alley. He easily evaded them, being more familiar with the area than they were.

"Where did he go?" Emma gasped in exasperation, looking around for the missing clerk.

"Not here," Cole replied, taking out a handkerchief to wipe his brow. "Emma, I'm sorry, I didn't think he'd do that."

"I understand." She fumed, still looking around.

"Who do you think he is?" Jeremy asked.

"Based on his reaction, I think he's a lookout for John Harden," Emma said. "He probably has several people watching Coreen. When we showed up at the hotel, he must have tracked us to the other location and saw me questioning her."

"So, John will know before we get there that we talked to Coreen," Jeremy said contemplatively.

"Yes," said Emma.

Cole looked at the two of them and said, "Let's head back to the hotel. We need to get our bags and arrange for a carriage."

Their bags were where they'd left them in the lobby of the small hotel. They grabbed them, exited, and found a carriage a few blocks away.

"Take me to where I can rent a wagon, please," requested Cole.

The driver mentioned the address and Jeremy said, "We will meet you there Pops. We will get the food for our trip."

Cole nodded and motioned to the driver. While he organized their transportation, Jeremy and Emma left to find a small café to provide their lunches and dinner for that day.

"Some fruit, also," Emma said to the waitress, picking up the bananas from the counter. The waitress nodded and continued to compile their order.

Jeremy held up some cans. "We can use these to take the food."

The waitress took them from him and packed them with their other supplies. The food was paid for and they exited toward the wagon rental location, where Cole waited in the driver's seat, holding the reins for the two horses.

"We got lunch and dinner," said Jeremy, holding the supplies up.

"Climb in. We'll be stopping at a few locations before heading out of town."

The first stop was the telegraph office. Cole called to Jeremy, "Take my place while I go into the office."

"Sure, Pops!" He moved to the driver's seat of the wagon to take the reins.

While Cole was in the office, Emma stood behind Jeremy and wrapped her arms around him. He took her hands in his and held them.

"Will it be a problem for you to see him again?" he asked.

The last time she had seen John hadn't been pleasant; she had killed his partner to save herself and a close friend, Thomas.

"I don't know," she said into his back.

They stayed in that position until Cole returned. He climbed up and took the reins from Jeremy so that he could move to the back with Emma. Turning to them, he said, "I got the note sent off to Sing Sing. The warden will be expecting us."

"Do you trust him not to say anything to John?" Jeremy asked.

"Oh, I fully expect that John's aware we're on the way. This was just a courtesy." Cole waited until they were settled and clicked at the horses to get moving. They stopped a few blocks into the trip at a nondescript building. He looked over at Jeremy and asked, "Can you go in and pick up my bag?"

Jeremy had an idea of what they were picking up. "You have a list?"

Cole handed it to him and Jeremy headed into the building. A few minutes later, he returned carrying a large dark bag. He placed it in the back of the wagon without comment and jumped in to sit beside Emma. "Ready," he said and, with that statement, Cole moved the wagon back onto the street.

As they were bumping along, Emma gave that dark bag a long look and thought, *Cole's expecting trouble.* Instead of inquiring about what the bag held, she asked, "How long will the trip be?"

Jeremy answered, "It should be about thirty miles north of New York City on the east bank of the Hudson River. By horse and wagon, we should be there in maybe a day and a half."

She settled down in the back with a bedroll under her head. Jeremy sat next to her and read as Cole drove. They would trade off the driving responsibility as they made their way. The carriage moved swiftly but would take time to get them to their destination.

CHAPTER 2

$\mathcal{E}$mma woke abruptly when the motion of the wagon stopped. "Is something wrong?" she asked, yawning.

"We stopped to give the horses time to rest and for us to have lunch," Cole replied over his shoulder.

Jeremy helped her down while his father unhooked the horses and walked them over to a small stream. The lunches were retrieved by Jeremy and Emma. They unrolled a blanket for them to sit on and all three ate, enjoying the quiet.

After a few minutes, Cole broke the silence. "Let's talk about what we want to get from John."

"Our main goal is to find more of the missing children," stated Emma. "I don't care about his other activities unless we can use them to make him talk."

"Yes," Jeremy agreed. Cole nodded.

"So, how are we going to approach this?" she asked.

"Use your instincts in the interview," Cole said. "They've worked well for us in the past."

Emma nodded. They finished lunch and, when the horses had adequately rested, they started on their way again, with Jeremy driving.

"Emma, would you mind if I borrow your lighter?" Cole asked.

"Sure," she said and pulled it out. It was a kerosene repository that had a flint to light the wick. She handed it to him and he placed it in his pocket without comment. When he didn't give it back, she frowned but didn't ask any follow-up questions. She sat back and picked up her book.

"Pull over to the side of the road," he directed Jeremy.

Emma sat up and laid her book down. "What's up?"

"Pops is looking for something," Jeremy responded.

Cole jumped down and ran down the road. He hastened back and climbed into the wagon and opened the bag Jeremy had retrieved earlier. Two pistols were withdrawn from it and he handed one of them to Jeremy.

Emma held out her hand, expectantly.

"Emma, I know you're good with knives..." Cole started.

"I can handle a gun," she said firmly.

"Let her have it, Pops," Jeremy said, checking his gun. "She knows how to use it."

Taking him at his word, Cole handed her a pistol and pulled out several rifles for himself. Jeremy started to move towards them to help.

"No, stay where you are and get us back on the road," Cole said.

Jeremy did as he was instructed and got them moving again.

Emma looked over at Cole, watching him load the guns. She started to do the same and found hers was already loaded. "Did you see something or are you just expecting trouble?" she asked him.

"Right now, I expect trouble."

"The clerk. Could he have sent someone after us?"

"Yes. He's one of John's men and I think we can expect someone soon."

"Or many someone's," she murmured, looking at the road behind them.

For the rest of the day, all three continued to monitor the road behind them. As the sun started to go down and still no one had been spotted, they pulled the wagon over for a dinner break. The horses rested for a long while and then they began their trip in the dark. Emma started to nod off against the side of the wagon. She was startled into full awareness when they heard hoofbeats coming up behind them. It was hard to make out how many men were following them.

Cole snatched up his rifle and yelled to Jeremy, "Keep going!"

Jeremy snapped the reins and got the horses moving at a faster pace.

The sound of gunfire exploded around them.

"Keep down!" called Cole, returning fire with his rifle.

She sent him a side glance and then fired the pistol in quick succession. One of the men fell off his horse. "As I said, I can use a gun. I just prefer a knife."

About a year ago

"I prefer my knife," she complained, feeling the heavy gun in her hand. "Why do I have to learn how to use this?"

"Emma, you might get into a situation where your knife isn't the best weapon," Jeremy explained.

"I can't think of one," she muttered, thinking he sounded like his grandmother, Miss Marjorie, when she'd taught Emma to throw knives.

"I can," he mentioned. "Not everything is going to be hand-to-hand combat."

"I'm not comfortable with this."

"That's why we practice," he reasoned. "Let's get started." He stood behind her and tapped her leg to widen her stance. She had the Colt gripped in her hand. "Remember, this is a double-action pistol. All you need to do is pull the trigger."

She nodded, keeping her fingers away from it. They faced the target; he moved her hands to the proper position and told her to fire the gun. "Brace yourself. There's going to be a kick."

She fired and the pistol spat out the bullet. The kick pushed her into Jeremy. He helped her reposition, and she shot until the gun was empty. Jeremy retrieved the target; her bullets hadn't hit the center but it was close.

"Doesn't seem all that hard," she said, examining the weapon.

Back to now

"I guess that answers that," Cole murmured as he switched to another rifle and continued to shoot toward the ever-approaching men.

Emma didn't spare him a glance and continued to fire. The riders pursued them, getting closer. She loaded more bullets and looked over at Cole. He had put his rifle down and pulled out some cans that had a bit of wick sticking out of the top. He lit the wicks and threw them quickly toward the marauders.

The small cans exploded in the distance, and white smoke expanded, overtaking the men. Their horses reared, preventing the men from following them.

Jeremy took advantage of the confusion and pulled ahead of their attackers. They went a couple of miles down the road and he yelled back, "I think they stopped."

"Keep going!" Cole yelled.

He and Emma kept their guns pointed behind them and, after a few minutes, Cole called to Jeremy, "You can slow down and go behind those trees."

He followed his father's direction and pulled behind a group of trees just off the road to the left.

"Are we safe?" Emma asked breathlessly.

"I think we did significant damage; we slowed them down."

"Cole, what were those cans you threw?" Emma asked as the wagon pulled to a stop.

"They were homemade grenades."

"Grenades?" Emma asked, the term was unfamiliar to her.

"A grenade is a small explosive device that was used occasionally in the war. It consists of a can full of powder, old twisted metal, nails, or any other sharp or cutting thing. A wick is added and has to be lit. It works pretty well, mostly as a surprise. Horses get spooked, men get thrown, chaos ensues."

"They were certainly effective."

"What now?" Jeremy asked.

"They may regroup. We need to keep watch," Cole said, looking toward the road. He motioned to them. "Spread out." They entered the wooded area and waited. Emma went to the right and Jeremy to the left. Cole stayed in his location.

"Where did they go?" They heard a man's voice call. "We have to find them!"

"I don't know, but be careful. They took down six of our guys," another man said.

"You go that way," the first man indicated.

Jeremy waited until the men separated; he went up behind the figure nearest him and knocked him out. He pulled his body back into the woods.

"Will, where are you?" the other man called loudly. "Don't hide from me!"

Emma stepped out behind him and pressed the gun to his head. "Drop your gun."

Instead of following directions, he made a sudden move and lifted the gun he held. "I wouldn't," Cole said, as he stepped out of the trees and pointed the rifle at him. "Do as she says and drop the gun."

He dropped it and stayed silent.

"Jeremy!" Emma called. "We have the other one."

He came out of the trees, dragging an unconscious man with him.

"Did you kill Will?" the man asked, his voice shaking.

"No, he's just out," commented Jeremy, nudging the man with his shoe.

Cole said to the man, "We have a few questions for you. Who sent you?"

He looked mutinous.

"You don't have an option here. Your crew's gone and the only person who can help you is unconscious," Jeremy said as he walked over to take the gun from Emma. She stepped back, watching the man closely.

"I have another option," the man said and went for his clutch piece. He turned quickly, pointing the small gun at them. Before he could cock the weapon, Emma pulled her knife and threw it, hitting him in the shoulder.

"I told you the knife was a better weapon," Emma commented smugly as they listened to him scream.

"Now, we want some answers from you," Cole said firmly.

"You won't get any!" the man screamed.

"Stubborn," murmured Emma. "Do you want me to help you with the knife stuck in your shoulder?" she asked and stepped toward him.

His face had a look of terror. He opened and closed his mouth, shaking his head.

"Who are you working for?" Cole asked, using the man's fear of Emma to his advantage.

The man stayed silent. Jeremy prodded him with his gun. "Talk!" he said curtly.

He finally said, "I can tell you who the main guy is, but I don't know who is running things for him."

"Who is it?" asked Emma.

"John Harden."

"One more piece of the puzzle," Cole said.

"What do we do with him?" asked Jeremy.

"Just leave me here. I won't tell them where you are going, I promise."

"And we just take your word?" Emma asked, her voice hardening.

"He's coming with us," Cole said. "Emma, get the rope; it's in the bag." When she didn't move, he said again, "Get the rope."

Jeremy saw her expression and said, "Pops, take the gun. I'll get it."

Cole took Jeremy's gun and kept an eye on both Emma and the man.

Jeremy came back with the rope and tied him up. "What do we do with him?"

"There's nothing we can do. We'll have to bring him with us."

"But where do we put him?" *I don't think he should be near Emma.* Jeremy thought. He looked at the wagon. "We need to adjust the luggage and roll him in the back."

Emma smiled suddenly. "Yes, that's just the location. We don't want him too comfortable."

Cole let the comment pass and said, "Emma and Jeremy, be sure to dress his wound. I assume Emma wants her knife back." He turned to walk back to the wagon to get the horses' food and water.

Her lips curled up in a feral grin; she didn't say anything.

"What's happened to you?" Jeremy asked her in a low voice as Cole left them. "Normally, you have more compassion."

"That person's mixed up in this. The kids have had to survive by any means possible or die. I think he should have the same opportunity; survive on his own or die."

He just shook his head. "Emma, he could be of use later. We need to make sure he's alive."

Emma cocked her head. "That's thinking I can get behind. Get out one of your shirts. I'm not wasting a petticoat on this man."

He hesitated to leave her alone with him and a gun.

"Don't leave me alone with her!" the man screamed.

She saw Jeremy's face. "I won't do anything to him." *Unless I am pushed.*

Jeremy nodded and went to fetch a shirt from his luggage. She could hear the fabric ripping as he returned. He handed her the strips of material and a bottle he'd retrieved from the wagon.

"We need to move him over to that tree." She indicted the large tree behind them. They each took an arm and sat him by the tree. Once there, Emma said, "I need to look at the wound. And I want my knife back. "

He shrank back from Emma. "Stay away from me! You just want to hurt me again!"

"Don't be such a baby," said Emma. "Stay still!" He sat and watched her as she moved closer. Before he could react, she pulled the knife from his shoulder. He screamed in pain.

She didn't spare him a glance as she used the knife to cut his sleeve off to view the wound. He grimaced as she pulled him toward her to check his back.

"It's not that bad," she murmured, "but I will enjoy this part." She picked up the alcohol and poured it on the wound. He screamed again.

She wrapped it quickly. "I'm not doing this for you. We'll keep you with us in case you have other information that can help."

His eyes were glazed, the shock keeping him quiet.

"Tie him back up, Emma," Jeremy said. She did so, none too gently, and pushed him back against the tree.

Cole returned from tending the horses. He had tied them loosely so they could reach the stream and grass.

"Has Will woke up yet?" called the tied-up man as he regained his senses.

Jeremy paused briefly as he set up the fire. "Will didn't make it. He'd been shot during the gunfight." He'd gone back to check on him after they treated the man's wound. Will's injury had been life-threatening and there was nothing he could do for him.

"But you said he was asleep…" The man trailed off. Everyone was gone. What would he do now?

They prepared a late dinner of hard bread, canned beef, and beans. After they finished, Jeremy tossed each of them an apple.

"Hey, what about me?" the man called. "I need to eat."

Emma took a slow bite of her apple and didn't look his way.

"Jeremy, take a roll and some meat over to him," Cole said.

"And some water. We don't need him getting sick on the way. That will just cause delays," Emma said. She really didn't care about the man, unless he got in their way.

Jeremy did as he was asked and held a gun on him while the man ate. He looked at Jeremy and said, "Thank you. My name is Earl Snyder."

"No funny business, Earl," Jeremy warned. "I need to tie you up again." Earl was compliant and held out his hands.

After Jeremy tied the man up, he walked back to the fire and sat by Emma. "Are you okay to continue with this case?" He was concerned about her mood. It had increasingly become more negative. The missing children had affected her; it had affected them all.

She looked over at him. "I'm the same person I've always been. I just don't like to give the enemy too much aid. He's a bad guy who tried to kill us. I understand we need to keep him alive, but if I get a chance to make him uncomfortable, I will."

He gave her a considering look. "Just don't take it too far."

"I won't," she promised and glanced to where Earl was sitting. *Unless he gives me a reason,* she thought to herself.

Jeremy reclined on his bedroll. "What are the plans?" he asked his father.

"I think we should try to get some sleep. We're relatively safe here and the horses need time to rest."

"What about him?" Emma asked, indicating Earl with her hand.

"We take turns keeping watch on him or anything else that might come upon us tonight."

Cole took the first shift while Emma and Jeremy settled down on their bedrolls.

Much later, Jeremy woke Emma for the final shift and wearily went off to his bedroll.

Shaking her sleepiness off, she walked the area and looked at Earl. He was sleeping soundly. They had secured him to the tree so he could lie down. *He looks a little too comfortable,* she thought, resisting the urge to kick him. "Pig," she muttered and continued to patrol the area. When she confirmed everything was quiet, she took her seat about three yards from him, keeping Earl and her team clearly in view.

The hours dragged by and her routine remained the same: walk the parameter and check on Earl. She returned to her base and sat down. *Buzz. . . crack!* A bullet sailed by her ear. She immediately turned toward where the shot had come from, pulled her gun, and started firing. When there was no return fire, she stopped.

Jeremy and Cole ran up, their guns drawn. "What happened?" Jeremy asked.

"Someone was shooting." She indicated the direction the shot had come from with her gun.

"Spread out, we need to see if they're still here," Cole said. They separated and went through the area. They met back and made their reports. They had found no one.

Cole walked over to check on Earl. "Jeremy!"

He ran to where Cole kneeled with Earl. They turned him over. Blood was spreading quickly. He had been shot, and the bullet had gone into his chest. There was no hope for him, his eyes wide open in death.

They looked at Emma.

"I didn't do it," she responded heatedly.

Cole and Jeremy's faces held no expression. "Hand me your knife," Jeremy said, not responding to her statement.

She took it out of her pocket and walked it over to him, handle up.

Taking it carefully, he moved Earl's body away from the tree. He traced the bullet's exit to the tree behind him. After he dug it out, he said, "Definitely not Emma's. This was a different caliber."

Cole had suspected Emma may have become impatient with their guest. He was glad to hear she hadn't killed him. "We need to get moving," he said. "They know our location."

"They know we're here," said Jeremy. "Why not kill us?"

"John," murmured Emma. "This type of behavior sounds like him. Take out the informant, but he still wants to know what we know."

Jeremy and Cole looked at her. She knew him better than they did and would follow her lead. "We can't take the chance he won't try again before we make it to the prison," Emma said.

They started to clear the site and got organized. Emma was quiet as she helped.

Jeremy asked, "What's wrong?"

"You didn't trust me," she said simply, not looking at him.

"You're right, I didn't. You'd made up your mind about Earl and I thought you took the opportunity to get some justice for the missing kids.

She nodded. "That's true. But, Jeremy, I would've told you if I had shot him. I wouldn't lie to you."

"You're right," he said, coming over to her. He took her in his arms. "It won't happen again."

She hugged him back. "What do we do with him?"

"We can't take him with us; he'll start to smell," said Jeremy.

"We'll cover him and the other one up with ground debris," said Cole. "I'll have someone take care of the burials."

Jeremy and Cole dragged Earl and lay him next to Will in the brush. Emma gathered up branches and brought them over to cover the bodies.

Once they finished, it was time to pack up the camp. Jeremy gathered the horses while Cole and Emma helped to harness them. Once completed, they climbed into the wagon and pulled out onto the road. Jeremy drove and Emma and Cole held their guns at the ready in case there was another attack. They went on for about fifteen minutes when Jeremy called back. "We might be in the clear for now." They finally set the firearms in the wagon next to them.

We're being allowed to go to the prison. John, what are you up to? Emma thought. She mulled that over as she settled back, stretching her legs.

Cole looked over at her. "Emma, get some rest. We'll wake you when we need relief." They were only about halfway to their destination at that point. "It could take another day."

The rest of the trip was uneventful; only stopping to rest themselves and the horses. By late the next day, they were near the prison and stopped by a local hotel to freshen up. Emma stayed clothed in her pants and long black coat. Her bowler hat was in place but the lace and dashing feather removed. She needed to fly under the radar and not be seen as a woman. Her long hair was tucked inside her black shirt and the collar flipped up to hide it.

Jeremy nodded approvingly when he saw her. He gave one last yank on his boots and stood up. "Time to go meet Pops. Are you ready?"

"I am," she said confidently.

"Keep your head down as we go in. Oh, and leave the knives here. The warden won't be patient if we're found carrying weapons."

She took off her bowler and removed her long sharp knife from its hidden compartment. Next, she reached into her pants pocket and removed her hidden knife. Lastly, she bent down and removed a knife from her ankle boot, then stowed all weapons in her bag.

"Did you get them all?" he asked laconically.

She tilted her head and coyly answered, "I think so, want to search me?"

He laughed. "Maybe later," he said, pulling her to him. A knock on the door interrupted anything that might have happened next. They looked at each other regretfully.

"Ready to go?" called Cole through the door.

"I am," Jeremy called back.

"Me too," Emma called. She picked up her hat and placed it jauntily on her head. She offered Jeremy her elbow and they exited the room. Cole noticed the mood had lifted and was glad to see that they had worked out their differences.

Their horses and wagon had been dropped off at a local stable. They needed rest, food, and the gunfire had also made them skittish. It had been a long trip.

Cole arranged for a carriage to take them to the prison. He had vetted the young driver and felt confident that he wasn't going to try to kill them before they got there. They had a plan on how to approach John and they'd stick to it.

They pulled up to the imposing prison entrance. Jeremy didn't offer Emma a hand as she descended from the carriage. As a gentleman, she was expected to get down on her own. Her walk and mannerisms became more masculine as they entered the prison gate. The air was oppressive as they entered, the gates swinging closed behind them.

As they made the long walk to the main building, Jeremy looked around with interest. "Where did the name of this place come from?" he asked.

Cole answered, "The land was purchased from the Sintsink Indian tribe in 1685. It evolved from there."

Jeremy said, "I heard the prison is trying to rehabilitate the prisoners for new lives when they get out."

Emma raised her eyebrows and said, "Sounds like John isn't taking to the rehabilitation."

They laughed, helping to relieve some of the tension.

"There are plenty of access ways into Sing Sing," Jeremy remarked, noting the railroads and the Hudson River surrounding the prison.

"This is not a small facility," commented Emma, looking at the many buildings inside the fences. They continued to the main administration building.

As they watched the heavy door on the main prison building being opened for them, Cole said, "I wonder if John is being kept in the same cells as the other prisoners. They are not comfortable; the inmates barely have enough room to move around and no windows."

She again thought, *Why does he stay?*

The warden met them at the main building entrance. "Cole, it's nice to see you."

"You too," Cole said, taking his hand. "We appreciate you letting us visit." He turned to Emma and Jeremy. "This is Warden Augustus Brush. Warden, my son Jeremy, and Emma Evans."

The warden nodded and led them into the room where they would be searched. Cole whispered to the warden, reminding him about Emma.

Brush nodded and said, "I've arranged for our head matron to conduct your search." A large woman entered the room and motioned for Emma to follow her. She was suddenly glad she had left her knives behind.

Jeremy caught her arm as she started to follow the matron. "Do you want me to come with you?"

Emma looked over at the rather sturdy woman. "No, I'll be okay."

They moved to another room down the hall. Once inside, the matron spoke in a firm voice. "I'll pat you down and then check your pockets."

"That's fine," Emma commented, following the woman's directions. It was painless and a little embarrassing, but the matron found nothing. When the search was completed, the woman smiled suddenly, changing her whole continence, and said, "There now. That wasn't so bad."

"No, it wasn't. Thank you for doing this for me."

"Just keep that hat pulled down," the woman warned. "We don't want a ruckus in here."

"Understood," commented Emma as she smoothed her hair into her shirt and pulled her hat low over her eyes. She eyed the matron and asked, "Are there female prisoners here?"

"Yes, Sing Sing is the first institution to have one prison with separate housing for male and female offenders. We have women wardens there."

The matron escorted Emma back to the room where the men were located. Cole and Jeremy put on their coats and looked over as she entered. Jeremy raised an eyebrow and she mouthed, "It's fine."

The warden saw her return. "If you're ready, we have Harden in an interview room waiting. This guard will take you." He waved to the man next to him. The guard stood silently and used his stick to indicate the direction they should take.

They walked down the long hallway. Emma didn't know what to expect.

CHAPTER 3

They went into the room indicated by the guard. John was already there and handcuffed to the table. Jeremy stepped from in front of Emma and revealed her to John.

"Emma," he said. She saw real pleasure in his eyes. He focused all attention on her, ignoring Cole and Jeremy

Her confidence showed as Emma stepped forward; she was no longer the same sixteen-year-old girl she had been the last time they were together. It wasn't just age that had changed her, but her life experience.

"You've changed," he observed.

"Have I?" she murmured, watching him as closely as he watched her.

"It's nice of you to visit me," he said as she removed her hat.

"This isn't just a visit, John," she said quietly. They had agreed that she would begin the questioning. Her prior relationship and the fact he owed her a favor would be part of it.

"May I sit?" she asked, motioning to the chair on her side of the table.

"Please, forgive me for not getting up." He held out his hands, showing the cuffs that attached him to the table.

Emma sat. The guard was behind her at the door; Jeremy and Cole stood on either side of the table, observing the persons in the room. "You don't seem surprised to see me," she said.

"I don't?" he said, answering her question with another question.

She let that go by. "John, we're investigating the child kidnapping ring that began two years ago."

He sat back and smiled, "You caught the person in charge, right? I thought she died very publicly."

"That's right." It was time to drop the first fact on him. "We did find out your sister was the person in charge."

All of Emma's attention was on John and his response. He didn't move.

"Sister?" John cocked his head and said, "No I don't think so. What did you say her name was?"

"Candace." Emma gave the birth name provided by Coreen. "And that would make you Christopher O'Leary."

His eyes narrowed. She knew details that were not public knowledge. "If this is true, where did you get the information?"

"I can't share that at this time."

"Can't or won't? How is Ma doing?" he asked, always a step ahead.

"John," she chastened, "you know I can't say anything further on that topic."

"In that case, I'm not sure what I can do for you," he responded, looking bored.

She continued with her questions. "John, did you know that the kidnappings have started again?" This time she sat back and waited for his response.

His face hardened. *Had she told him something he didn't know?* His eyes flickered. *What is he looking at?* she asked herself.

She went on. "I think you didn't approve of Candace's involvement with the children, given the way you took down the first organization. I'd assume your underlings know your wishes and wouldn't go into business for themselves." Emma played upon his ownership of his organization. In prison or not, this business was his to run.

"I don't wish to talk anymore today," he said. His statement was final.

Jeremy stepped forward, intending to say something, to make him talk. Emma held up her hand to stop him; she didn't look away from John.

"We'll be staying nearby when you wish to have another conversation." She stood.

John watched her silently as she placed her hat back on her head and adjusted her shirt collar higher to hide her hair.

"Emma," John said suddenly, "I really did enjoy seeing you again."

She dropped her coin purse near her leg and bent down to pick it up. As she came up, she murmured, "Remember that favor you owe me."

She didn't wait for a response but walked toward the guard. He sent a glance to John and then opened the door for them. The guard on the outside of the room told his companion, "You can take him back to his cell."

Jeremy, Cole, and Emma made their way out and the door slammed shut behind them. That sound stopped them for a moment, then they continued down the hallway. They exited the facility and located their carriage for the ride back.

All sat quietly in the carriage. When Jeremy started to talk, Cole cleared his throat and shook his head. There would be no discussion in front of a third party. Jeremy nodded and settled with his arm around Emma.

It was noon when they arrived at the hotel. Cole said, "Wait here." He strode to the desk and ordered lunch brought to their room. Once the three were back together, they headed up the stairs. It wasn't until the door to their room closed that they spoke. "Finally, we can talk," she said as she took off her hat and jacket, dropping down on the settee.

"Yes," Cole said. "This case could involve almost anyone. If we don't want to be overheard, we'll have to be cautious about what and where we share."

A sudden knock at the door startled them. Jeremy went to it and called back over his shoulder, "Just the food." He allowed the man into the room to set up the cart. Once completed, Jeremy escorted him out.

They filled their plates and sat down at the table. "Let's start the review of the interview," Cole suggested as they ate.

Emma and Jeremy nodded their heads in agreement.

"I can start," said Emma.

"Go ahead," encouraged Cole.

She picked up her glass to take a drink and then put it down slowly. "I am not sure if John's reaction to my question meant he knew about it or not. His eyes flickered when I mentioned the kids. What happened behind us at that time?"

Jeremy smiled. "I wondered if you saw that. His gaze shifted to the guard."

"What did he do?" she asked.

Cole said, "Nothing. He didn't move at all."

"He responds and he's dead. That must be our guy running things on the outside," said Emma.

"Exactly," stated Jeremy. As John's guard, he could move around unmonitored.

"What next?" Emma asked.

"We find out where the guard lives," Cole said.

"We could follow him," suggested Jeremy.

"That we can," said Cole.

"We'll have to keep our distance; he could be dangerous," Emma said.

"We'll be needing to go at 6pm," Jeremy said.

"Why's that?" Emma asked.

"Shift change at the prison."

"Yes," Cole agreed.

They cleaned up the plates and placed them outside their room. "We have enough time to rest and then head back to Sing Sing," said Cole.

Emma walked with Jeremy to their bedroom and Jeremy turned to her. "What was it you said to John just before we left?"

She smiled widely. "I reminded him he owes me a favor."

Jeremy grinned and escorted her to their room for some rest.

CHAPTER 4

As they followed the guard home that evening, he took a circuitous route. He stopped at several establishments, exiting each with a bag and a self-satisfied expression on his face.

"I guess he convinced John he wasn't involved," Jeremy suggested, watching from behind his paper.

Cole sat outside the cafe across the road from them.

"Oh, no?" Emma asked. "Take a look at his eye."

Jeremy followed her direction and noticed the man had pulled his hat low; his right eye was blackened.

"John must have been concerned," murmured Emma.

"He's acting normal," Jeremy said, continuing to watch him.

"Is he, though? I think we have a runner," she said in the same tone.

"If he's going to run, he wants something to take with him."

"The bags," murmured Emma.

The guard walked along and they followed, hanging back so as not to be seen. They needn't have worried about being spotted, though; his attention never wavered from his task. Cole gave up pretending and walked boldly over to them.

He seems to be unaware of the parade he's leading, Emma thought. He *has too much on his mind.* They continued to follow him into a residential area.

"The area is affluent," Cole commented. "I would've expected something much smaller based on his actual income."

"He's spending John's money and living like he's in charge," Emma observed.

"Hmm, this isn't something he'll want John to know," Jeremy commented.

"No, and normally he may not have led us directly here," Cole replied.

The guard went into an apartment building, they followed and saw him make his way up the staircase. Once he was out of sight, Cole went to see the doorman. Emma smiled when she noticed the handshake and the transfer of money.

Cole left him and approached them. "4th floor—large apartment." They went to the stairs and made their way up.

They studied the door. "Do I pick it?" Emma asked in a low voice.

"No, I think we knock," Cole said, thinking over the man's behavior. "We need to use his panic for our own purposes."

"Think he'll go out the window?" asked Jeremy, running scenarios.

"We'll be ready for that, but I don't think so. The man living here has been taking chances for a while now. He has to know he had a limited time in this role."

They agreed Emma would speak for them. Jeremy knocked and stepped to the side. "Yes, who is it?" the man's voice called. He sounded impatient.

Emma pitched her voice higher and said, "Towels, sir. I was told to bring you towels."

"Towels?" he called back. "You can take them back, I don't want them."

"But, sir, I'll get into trouble if you don't take them."

"Oh for…" he started to say as he swung the door open. He saw them and immediately tried to push the door closed. Cole, Jeremy, and Emma pushed back, causing it to slam into the wall. The man fell backward onto the floor and started to crawl away from them. Jeremy jumped on him to try to secure him, but he got loose and ran to the opened window.

Emma jumped on his back and Jeremy grabbed his legs. The guard stumbled and fell hard, taking Emma with him. She took hold of his hands and began securing them.

"There wasn't an easier way?" she asked over her shoulder.

"Not that I could think of in the moment," said Jeremy, breathing hard.

The man lay groaning on the floor. "Why are you here? What did I do to you?" he whined.

"Let's get him secured," Cole directed.

He and Jeremy took his arms and dragged him to the sofa. Once he was in place, they formed a half-circle around him. The man looked at all three of them but stayed silent.

"We are curious about something," Jeremy started.

The guard looked unyielding and didn't open his mouth.

"How can you live here on a prison guard's salary?" They watched him closely but he still didn't talk.

"Don't you want to brag about your beautiful apartment? The wonderful furnishings?" Emma asked as she stood and walked over to the mantel. She picked up a vase. "Maybe it isn't yours? If I just drop this, would you care?" As she tossed it into the air, he screamed. She caught it deftly and asked. "So, you do care. Are these your things?"

He struggled against his restraints and finally snapped, "Aarg! It's mine, all mine!"

"All yours," commented Cole, stroking his goatee. "Tell us how that's possible."

"I'm not just a prison guard," he said importantly as he sat straighter on the couch.

"You're not? What else do you do?" Jeremy asked interestedly.

"I run businesses. I have many things I'm involved in," he said.

Emma started to look around, opening cabinets and closets. Then she moved to the bedrooms.

"Where's she going? What's she looking for?" he asked, his tone changing to one of desperation as he watched her walk around the apartment.

"Oh, she's just curious about what you might be hiding," commented Cole.

"I'm not hiding anything!" he screamed.

Emma walked out holding several cloth bags. "What's in these, I wonder?" She upended one and dumped it on the table in front of the man. Money tumbled out and onto the floor.

"How much do you think is here?" asked Jeremy idly, picking up one of the bundles.

"Don't touch that," the guard sputtered.

"This?" he said and slipped it into his jacket pocket.

"Put that back! You can't have it. That's mine!"

"What kind of business gives you bags of cash?" asked Cole contemplatively.

He didn't seem to know how to answer that question.

"Do you run the business for John Harden?" Emma asked bluntly.

"If I give you that information, will you leave?" he pleaded.

"His bags are out and his clothes thrown into them," Emma said to Jeremy and Cole.

"Leaving town?" Jeremy asked.

"Yes, I need to leave today," he said desperately.

"That black eye, how did that happen?" Jeremy asked.

The guard moved his hand to touch his face, but the restraints stopped him. "Just an altercation at work. It happens occasionally."

The day before:

Jeremy, Emma, and Cole planned out their confrontation with the security guard.

"Tomorrow in his room, what are we looking for?" asked Cole.

Emma stood and walked around, thinking. "First the businesses, there'll be accounting books."

"They'll be hidden. Under a floorboard, inside a wall, or a safe," suggested Jeremy.

"Emma, you look for those and any other hidden papers," directed Cole. He looked over at Jeremy. "You'll be the primary interviewer."

"This will be quick; we won't have time to build a case on him," Jeremy said, frowning. "Questions will have to come through observations." Emma was better at that than he was. He looked over at her, and she sent him a smile showing her support.

They nodded, set in their plans for the next day.

"Was the altercation with John Harden?" Jeremy asked, his eyes narrowed.

"Him? Why would he hit me? Untie me!" he demanded.

Jeremy ignored that and continued to question him while Emma returned to searching the rooms.

"What's she doing in there? What else is she looking for?"

"She's just looking around," Jeremy replied.

"She won't find anything." The guard swallowed and his eyes darted to catch a glimpse of Emma.

"Hidden that well?" Jeremy asked, seeing the doubt in the man's eyes.

"Nothing's hidden," he said, but he didn't sound so sure this time.

"Ah ha!" Emma's voice floated in from the other room.

Cole stood up and went to see what Emma had found. The man's panic increased and he struggled with his bonds. He moved around until he threw himself on the floor.

"Hey now, what's the matter?" Jeremy asked as he gripped the man by his collar and dragged him back to the sofa. "We still have more to talk about."

The guard growled.

"You think you scare me?" Jeremy asked, his voice low and threatening. The man must have seen something in Jeremy's eyes and sat back, looking away.

There was a delay, then both Cole and Emma exited the bedroom, their hands full of books.

The guard froze and stopped struggling.

Emma started opening up the small books first. She read the owner's name and said aloud, "The bank accounts are all in your name. That is your name, isn't it? Jacob Smith?"

He screamed, "It was him and not me! I only took orders!"

"John's orders?" asked Emma, her voice ringing through the room.

"Yes," Jacob said desperately. "This is all him! He had me do it! He said it had to be in my name!"

She tossed the bank books down on the table in front of him. "I don't care about those. What I want is the children, the ones taken before and the ones you've taken since that time."

"Kids? No, no. That was finished when Candace died. I've no involvement in anything like that. That was all her."

Cole was reading through the journals. "This one is the one John must see. It's related to businesses and other types of deals." He picked up another one and read through it. " This one has information concerning events you claim to know nothing about."

"The kids?" asked Emma, her voice going high.

"Yes."

The blood drained out of Jacob's face. "There was too much money involved. They kept throwing it at me and I just gave in and set the networks back up," he said, his tone dull.

"You aren't using schools to find the kids now?" Jeremy asked. The prior kidnappings had been related to Candace masquerading as a school nurse.

"No," Jacob said, "became too hard after you caught her. We had to start grabbing them as they walked to school, went to the park, or played in the streets. It was extremely easy. No one lifted a finger or took notice when one child would go missing. How did you know it was going on?"

"Your people got greedy and took a group of children all at one time. They were reported immediately. It started us on the path here," said Emma.

He grimaced. "I told them we have to lay low, take one at a time."

"Where are they?" she demanded. They all leaned in toward him, their patience at an end.

"No, no, that will get me killed," he said and shook his head.

Emma reached into her pocket, pulled out her knife, and grabbed him by the hair. "This time," she growled, "we will kill you! Right here and right now! I could take care of you and no one would lift a finger to stop me. So, I want you to think long and hard about that answer."

Cole started to move toward her, worried about what she might do; Jeremy took his arm and held him back. "She knows what she's doing," he said in a low voice.

Jacob looked into her eyes and saw she would follow through with her threats. "I have a list of locations where the children might be," he admitted.

"Might?" she echoed, pulling his hair again.

"Yes, *might*. They could be almost anywhere after a few days," he explained quickly.

"Then you will give us the locations you know of," Cole demanded.

Jeremy looked at Emma. "I think he's ready to help us."

Emma slowly released his hair and reluctantly withdrew the knife. She glared at Jacob and said, "People who do this to kids deserve no mercy. Tell us a lie and I will cut you."

His eyes followed her to the chair where she sat down.

Jeremy cleared his throat to get his attention. "The locations you mentioned?"

"Yes," Jacob said, pulling his eyes from Emma. He listed a number of bordellos located from New York to Chicago. "That'll be your first stop. From there, they could be sent anywhere, including overseas."

Emma's expression didn't change, but her spirits dropped. They may find some, but not all.

"Who are your people on the streets, taking the children? We also need the holding facilities," Jeremy directed.

Jacob was hoping to keep those to himself. Wait until the heat was off and start again. The money available in this business was too good to not start again.

Jeremy waited for the answer to his question. When it didn't come, he turned to Emma. "Emma," he said. She started toward Jacob.

Jacob saw her face and the knife in her hand and immediately started to provide the answers they were looking for. Warehouses were the building of choice as holding spots before moving to bordellos.

Cole spoke up then. "We need specific names of your groups at each location."

"Wait," Jacob said suddenly. "What am I getting out of this?"

Emma and Jeremy sat back; it was Cole's turn to talk.

"You'll be going to prison, probably the one you work at now," Cole said bluntly.

"How is that fair?" Jacob asked indignantly.

"Fair?" Cole said. "Fair is not putting you in the general population and, if you keep pushing, we'll make sure that is where you end up."

His face whitened considerably at that remark. *Yes, that would be worse.* He gave them the names and locations. He had to try one more time. "You could just let me go."

At that moment, there was a knock on the door. Jacob tried to get up from the couch and run. They grabbed him and sat him back down.

Emma said, "I'll get it." She went to the door and opened it.

The local police came in. The lead man looked around. "Nice place."

"Jenkins," Cole said and walked over to him.

"What is going on?" Jenkins asked. "I got your message to meet you here."

"You're right on time," Cole responded.

The two men talked in the corner while the other officers took Jacob into custody.

Cole and Jenkins returned to the group. "We'll book him with this evidence," Jenkins said. "You'll retain the other information on the missing kids?"

"Yes, we'll continue to investigate the children," said Cole.

Jenkins nodded and turned to his men. "Let's take him in. We'll need to sort the charges out."

"But what about John? Will he be charged also?" Jacob cried, distraught at being taken into custody.

Jenkins looked at him. "John Harden is in prison. There's nothing on these papers that indicates he was involved. I don't think we need to bring him into this."

Jacob looked at him in terror and screamed, "He's one of John's men! You have to listen to me!"

Emma, Cole, and Jeremy watched as Jacob was dragged from the room. "Do you think he is one of John's men?" Jeremy asked.

Cole shrugged, "There was nothing that pointed in that direction. Jenkins will use the evidence he has to convict him."

Emma wondered how far John's reach was. In the carriage on the way from Jacob's apartment, Emma looked at Jeremy. "Were we played? Did John use us to get rid of someone who was getting too strong in his organization?"

"Does it matter?" asked Jeremy.

"No, not really," Emma said as she sat back. "The kids are all I care about."

CHAPTER 5

$\mathcal{C}$ole had arranged for John to be moved to a room for them to speak to him at Sing Sing. The guard accompanying him kept his head down and secured John to the table. *Is he Jacob's new replacement?* Emma wondered.

"Well, this is a surprise. I didn't expect to see you here, Emma. Are you back for that favor?" Harden asked mockingly.

Her head whipped toward him when she heard her name. "No," she said quietly. "It turns out we didn't need your help after all."

He laughed out loud. "How can I be of help from here?" he asked. "After all, I am in prison."

Cole spoke next. "We know that your business activities have continued since your incarceration."

Harden turned his gaze from Emma to Cole. "And you are?"

"Cole Tilden."

John looked at Jeremy.

"Jeremy Tilden," he supplied.

John tilted his head. "Now we know who we are, what do you want?"

John's conversation with Jacob the day before.

Once Emma and the Tildens exited the room at the prison, Jacob stepped up to John to disengage him. "It's time to go back to your cell."

John sent him a look and didn't address the comment. The guard got impatient and grabbed John by the arm. "I said it is time to go."

John appeared to have had enough rough handling and reached up to take him by the collar and pulled him down to his eye level. "You think you're in charge now? That you have something to hold over me?"

Jacob went still. "Yes, until we get what we want."

"Take me back to my cell," John said releasing him. He had settled and looked almost relaxed.

Jacob took a deep breath and released it before undoing his bonds.

John took the opportunity, rolled his hand into a fist, and hit Jacob in the eye.

"You can't do that!" Jacob cried, holding a hand to his eye.

"You will regret trying to take over my business. And if *she* is hurt in any way, you will not survive," John promised.

Taking her had controlled John, but was it worth it? It's time for an exit strategy, thought Jacob.

John had an idea of what the other man was thinking and would not stop Emma and her team from taking him into custody. Jacob would pay for taking someone who meant the world to him.

Present day

The new guard moved Harden back to his cell. Once he was secured inside, he said, "I have taken over all of the businesses."

"Then we lay low for a while," said John. He wanted to wait for news on the children. *She must be found.*

CHAPTER 6

*B*ack at their hotel, Emma was studying the information they had gotten from Jacob. "Where do we start?" she asked.

"We map it out and get the Pinkerton offices in those areas to begin their reconnaissance," Cole said.

"Will we be involved?" asked Jeremy.

"Yes, we'll see this through."

"I'll notify Clair that we'll need safe houses in each area fully staffed with medical professionals," Emma said.

Cole nodded. "We'll start with travel to the closest location and then we'll send telegrams from there."

"Not from here?" asked Emma.

"No, it's better that we're far away from this area before we send anything. Get organized; we'll be leaving soon."

They retrieved their gear and went down to the lobby. Their wagon was parked out in front of the hotel; they would drive themselves.

"Dinner?" Jeremy asked.

"We will get food for the road. Better to camp out. It'll probably be safer," said Cole.

They took turns driving the wagon. While Cole was handling the horses, Jeremy and Emma sat in the back talking.

"You were pretty angry back there," he commented.

"I know. It's the kids. Their involvement heightens my emotions."

"Are you sure you want to be in on the raids?" He was concerned about the things they would see.

"No, I want to be there. And the others..." Her voice trailed off.

"Others?"

"The ones who have been sent outside the country," she explained.

Jeremy shook his head. "We don't have the resources for that. We'll turn that over to the agencies in those locations."

"Jeremy, even if it's only one child at a time, we need to continue."

He took her hand tightly in his. "We'll do that," he pledged. "We'll follow every lead we get from our raids."

"We need the other teams to be briefed on what we're looking for. If we waste this opportunity, we may never find them."

They mulled that over and when they stopped for the horses to get a break and for them to have a snack, they discussed the information with Cole.

He nodded. "This may take years."

"Yes," Emma said as her eyes teared up. She wiped them away quickly and took the sandwiches Jeremy handed to her.

"Pull out the list," Cole said. They looked at it. All the towns outside of New York City were listed; those would be their first stops.

At the first town with a telegraph office, they stopped and Cole arranged for Pinkerton agents to start watching the houses they were targeting. They arrived at the first location in Newark, NJ, an empty warehouse a few blocks from the bordello, for a meeting with the area Pinkerton agents.

Emma dressed as a boy and kept her hat pulled down low. These men didn't know her and she didn't want any arguments about her role in the raids.

"Patterson," Cole started, "where do we find them in the house?" The men had been watching the bordello.

"Cole, it is good to see you," Patterson said and pulled out his notebook. "We could use the support. We have a large number of areas to cover. The bordello we are targeting has a basement. The only way in is through windows. We think it might be where they are keeping the kids. But there's a problem."

Cole frowned. "What's that?"

"It's the size of the windows. We don't have any men small enough to get in," Patterson explained.

"I think I have the right person for that." Cole looked over his shoulder and he waved Emma over to them.

"He is the right size," Patterson said. He then realized the person in front of him was not a man. "But..."

"Yes?" prompted Cole.

Patterson lowered his voice and exclaimed, "But he is a she! How can we send a woman into that environment without backup?"

"You'd be surprised; she's quite capable," Cole replied.

"And she won't be alone," Jeremy said, walking up beside her.

"I am Jeremy and this is Emma."

"Patterson," he said. If Cole recommended them, he wouldn't question them. "We'll wait for you to report back before we make any plans to enter."

"Do you have drawings of the building?" Emma asked.

"We were able to get them." Patterson turned and pulled out a set of drawings and walked to their makeshift desk. He pointed to it and said, "You see the basement windows here? They're located at the base and go around the building."

"They'll be locked," said Jeremy.

"We should be able to take care of those," Emma commented. "Has anyone tried to look into the windows to see if anyone is there?"

"They keep them covered or painted," admitted Patterson.

"Then how do you know Emma and Jeremy won't be crawling into an area where people will see them?" asked Cole.

"We don't," Patterson admitted. "We are hopeful, given the nighttime entry, that we will not have any trouble. Also, this is not a rescue mission—reconnaissance only. Once we have the information, we will return and get any children out."

Cole considered this plan without comment.

"Are we ready?" asked Patterson.

Emma looked at Jeremy and held out her hand. Jeremy took it; they would do this together. "Yes," Jeremy said. "We're ready."

They looked at Cole. He didn't like the plan, but he wouldn't stop it. "Okay."

Patterson, Cole, Emma, and Jeremy approached the targeted bordello. Emma and Jeremy had their hats pulled down low as they got their final instructions. "Go over the back fence; there's a spot where the guards don't walk. There are four windows in that area at ground level." Patterson handed them a rope with knots to help with climbing.

Emma and Jeremy nodded and started toward the fence.

Cole stopped them. "If it gets dangerous, stop and back out. We can take it from there."

Emma and Jeremy nodded, understanding his concern, as the Pinkerton agent wished them good luck.

The agent had told them there were guards on the front door but this side was unmonitored. As they reached the fence, Jeremy cupped his hands to allow her to stand and get a view over the fence into the small yard.

"We're good," she whispered.

He took that as an okay to give her a push up and over. She

grabbed the top, swung her legs over the tall block fence, and jumped down. The rope weighed heavily on her shoulder; she took it off and threw it over for him. Bracing herself, she held onto one side of the rope while he climbed over. Once he was on top, she retrieved the rope. He jumped down and helped her gather it up.

Keeping their heads lowered, they looked around for any additional guards. They heard voices and stayed close to the fence, but the guards didn't walk into the area where the two were hiding. When the voices could be heard drifting away, they moved silently, crouching down, staying in the shadows as they made their way to the house. Bushes were bunched up around the base of the home. Emma put her hand behind them to see if she could find the windows. They went about five feet from the back left corner and she whispered, "Got it. That means the next one is probably about five feet down."

Jeremy nodded and knelt to look. "Help me pull this back," he said, indicating the bush. They gripped it and pulled it toward them. It gave her enough room to check out the window.

"What do you think?" he asked, still holding the bushes away from the window.

She pressed her ear against it. "I don't hear anything."

"Let's check the ones down this wall," he suggested. They went to each one and she checked—still nothing.

"The front is quite busy. They may be keeping them quiet with drugs."

"Shall we chance it?" he asked.

"Weren't we supposed to let Pinkerton know before we go in?" Emma reminded him.

"We don't know anything yet," he reasoned. This was supposed to be a fact-finding mission.

"We'll go in." They went back to the first window and she looked at it. "It isn't meant to open," she observed.

"No lock?"

"No." She pulled out her knife and dragged it around the sash to remove the paint sealing the window. The glass was old and it popped out rather easily. "Shh," she whispered and reached in to pull the inside covering back. The room was dark and she couldn't see much from her location. "I need to go in." The window would allow someone her size, but Jeremy wouldn't fit.

"I'll be here. Don't take any chances. Just get information and come out. Our men are waiting."

Kissing him quickly, she said, "I will." Jeremy handed her the rope, and she dropped it inside the window and climbed down into the dark room. As she lowered herself, she tried to find a foothold when she felt something soft. She eased back, trying to find something more stable. When a solid surface was found, she bent down and felt the soft material. She took a moment to light her portable kerosene lighter. When the room was illuminated around her, she was shocked at the number of children. There were so many that there were no pathways to walk.

Are all of them sleeping? she thought. Then the smell hit her. She wrinkled her nose. The odors in the room were not pleasant: urine and other bodily waste smells. The kids were so drugged they were messing themselves. *Horrible people,* she thought again.

"Are you here to help?" a small voice reached her ears.

She turned toward it and found a tiny girl. Emma made her way over to her, careful not to step on the other children.

"Hi, little one," she said, kneeling down and pushing the girl's brown wispy hair back on her forehead. "How are you not asleep?"

"The medicine they give us makes me throw up." The girl started to cry softly. "They'll be mad and hit me for throwing up again."

"No, little one, they won't. We'll be taking you out tonight."

She stopped crying suddenly. "Tonight?"

"Yes. I'm going to go back out through that window and we'll come back for all of you."

"No!" The girl started crying again.

"Shh, we don't want to be heard," Emma cautioned softly, looking around.

"*Please* take me with you!" she begged in a rush. "I can hang on tight. My brother could tell you. I clung to his back all the time when he was climbing trees."

Emma looked doubtful but said, "We'll try." She pulled the cover down, looking for restraints on the girl. *They don't appear to tie them up; the drugs must be very strong.* Emma sat the girl up and turned her back to her. "Wrap your arms around my neck," she said softly. The girl did as she was asked and Emma wrapped her legs around her body.

"I'm going to stand up now, and you must hang on tight."

"I will." The little girl's grip tightened, almost strangling her, but Emma didn't stop.

Emma pulled twice on the rope to let Jeremy know she would be climbing up. He would start pulling when he felt the rope go taut. It was harder with her added companion, but Emma resolved to get them both out. Her muscles strained as she reached the window. She said over her shoulder, "I'm going to boost you up. The man's name is Jeremy. Give him your hands."

Emma stopped and boosted the little girl on her back up to the window. Her muscles strained as she clenched the rope with one hand and pushed the girl up with the other.

Jeremy saw movement and reached in to help Emma come out. The size of the hand surprised him, but he didn't question it and pulled the little girl through the window. He moved her behind him and held a finger to his lips. She nodded and waited. When Emma's hands could be seen, he grabbed them and pulled her through. Once she was out, Jeremy bent down, took the girl onto his back, and whispered to Emma, "Ready?"

"Yes," Emma said and rolled up the rope.

They ran for the fence, where Emma threw the rope over and looked at Jeremy.

"You first," he told Emma. He boosted her to the top. Once she was there, he held up the little girl to have Emma take her. She reached out and pulled the girl up and put her on her back. Next, Jeremy jumped up. She swung the rope over and climbed down, with Jeremy holding the rope taut for support. They pulled it down and the three of them made their way down the long alleyway. They ran the blocks back to the warehouse. The men outside opened the door and let them in.

"Mr. Patterson!" Emma called. He turned with a smile on his face, happy to see them. That smile faded when he saw who was with them. "Emma, we told you to look around only!"

"I couldn't just leave her." Emma knelt to put the girl down and moved away so he could see her.

Patterson ran over to them. "Sophy!" he said in disbelief.

"Uncle Lucas?"

"Oh, Sophy," he said crying and taking her into his arms.

"Uncle?" mouthed Emma.

Cole had walked up and seen the reunion. "Yes. He's been looking for her and volunteered for this position."

Emma watched them. She looked over at Cole. "We have to move soon," she said. "There's a limited window of time to get the kids out."

Mr. Patterson hugged Sophy to him tightly and then called out, "Ted, come take her. Have the doctor check her out."

There were medical services arranged in the warehouse so the children could be cleared before being transported to a safe house. Cole had gotten in touch with Clair and she had quickly arranged homes in the areas where the children could be housed safely until their parents were found.

"But I don't want to go," Sophy said. These people were strangers to her.

"Just for a little while and then we'll get you home. Okay?" he implored.

Sophy nodded slowly and went reluctantly with Ted. They only made it a few feet when she stopped and turned. "Wait!" she called. "Emma!"

"Yes?" Emma asked and went to her. She bent down and listened intently.

"The woman with the tall hair, with white running through it and a large bosom. She's in charge. And she's mean."

"Is she the one who did this to you?" Emma asked, touching the bruises on the girl's arms.

"Yes. She likes to hit us."

"We'll look for her. Thank you, Sophy," said Emma sincerely.

"I held on tight," Sophy said.

"Yes, you did, little one, you did," Emma said and touched her face. "You go with Ted now."

Sophy nodded and took his hand. Ted's nose wrinkled as he got a whiff of her. Emma's mouth turned down and she mouthed, "Throw up and urine."

He shook his head and took her to the doctor.

Patterson looked at Emma. "Why did you bring her out? Why her?"

"She was lucky. She couldn't tolerate the drugs. She was the only one awake. I don't think she would've survived the night."

"Thank you for going against my orders and bringing her here," he said sincerely.

Emma nodded.

He shook off the worry for Sophy and said, "Tell me how many."

"At least twenty boys and girls, various ages. They're being kept heavily sedated. Maybe with morphine."

"Are they restrained?"

"No, I think they're counting on the drugs to keep them quiet."

"Guards in the room?"

"No. Again, I think they are counting on the sedation." She frowned.

He noticed and asked, "What is it?"

"The last kidnapping case, several overdosed. I hope we get all of them out alive."

Plans were made and the men dispersed around the house. "Once we get through the front doors, here," Patterson said, pointing to the drawing, "Emma and Jeremy, you'll need to get to the basement door. You'll have a team with you."

He eyed everyone. "One thing, there might be children upstairs in the rooms."

"Horrible, but you're right," agreed Cole. "Once we get the basement under control, Emma, you, and Jeremy search the rooms. We'll hold everyone downstairs."

Their plans in place, they approached from the front and the back of the house, expecting guards at both entrances. Emma, Cole, and Jeremy were with the group entering from the front. A large group of armed men went in first, crashing the door open.

The door splintered open and they rushed in. The foyer and sitting room were full of couples, some dancing, some talking. At the first sound of the door, the people stopped and stared before running toward the exits. The agents grabbed them easily and contained them in the room. The other agents could be heard coming in through the back of the house, gathering up people as they made their way forward.

Emma and Jeremy came in behind them and ran toward the basement door.

"Wait right there, this is a private residence!" called a voice.

Emma turned slowly toward the voice and saw a woman with a tall head of hair and a white swatch running through it.

Her gaze shifted to her chest. *Sophy was right, that is an impressive bosom.*

"You think so?" Emma asked as she strode three steps toward her, then jumped and kicked her in the face. She went down like a rock. One of the detectives nearby whistled and went to take her into custody.

"Let's go," Jeremy said.

Emma went in first and the others followed her down. She turned up the gas lamps and saw there were more than twenty children.

"We need to get them out of here. The doctor can check them at the warehouse." They had twenty men but would need at least ten more.

"I'll go up and tell Pops we need more people," Jeremy said.

"I'll come with you." Emma followed him upstairs and saw Cole was speaking with local law enforcement, directing them.

"Pops!" Jeremy called. "We need ten more men to help move the kids."

"We have additional officers from the local police station who can help with that," his father called back.

Jeremy nodded and waved the men over to the basement. As the children were brought up, the people in the room watched in horror as babies were moved past them.

"We need to get upstairs," Emma told Jeremy, distracting him from the children.

"Yes. Have you got your gun?" he asked.

"Yes."

They approached the second level and split up. The adults appeared to have exited. *Probably due to the ruckus downstairs.* What they were looking for were scared children.

They checked in closets and under beds, speaking softly, trying to find anyone who might be hiding. There were none on the second floor, so they headed up to the third floor and split up again. Jeremy called down the hall, "Emma, over here."

When she entered the room, she saw him holding up a bed skirt.

"There's one under here," he directed.

"I'll take care of this one if you want to check the other rooms," she said.

Emma bent down and what she saw broke her heart. It was a girl of about seven wearing a negligée meant for an adult. She was huddled in the corner, shaking like a terrified rabbit.

"Honey, come on out," Emma called softly, lying on her stomach to slide under the bed.

"Don't call me that. They call me that," the girl stuttered.

"Okay, can you tell me your name?" Emma asked, her voice soft.

"Mary," she said, her answer so low, Emma had to strain to hear it.

"My mama's name was also Mary." When she didn't move, Emma started again. "Mary, I'm not with those terrible people. I'm with the Pinkertons and the police. We've found the other kids downstairs and we're moving them to a safe place."

"Safe place? Away from here? Away from those men and women?" Mary asked, hope sounding in her voice for the first time.

"Yes, away from them. Can you come to me?" Emma asked and put out her arms.

Mary crawled to Emma and allowed herself to be pulled out. Once she had hold of her, Mary plucked at her garment "Is there something else I can wear?" she asked. "This is the only thing they would give me."

"I think there must be something. Let me check." She looked in the closet and found a man's shirt. "I think this will work."

Emma walked to the bed and, while she helped Mary change, she noticed the bruises covering the girl's body. She so badly wanted to cry but she held it in as she helped her put on the large shirt. It reached past the girl's knees. She rolled up the sleeves and asked, "How is that?"

"Better," Mary admitted.

"Let's head down."

Mary gripped Emma's hand tightly and kept her face buried in Emma's side. "Don't worry, they won't get you," Emma reassured the girl.

"You think not?" said a male voice from behind them. Emma kept her hand in her pocket and turned, keeping Mary close.

The tall thin man demanded, "Give her to me."

Mary was muttering into her side, "Not him, not him, not him!"

Emma just pulled her closer. "I will not give her to you. I suggest you leave while you can."

"Or what," he sneered.

"I'll have to kill you," she said fiercely.

"You kill me? I don't think so." He pulled out a knife and started toward her.

"Don't think you weren't warned," Emma said and fired through her pocket. The bullet met the mark and the man went to his knees with a startled expression

"You shot me!" he said, looking at the bloody hand he pulled back from his chest.

"Yes." Emma made no move to help him as he fell forward. She didn't stop to see if he was dead; she didn't care.

"Jeremy," she called and when she didn't hear him, she and Mary went room to room. They found him in the last room with a little boy of about five. The boy looked dazed, not quite aware of his surroundings.

"We'll have to carry him. I don't think he knows what is going on," he said and picked him up, motioning for her to go in front of him. They made their way out.

"What about the fourth floor?" Emma asked, looking up at the next set of stairs. She didn't want to put the kids they had with them in additional danger. "Do we leave them here in a room?"

"No! I want to go with you!" Mary cried out and the boy with Jeremy clung tightly to him.

"We go up together," said Jeremy.

They headed up and found several locked rooms. Jeremy kept the children and watched as Emma picked the locks and opened the doors. There weren't any children, but there was morphine and a lot of it. Each room contained more supplies but no more children. Emma let out the breath she was holding. "That's all of them. Let's go."

"No," Mary protested. "There's one more. I hear it at night."

"What do you hear?" asked Jeremy.

"A baby crying."

Emma looked at Jeremy, her eyes wide. She bent down to Mary. "Do you know where the baby might be?"

Mary walked to the closet, tapped the wall, and knelt down in front of it. Emma went to her and asked. "What is that room?"

"It's the punishment room. If you don't do as they ask with the men, you got put in there."

"Emma, Mary, come away from there." Jeremy handed the boy he was holding to Emma and directed them to back up. He kicked the door and kicked again. It came apart and he removed the remnants. It was a small closet, and dark. He stepped a few feet in and Emma handed him her kerosene lighter.

He lit it and examined the room. It was covered in feces and there was a small pile of rags in the corner. "Nothing here," he said, "just rags."

She peered in and saw something. "Jeremy! The rags moved!"

He stepped carefully, trying to not step on them. He moved them around and found a tiny girl who appeared less than a year old.

"Emma, there's a baby girl here." *They must have left her here to die,* he thought. He picked her up carefully and she whimpered. "It's okay, we'll get you out."

They walked downstairs with their bruised and broken children. Emma and Jeremy were barely holding in their emotions as they cradled them. Mary had become a permanent appendage on Emma's side.

Cole saw them on the stairs and ran up. "Any trouble?"

"I left a man on the third floor," Emma reported.

"What happened?"

"A gentleman had a notion to keep little Mary here with him."

"And?"

"I disabused him of that notion."

"I will check it out." Cole headed upstairs.

Jeremy looked over with raised eyebrows.

"Later," she mouthed and hugged the two children close to her.

Jeremy continued to cradle the baby.

A detective downstairs was taking names and arranging for transport to the safe houses. "Three more?" he asked. "Do you want us to transport them?"

"No," Jeremy said, surprising Emma. "We'll take these three over."

"Okay." He noticed how small the child was that Jeremy carried. "How old?" he asked.

"I think less than a year."

His face twisted. "And this is just the start." They had been told there would be many more raids that night, possibly more after that.

"Yes," Emma said. "See if you can find any accounting books in the manager's office. I'd expect these transactions had to be recorded. There'll be a significant amount of money to be tracked."

Jeremy stayed quiet, holding the baby close as they headed to the warehouse. The children needed a doctor's care.

"You heard the guard, Jacob, say they didn't even have to use the schools, that kids were just there for the taking," muttered Jeremy.

"So many immigrant communities don't trust law enforcement, so they may also be under-reporting the kidnappings."

"Yes." They finished the last block and the men at the warehouse door held it open so they could enter.

They were waved over to the large area where the children had been staged. The doctor was shaking his head and covering one of them as they walked up. Emma and Jeremy averted the children's eyes. The body was moved out of the area.

The doctor walked over to them. "Who do we have here?" he asked in a kindly voice, his eyes showing worry.

"This is Mary," Emma said. "She is a brave girl."

Mary kept her head hidden in Emma's hip. "Well, Mary, will you come to me?" The doctor asked, "I need to make sure you're okay."

Emma leaned over and whispered in the doctor's ear. He started visibly at the news. "Yes. I'll have to check that." *Sexual activity in a child that age could be damaging.* He could only hope she would be able to have children later. "And the other two?" he murmured.

"We aren't sure. They'll have to be checked," she said.

"Can you stay so they feel secure? I don't want to scare them."

"Of course." The small boy she held was coaxed away by a nurse.

Mary went with the doctor and another nurse.

Jeremy continued to hold the baby. Emma watched him, concerned about his intense concentration. The doctor distracted her and called, "Emma, can you follow me? Mary is asking for you."

"Of course." She went over to the room where they were going to examine the girl.

Mary looked at Emma. "Will you stay with me?" she asked. She had been left alone with too many men to trust the doctor. She held her hand and Emma took it. The doctor walked over to them and gently asked, "Mary, can you tell me what happened to you?"

"No, no, no," the girl moaned.

"Did the men touch you?"

She nodded, not raising her head from Emma's chest. "Can you tell me where?" She pointed to her chest and between her legs.

"Just touch?"

"Yes, they said something special was planned tonight."

Emma wanted to crush the girl to her. She held off. All she could think about was, *What if we had delayed our arrival by even a day?*

As they finished up, the doctor asked, "Mary what's your last name?"

"Connelly."

"Do you know where you were taken from?"

"I was in the front yard of my house. They grabbed me and put a bad-smelling rag over my mouth. I woke up in a building like this one."

"Do you know what city or town you were taken from?"

"Buffalo, New York."

"Do you know your parents' names?"

"Mama and daddy," she said and sniffed.

"That's all I need for now. I understand there's food if you're hungry." Her stomach rumbled in response.

"Yes," she said, turning red. Mary and the nurse went to find some food.

Emma went back to where Jeremy sat. He still had the baby in his arms.

The doctor walked up to them. "Let me see the little one." Jeremy's eyes were wet and he continued to rock the baby.

"Jeremy?" asked Emma quietly.

He shook his head and said hoarsely, "She isn't breathing."

"Jeremy, can you bring her over here? I need to check to make sure she is okay," suggested the doctor.

Jeremy cradled the girl to him and walked to the doctor. There was a bit of a struggle to get the baby from him. Once he released her, the doctor laid her on the table. He listened for her heartbeat and started to palpitate her chest.

Jeremy couldn't watch and put his head on Emma's shoulder. There was a sudden gasp from Emma. Jeremy lifted his head and turned back toward them. The girl's chest was rising and falling.

"Is she ok?" asked Jeremy, wiping the tears from his eyes.

"This young girl has had too many drugs, and it depressed her respiratory system. We will have to monitor her and give her a number of massages. Nurse!" he called. He gave her instructions. "And make sure she is fed."

"Thank God," Jeremy whispered, shuddering against her.

"Yes," Emma said, crossing herself.

They went to help monitor the other children. One had perished but they had managed to save so many.

A couple walked into the warehouse. "Emma! Jeremy!" They heard a voice call out. Turning toward the doorway, Emma called, "Clair! Thomas! When did you get here?" Jeremy and Emma ran over to greet the new arrivals. Even in these circumstances, Clair was elegantly dressed and her hair coiffed.

"We were here earlier but we wanted to get the safe house ready," Clair explained.

Thomas said, "We have staff coming in from our New York residence until we can staff locally."

"How many?" Clair asked grimly, looking around.

"Close to thirty," Emma replied.

"Any deaths?" she asked quietly.

"One," Emma said bitterly. "The others will have to be monitored closely as they are coming off the morphine."

"Yes," Clair murmured. "We have a group of five nurses secured for the house."

The doctor walked up to the group. "I'll be accompanying them. I'm Dr. Phillips, and you are?"

Clair held out her hand. "Clair Callahan and this is my husband, Thomas. We run a charity that helps people who need it."

"These kids will need it. How far is it from here?" Dr. Phillips asked.

"We managed to secure a location in residential areas, about five miles from here," said Thomas.

"Will there be enough room for all the children?"

"Yes," said Clair. "We hope to keep them together in case the older children may be able to identify the younger ones."

Dr. Phillips nodded and said, "We will let you know when they are stable enough to travel."

"Thank you, doctor," said Clair sincerely. They watched him go back to caring for the children.

"I'm so glad you were local," Emma said to Thomas.

"Us too."

"Is Mary Elizabeth with you?" Emma asked. They had a baby the same age as her niece.

"Yes, she is with her nanny at the house"

"Oh, nice—how is she?"

"She's busy. Running everywhere. Running all of us ragged."

"And she has you wrapped around her finger."

"Yes," he admitted with a laugh.

It was nice to have a conversation not related to kidnapped children. Jeremy seemed to relax as he listened to the news. They hugged and said they would see them soon. At that time, Clair and Thomas departed to the house to meet the first group of children. Jeremy and Emma stayed behind and only left when the final child was moved to the safe house. The children would stay there for weeks, possibly months, until the families could be located.

The two couples met the next day at Emma and Jeremy's hotel. It was safer for them to meet away from the safe house. The fewer people coming and going, the more likely they could keep its location a secret.

"Thomas and Clair, come in," Emma greeted them. "I've ordered tea for us."

"I'm missing home, but we need to be here," Clair said, sitting down.

"How did the other raids go?" Thomas asked.

Jeremy sat back. "Cole sent several telegrams, and more kids were found at the different locations. They're being moved to the safe houses you have set up." He then added, "We expect that they'll have similar setups. You got the list we sent?"

"Yes," Clair said, "Thomas is managing that for us."

Thomas took over from there. "I've located houses in each of the areas. We've dispersed staff to those cities to do the setup and wait."

"If they're not needed?"

"We'll close down and move to the next location."

A knock sounded at the door and Jeremy got up to answer it. He showed the waiter into the room with a tray of tea and cakes. When the waiter left, they began to speak again.

"These are just lovely," Clair remarked as Emma poured the tea and handed the cakes out. "I'm hoping we don't have any cases involving children in the future."

"Agreed," Emma said, watching Jeremy. She was concerned about his reaction to the baby last night.

Jeremy said, "The baby…"

"The small baby girl?" asked Clair.

"Yes. How is she?" he asked, averting his eyes.

"The nurses stayed with her all night. Her breathing became steadier and they got some milk into her. The doctor thinks she'll make it."

Jeremy let out a breath he didn't know he was holding. "Good."

The conversation moved on to other things. Thomas and Clair said, "We need to head back to the house to check on the kids."

"Oh, we'll be in the area for at least a few weeks. Can you send Jake to us?" Thomas asked. "Pictures would help with the child/parent identification."

"I don't think Jake will be able to be away from home that long," Emma replied.

"Even if Tim was with him?" asked Thomas. Tim, Emma's brother-in-law, could be a stabilizing influence on Jake. When circumstances changed beyond Jake's control, Tim could settle the young man down and help him accept what was happening.

"I don't think it would be fair to pull Jake from his work for that long. Can we find someone local?" Emma asked.

"Is there someone Jake can recommend?" asked Clair.

"He might. I'll see if he can recommend anyone or several people so there won't be a delay," Emma said.

"I'll be happy for this to be over," said Jeremy.

"Yes, but I'm afraid it's just beginning," Clair said, thinking of the damage that had been inflicted on the children.

"Clair," Emma said thoughtfully, walking her out. "Where did you get the people to run the safe-houses on such short notice?"

"My women," Clair said simply.

"From your previous employment?" Emma asked, surprised. Clair had been a Madam at a bordello in the past.

"No." She chuckled. "Though some of them might help if we need them," she said thoughtfully. "It's the women we've helped in our Chicago safe house."

"How did they know we needed them?"

"I told them. As soon as I found out we would need support, I sent telegrams."

"Some of them said they would help?" asked Emma.

"All of them. There was no hesitation. They just needed to be told where to go."

Emma's eyes teared up. "I can't believe it."

"I can. They're strong women who got through something horrible and want to do the same for these kids."

Jeremy stood at the door with Thomas, "Everything's in place?" he asked.

"Yes. We'll handle this one and, hopefully, get the kids home."

Clair and Emma joined them. Jeremy asked quietly, "Would you mind if we check in on the girl?"

"Of course. This is the address." Clair wrote it quickly and handed it to him.

After they left, Emma turned to Jeremy. "Are you still worried about her?"

"Yes," he admitted. "I want to see her for myself. When that little body went cold," he began. He sat down heavily and cried. She went to him quickly and took him into her arms. They sat like that for a long time.

After a while, she said, "We need to do something fun after this. Just for us."

"What?" he said, laying his head on her shoulder. "Murder and kidnapping are not fun?"

She laughed shortly and said, "It certainly has its moments."

"I'll think about it," he murmured.

Emma sat back away from Jeremy and asked. "Did Cole go to the other locations?"

"Yes," he commented.

They didn't sleep much that night, waiting for word on the raids being orchestrated. The next morning, a knock sounded at their door. Emma looked hopeful. Jeremy walked quickly to the door and opened it. A bellman was there with a telegram. Jeremy tipped him quickly and opened it.

"Well?" she asked, following him.

"They were able to get into the targeted houses."

"Kids?"

"Found." He crunched up the telegram. "More dead and abused."

"Jeremy," she said carefully, "we were lucky. We only lost one here."

"One that we know of," he muttered.

"We've gotten into the operations and shut them down," she reminded him.

"They're like cockroaches. They keep showing up, even if we kill their nest."

"Yes," she admitted. "This is horrible and we will do what we can to stop them. Clair will continue to open up activity locations to keep children off the street."

"And still that will not be enough," he said bitterly.

"No," she agreed. "It won't be."

They got some rest before they headed to the safe house. On their way there, he stayed quiet, his mind on that baby girl. The location was in a neighborhood with older homes. There weren't any crowds or noise. It was chosen due to its quiet nature. Emma was dressed in her boy's clothes. She and Jeremy pulled their hats down and approached the door. They knocked. "The guards are well hidden," Emma murmured.

Jeremey nodded and said in the same tone, "Yes, one at the corner, a lady with a baby carriage in front of that house."

The curtains moved on the side of the front door. It opened quickly and Clair said, "Come in."

They followed her direction.

Emma smiled suddenly when she heard children's voices. "They're awake!" she said.

"Yes, and boisterous. All have eaten several meals. We've had to send out for more groceries."

"That is wonderful," commented Emma, relieved.

Thomas called from the stairs, "Were you wanting to check on this little girl?"

They turned quickly and saw the small girl turn and grin at Jeremy. She held out her arms to him and he immediately took her from Thomas. Emma grinned when she saw her grab Jeremy's hair and pull.

Clair watched them as she put her arms around Emma's shoulder and pulled her close. "That seems to be helping him."

"Yes," she murmured. "This has been hard on him. He thought the baby died in his arms. It just wrecked him."

"I'm glad you came by," Clair said as they watched him. "Come in and sit down," she requested.

"Have you started to compile the names and locations where the kids came from?" asked Emma.

Jeremy sat across from them, still playing with the baby. Clair started to speak when a loud argument interrupted her. "Just a minute," Thomas said and he left to settle a fight that had erupted between the children.

"Yes," Clair continued, answering questions about the children. "I have them here," she said and handed it to Emma.

Emma flipped through the pages. "Most are from around here. That's good."

"I wish we could contact the families now."

"We need the pictures," Emma commented. "We want them to end up with the right families."

"Yes," Clair said regretfully. She was a parent and knew any delay could be heartbreaking.

Mary Elizabeth ran out of the kitchen toward Emma. She picked her up. "How wonderful to see you!" Emma exclaimed.

"Where are you headed after this?" asked Clair, watching her play with the small girl.

"It sounds like Cole and you have the other houses under control and I think Jeremy needs a break from cases involving children."

"Yes, do you have something in mind?" her friend asked, thinking it would be a vacation.

Emma said, "No, I was looking at this." She juggled the girl and reached into her pocket for a folded article.

Clair took it and began to read. "A serial killer, Jack the Ripper, is under investigation." She noticed where it was and asked, "In London?"

"It wasn't that. I saw that they're using new investigative skills. I thought we could look into that."

"And this would be a vacation with you not getting involved in the case?" Clair asked doubtfully.

"I need a break also," Emma said.

"What will you do first?"

"Go home," Emma said simply.

"When will you bring this up to Jeremy?"

"On the way there. A nice long train ride where he won't be able to avoid me."

"Good luck with that."

Jeremy was playing with the baby and Thomas sat down next to him. "The women are talking," he commented.

Jeremy looked up. "I see that."

"You think it's about us."

"Maybe," he said, watching Emma smile and put her fingers to her lips. *She's planning something*, he thought.

Clair and Thomas went to look in on the children. Emma and Jeremy sat in the sitting room. "Where are you thinking after here?" he asked

She had thought to wait but told him her plan. "I was thinking we might go to London." She went on to describe the trip.

Jeremy listened. Normally, he was on the same page, but an

overseas trip was not what they needed. "Emma," he said stopping her. "No."

"No?" she asked, confused.

"No. I want to go somewhere secluded, a beach or something like that where we can just hang out, watch the water, and be together."

She thought about it. "I think you're right. Do you have a location in mind?"

"No," he admitted, "but Pops might."

"Hmm, I think it sounds wonderful," she said sincerely.

He grabbed her in a hug and swung her around. "I'm so happy you are with me," he said.

"Me too," she said, returning his hug.

The nurse listened to the conversation and stepped back with a small smile.

CHAPTER 7

$\mathcal{J}$eremy and Emma finished up their day and headed back to the hotel. They had just settled in for the evening when there was a knock on the door. She looked over at Jeremy and saw lines had set around his mouth where they hadn't been before. Emma's mood had improved with the raids and the news that more children had been found.

She shook her head. *I have to get him away soon.*

"I'll get it," said Emma and went to the door, finding a bellhop with a package for her. She took it and gave him a tip. Turning it over in her hands, she walked back to the sitting room.

Jeremy sat up and rubbed a hand through his hair. "What is it?"

"I don't know, but I am going to find out." She tore it open quickly.

He closed his eyes again as he listened to her rip open the envelope, his mood still down.

"It appears to be a vacation," she said, looking through the papers. Included in them were train tickets and an address of a cottage on the beach.

"What?" he asked and moved to her side to read the documentation.

True to her word, it was a beach vacation.

"This is perfect," said Jeremy as he read the documents. It was just what they needed.

Emma frowned; it was too perfect. Everything was prearranged. *Why?* She looked over at Jeremy; his hands holding the package were shaking. She knew at that moment that it didn't matter where the trip had come from. She would do what he needed and go away with him. Smiling brightly, she asked, "Do we pack?"

He smiled back genuinely for the first time since the raids had started. "Yes, I do believe we do."

Once they made their decisions, their plans came together quickly. They sent a telegraph to Dora and Cole to let them know they would be going away for a week. In a few days, they were on a train to their destination. They eagerly jumped down from the train when it stopped and went to get their carriage. A man held a sign indicating he was there for them.

"Who arranged this?" she asked herself, not realizing she had said it aloud.

"Must have been Pops," he said, not willing to probe any more deeply. He wanted to just relax and not think for a while. The driver had been arranged and headed out to their rental house.

As they passed a grocer, Emma asked, "We should stop before we become hermits. We'll need food."

"True," he said. He directed the driver to the grocer. They walked into the small store and picked up a basket and got food for the week. Mostly sandwich makings and some baking supplies.

"What are you making?" he asked when he viewed her selection.

"I was thinking about bread and maybe a strudel."

"That sounds wonderful." He looked around. "The fruit is over there."

They finished gathering their items and walked to check out with the cashier. She was an older woman and had a pleasant smile. "Are you visiting the area?"

"We are," said Jeremy. "We'll also need ice delivered and milk and butter for the week."

"Where are you staying?" the cashier asked.

Emma bumped him when he started to answer. "Sorry," she said. She wasn't sorry and answered for them. "Down at the beach."

"There are several houses there, which one?" the cashier questioned. "I need to know for the deliveries."

Emma turned red and gave her the address.

As they were leaving, an older man moved slowly down the narrow aisle that led to the door and blocked their path. He turned toward them. "Well, hello, am I keeping you?" he asked.

"Just a bit," she answered. "We want to head to the beach."

"Grand day for it," he said. "I hear you're on vacation."

"Yes. We best get going," she said, dragging Jeremy from the store.

"What's the hurry?" he asked.

"Didn't you think they were asking too many questions?"

He chuckled. "No, I think they're very normal for people who live in a small town. They're curious when strangers arrive. Emma, not everything is a case."

"Really?" she teased. "You don't think the cashier had nefarious plans? Or that man outside, was he some kind of undercover spy?"

"Maybe," he responded. "The whole town is a fake, set up for us. Crafted when they heard we were visiting."

"Now that would be interesting," she said, looking back at the town.

He laughed, already enjoying himself. Pulling her with him,

he threw an arm over her shoulder and led her to their carriage. "We have our food; now we head to our beach house."

Back in the carriage, they waited expectantly for their destination. As they pulled onto the beach, there were many cottages spread out. "There, that must be it!" she exclaimed. The house looked like it had been there for a while.

"We can only hope the inside is better than the outside," he said.

"Agreed.'"

They thanked the driver and took the food in. He called after them, "I'll return to take you to the station in five days."

They turned back and nodded their agreement, sending him a wave goodbye. They entered the house with their packages and looked around. The house was surprisingly immaculate.

"Wow," Jeremy said.

"Indeed. I expected to spend the first two days cleaning." She laughed. "Let's head to the kitchen and see if a similar job was completed." The door to the kitchen opened easily, revealing an old but clean kitchen. They set their packages on the long wood table and looked around.

Jeremy walked over to the sink and turned on the water. "Running water at least."

"And an ice box," she opened it, "and it has ice."

He walked over and looked into the box. "Well, good."

"It is. Who set all this up?"

"Pop's may have..." Jeremy suggested again, but he was starting to doubt it. He pushed the thoughts out of his head. "Oh well, we're here and it's a vacation."

She put her fingers to her lips and stopped herself. Jeremy needed this week, no matter who planned it. She put on a smile and dropped her hand to her side "Let's go up for a nap."

He caught her meaning and smiled broadly as he took her hand. The bed upstairs was comfortable, and they stayed there for a while.

Afterward, she propped her chin on his chest. "How about a snack and a walk on the beach?"

"Now that's a plan."

She pulled on pants and borrowed a shirt from Jeremy, leaving it untucked. Jeremy pulled on loose pants and left his shirt untucked as well. They headed downstairs, barefoot and carefree.

It was three in the afternoon and there was plenty of time to enjoy a snack and a walk on the beach. The sun was low in the sky and the water was inviting. "Race you to the water," he said. They ran to it, sitting down on the sand to roll up their pants.

Emma splashed quickly into the breaking waves, enjoying the cool water against her legs. "Come on in!" she called. "The water's amazing." He didn't move; instead, he watched her. The picture she made with the ocean at her back.

"Come on!" she called again.

He ran down to join her in the water. It was perfect as he took her hand and walked down the beach. They stayed until the sun started going down. After, they were pleasantly worn out and returned to the cottage. Once on the shaded porch, they collapsed on the old wooden chairs that must have been there since the house was built.

"That was fun," she said, throwing her arms over her head and leaning back against the wall.

"It was," he agreed, "and something we needed."

"Yes." She knew it was too early to talk about the events they had witnessed and she wanted to rest and relax. Instead, she looked over at him and asked "Want some lemonade?"

"Yes, I do," he stated.

When she made to stand, he stopped her, "No, stay here, I can get it."

"If you're sure..."

"I am." He pulled himself up and headed into the house. The lemons and sugar were with the supplies they'd brought from the store. He made it quickly, juicing the lemons and adding water and sugar, tasting it as he went. Once satisfied, he organized the pitcher and two glasses for the porch

She rose when she saw him and went to help him put the tray on the table between the two chairs.

"Thank you," he said.

She poured him a glass and he took a long drink. "Thank you," she replied. "I needed that."

"We have to remember to stay hydrated this week; we aren't used to the heat."

They sat watching the sun slowly make its way down. Jeremy looked over at her. "Dinner?"

"Yes."

"I'll go," he said and got up to head to the kitchen.

She didn't argue, just smiled and sat back. It was nice to have a place to themselves. The boarding house was wonderful, but it was a shared home. She would have to encourage Jeremy to do this a few times a year. Looking around, she didn't think he would disagree.

The door slammed as he exited the house with sandwiches overflowing with ham, tomatoes, and lettuce.

"Yum," she said. "That looks amazing."

He handed her a sandwich and took his. He chewed and watched the water. "You know, I could get used to this," he said, mirroring her thoughts.

"I was thinking we could do this a few times a year," she said.

"Hmm," he said. "I was thinking we might buy a bungalow like this. For us to rent out when we aren't here."

"It would be amazing to have a place like this that's all ours."

CHAPTER 8

The next morning, Emma left Jeremy to sleep and took her coffee out to the porch to watch the sun come up. She sat and enjoyed the sounds of the water. Stirring herself, she stood and noticed something out of the corner of her eye. *What is that?* she wondered and headed over to investigate it. Bending down, she found a basket of baked goods and fishing poles, and—from the smell—she deduced what was probably a bucket of bait.

She straightened and went over to the basket. There was a card attached to the top. She opened it and read, "Welcome to our small town. Enjoy these. And try fishing today!"

So thoughtful, she thought. It was so nice the townspeople would do this and provide the fishing poles. The bait can wait until later. Baked goods first. She headed inside, where Jeremy was leaving the kitchen.

"What's that?" he asked.

"This?" She held up the basket. "Someone left it outside with fishing poles and bait."

"Fishing poles?"

"Yes. I guess they have our activity for today laid out for us." She started toward the counter with the basket.

"Let me help you with that," he said. He took the side opposite her and helped place it on the counter. "There's a lot of food here," he commented, looking at the variety of baked goods. He picked up a muffin.

"Yes, it was nice of them to send it," she commented but continued to study it thoughtfully.

"Emma? What are you thinking?"

She shook it off. "Nothing, just that I want that exact muffin." She smiled and took the one he was holding.

"Hey!" he protested, laughing.

"I told you, I found the perfect one!" she teased, keeping custody of the muffin and backing away.

He lunged for her and she dodged him, running into the living room. "You better not eat that," he warned.

"This?" She pretended to take a bite. Taking pity on him, she tossed it back and he ate it in one bite. She walked to the couch and dropped down. "Do you want to try fishing?"

"Have you fished before?" he asked.

"No, have you?" asked Emma. She hadn't had much interest in the sport.

"I'm a city boy. We get our fish from the market. But I guess we can try. Do we fish from the shore?"

"I think so. I don't think I'd want to be in the water with a hook."

"Okay then, we go fishing."

Emma went to the kitchen and grabbed some more muffins and scones. Lastly, she added a bottle of lemonade to her full bag.

"We need towels," Jeremy called from upstairs.

"Yes," she called back. "And wear the same clothes as yesterday; we don't want to get burned."

"Okay."

She gathered her items and walked out to the porch. Jeremy came out dressed in the same outfit he'd worn yesterday. He carried the towels. "Ready?" he asked.

"Yes." She picked up one of the poles and handed the other to him. She also handed him the bait bucket.

"What is this?" he asked. "And what is that smell?"

"I think it might be the bait. I'm not sure what type it is. "

"I guess we'll find out."

They walked down to the water, laid out the towels, and opened up the bait bucket. "That's what I smelled," he commented, his nose wrinkling.

The bait was added to the hooks on the fishing line. "Careful with that," he said as she went to cast it into the ocean.

"You're right." She walked a few yards away and cast her line into the water. Jeremy went next and they waited.

"You can move back and sit," he called.

She nodded, watching her line. When nothing seemed to take the bait, she walked back to the towels. They put the poles in the sand, watching the lines bounce in the water.

"I'm not sure I want to catch a fish," said Emma.

At that moment, her line went taut.

"It's too late to stop now!" He laughed. "Get your pole before it's pulled in."

She did as she was told and wrestled the large fish onto the beach. "That was great!" he said. They looked at it flopping on the sand.

"Now what?" she asked.

"Can you cook it?"

"I don't think so, can you?"

"No. Let's put it back into the ocean."

"Good plan." She reached down to pick up the wiggling fish. She removed the hook and tossed him back into the water. It swam away quickly.

"I think we're done fishing," he commented and removed his pole from the water and placed it beside hers on the sand.

"That's better," she said.

He nodded and watched the water.

Emma took that moment to ask, "How are you?"

He knew what she was really asking and said, "Better, I think."

"What happened back there?"

"My reaction to the baby?"

"Yes."

"When the life seemed to drain out of her... I just thought I was dying also." He looked over at her and said, "You seemed better the minute we got Sophy out. Why?"

"I think my frustrations were relieved when we started to find and rescue the children. And I did get to take a few of the bad guys down in the process."

He nodded and sat quietly. There was a subject he wanted to broach. "If the baby's not claimed, I would like us to take her."

"Us?" Emma had not expected this and turned her gaze toward the ocean. *What does he mean? Marriage? Adoption?* "Are we getting ahead of ourselves? She must have a family looking for her."

"I want you to know, that if she doesn't, I want us to adopt her."

She turned tear-bright eyes toward him and asked, "Are you unhappy with how we are now?"

"No, not at all!" He took her chin when she tried to turn away from him. "I just feel that I want to be there if no one else is. This isn't about our life or our decisions."

"This is about her."

"Yes."

She took a deep breath and said, "If this is what you want, I will support you."

They held hands and thought about their possible future.

CHAPTER 9

"This week has been ideal," Jeremy said. He and Emma sat on the porch, enjoying the sunset on their final day.

"I agree," she said and let the silence settle around them. A single thought was in her head. *Who set this up? Who was responsible for this ideal holiday? Could this really be Cole? He was busy closing down the houses.* She glanced over at Jeremy and thought whoever did it was worth it. "Jeremy, what are you going to do next?"

"You mean can I handle going back and helping get the kids home?" he asked, knowing she was asking a deeper question.

"I wouldn't have said it that way, but yes," she agreed.

"I just needed some separation, and this week was perfect. I also want to check on the baby girl."

"If her family has been notified and wants her?" she asked softly.

"I only want her to be safe and happy."

"Hmm." She smiled. "Let me know if any arrangements need to be made."

"What about you?" he asked.

"I need to head home. I have some things to work on, and I bet Mr. Pennington has some cases for me."

"Our tickets are for the morning," he mused, looking back out at the water, wishing they could stay longer.

Later, when she put Jeremy on his train, she headed into the town. Her train wouldn't be for a few hours. The town appeared abandoned; there wasn't anyone in the streets. *The store,* she thought, and walked quickly to it. It was locked down; she pressed her face to the window. "Empty? Where are all of the groceries?" she muttered and walked around, peering into different shop windows.

Who could have set something like this up? Who would have the resources to do this? Only one name came to her mind—John. But why the elaborate ruse? He got nothing out of it. She and Jeremy did, but John? She mulled that over and walked back to the train station.

John set this up. I know he did. He set the whole town up. Appeared and disappeared. What does it mean? Why do it?

She was still mulling when she arrived at the station. Her gaze found the ticket booth and she had an idea. "Hello?" she asked.

The clerk walked over. "What can I do for you?"

"Can I exchange my ticket for one to Manhattan, New York?"

"Of course." He processed the ticket and told her the new price. She nodded and pulled out the money. What was her plan? She had no idea. "The town here, is it normally empty?"

He didn't answer. Instead, he motioned to the train. "It's boarding soon," he said. She heard the train whistle.

"Oh, thank you. I'll go now."

She had a ticket in one hand and a bag in another and rushed to the platform. The trip would be longer than her trip home, nearly two weeks. Is *this a bad idea? Too late now,* she thought as she felt the jerk of the train pulling away.

Once she was settled in her private room she thought, *There's a connection. This wasn't about Jeremy and me needing time off. Why had John wanted them out of the picture? What didn't he want them to see?* She thought about where she'd been when she received the vacation information. They were in a hotel in the same city as the raid. What had happened? Who had she seen? Was there anything unusual?

One thing came to mind: the baby girl Jeremy had rescued. She was just a baby and very different from the typical children the kidnappers were known for taking.

Was the baby John's? The age of the child didn't fit for the time he had been in prison. Did he know something about the parents? It was one thing for him to run things from prison, but he wasn't free to leave.

She leaned her head back on the seat. *Could the girl be a granddaughter? His son or daughter would have to be young,* she thought.

She pulled a book out of her bag but couldn't concentrate on it.

Almost two weeks later, she stepped down off the train, wearing her boy clothes, and pulled her hat low. This time, she would be by herself and she didn't want any trouble. She would still have to contact the warden and request a special search.

The large gate swung open, leading to the foreboding buildings at Sing Sing. When she was led into the administrative building, she requested a meeting with the warden. There was a small room with wooden upright chairs near his office, and she was told to wait.

"You're back," Warden Brush said warmly, recognizing her. "Cole didn't let me know you were coming."

"No, I wanted to follow up on something on my own," Emma murmured. "Can I have the same person who searched me the last time?"

"Of course. Are you sure you want to see him alone?"

"I am," she said. "I also have a favor to ask. I need to leave my things with you until I come out."

"Of course. I can keep them in my office." He bent down to pick them up.

"And," she warned, "there are several knives and a gun in my bag." He looked at her in surprise, then down at the bag.

"Oh, okay, I'll lock it up." He took the bundle to his office and she heard the door click as the lock engaged.

He returned and motioned for her to follow him. Brush had sent for one of the lady officers to conduct the search before Emma went in to see John.

The search was completed quickly and she was escorted to the private visitor room. She entered and saw him at the table, looking much the same as last time. The same guard as last time was in the room with them. She nodded to him as she moved to the table.

"Emma, what a pleasant surprise. You look well rested," John observed.

"Yes, about that. Why? John, I just can't figure out why you did that," she said as she sat down across from him.

"The vacation?" He waited until she nodded before he admitted, "I thought you needed it. After all, you had just been exposed to a traumatizing event. I heard Jeremy especially had a hard time."

"One that was created by you," she accused.

He raised an eyebrow. "As you know, I had nothing to do with that business."

She sat back, took off her hat, and tossed it on the table. "You were involved initially," she stated.

"Was I?" he asked. "I thought we agreed that was Candace."

"Your sister," she reminded him.

"I had no idea she was involved in something like that. We haven't talked in years."

Knowing this line of questioning would not go further, she changed the topic. "Why the ruse?"

"Can't I just be nice?" he asked lightly.

"No, you have an agenda," she said, looking him in the eyes, trying to read his responses.

"Maybe I just want my favor canceled," he suggested.

"Is that it?" she asked and sat back in her chair.

"Yes, I find that it's like the sword of Damocles. I'd rather not wait for it to fall at an inopportune time."

She narrowed her eyes as she evaluated his statement. She didn't believe him; there was something she wasn't seeing. "I'll let that go for now."

He watched her but didn't offer anything more.

"I guess that's it then," she said, reaching over for her hat.

His voice stopped her. "I understand my previous guard got his hands dirty in that mess with the missing children."

She took the hat into her hands, dropped it on her head, and said, "As far as I know, that's under investigation."

"How is my former guard?"

"I don't know anything about that," Emma said noncommittally.

John laughed suddenly. "Will he be joining us here soon?" he asked.

She didn't answer this time and stood. "Bye, John. I hope we don't see each other for a long while."

She hesitated at the door, looked back, and said, dropping the information on him with deadly accuracy, "You have a lovely granddaughter, John."

His eyes widened, showing true emotion. She saw what she wanted to see and left the room. The heavy door closing punctuated her exit with a BANG.

Home, she thought.

Back in the room, John murmured, "Good." He looked at the guard. "Ma did good."

"Yes, she did. She played her part perfectly."

"Did Lidia have any trouble getting the baby and moving to your new home?"

"They are on the way and our baby is well," he said with a grin. "The nurse took care of her at the safe-house until she could be retrieved."

His gaze moved to his son-in-law/guard and said, "I think it's time for us to exit this locale." As he stood, he mused, "I still owe her a favor; this one was significantly bigger than the last one."

The son-in-law nodded his agreement. "Just let me know when and where boss."

"Though, thinking about it, we might wait—just a bit."

"What for?" He was eager to get to his family and away from the prison.

"Jacob is due here soon."

"So, he is. Yes, we should wait."

CHAPTER 10

There was nothing left for her to do but head home. Emma went to the train station and waited for it. *Another week by train,* she thought as she waited to board.

I need to send a telegram. She glanced at the time; it was 3:00, and the train was scheduled to leave at 4:00. *There has to be enough time.* The clerk was at his desk, and she ran and asked him for directions to the telegraph office. "Down there about two blocks. Don't be late," he called, watching her run in the direction he indicated.

She ran until she spotted the small shop, surrounded mostly by dusty roads. She went in and up to the desk. "I need to send a telegraph, please."

"Go ahead," the clerk said. He held a pencil to paper and waited for her response.

She realized where she was and thought about John's reach. *I'll have to send a specific one later.* "Yes, I would like to send it to Clair Callahan. It will read: Jeremy is on the way to you. Stop. He'll be on the evening train in two days. Stop. Please meet him. Stop."

He put down his pencil and asked. "Is that all?"

"Yes, thank you." She glanced at her timepiece and saw she should be heading to the train station. Paying him quickly, she hurried back in time to board the train before it departed.

Once settled, she thought about the events. *Why did Jacob take the baby? Blackmail? Was that the only way to control John and have the kidnapping operations stay ongoing?*

That telegram would need to be sent as soon as possible. At the next stop, she jumped off the train and ran to the ticket clerk. She found that they also were a telegraph station. "I need to send one out."

"Tell me what you want to say."

"Clair, the baby girl, is she still there? Stop. I think she's related to John, a possible granddaughter. Stop. It's important that I hear back. Stop. On my way home. Stop. Send information there. Stop. Emma."

The clerk took it down and read it back to her.

She nodded and asked, "How much?"

He quoted the price and she paid. *That will do it,* she thought and headed back to the train. Normally, she enjoyed the time alone reading and relaxing, but this time she wanted to know what was happening with that baby. *John must have someone on the way to get her. Jeremy! He got attached—how will he feel? Relieved she got her family or upset we couldn't adopt her? Could it be any baby or just this one at this time?* They would have to talk.

Days later, the train pulled into Chicago. Emma grabbed her bag and ran for the exit. She jumped the steps before anyone could start down. "Young man!" called the porter.

She didn't stop as she ran for the carriages. At the first one she saw, she jumped in and gave him her address. "There'll be a large tip if you get moving quickly," she told the driver. He immediately pulled out and started toward her home.

When they arrived, Emma paid the fee and the promised large tip. She took her bag, jumped out, and headed up the front stairs. She swung the door open and slammed it closed, announcing her arrival.

"What is all the noise?" complained her sister Dora as she came into the foyer. "Emma! You're home!" Dora ran over to hug her sister. After the hug, she pulled away and crinkled her nose. "Ugh. You need a bath."

"I agree," Emma said. "And I need to wash my hair!" She looked around. "But first, have I gotten any telegrams?"

"Yes," her sister said, walking over to a small table located by the staircase. "These came last week." She handed them to Emma and watched as she tore open the one on top.

"Who's that from?" Dora asked. She'd wanted to open them but had respected Emma's privacy.

Emma saw the first one was from Clair. She read quickly and looked at Dora. "I'd inquired about a baby we rescued. We were worried about finding identification on someone so little. Clair said the mother and father were able to identify several birthmarks on her. They took her almost immediately. That's a relief."

It seems *John can make things happen,* she thought.

Dora was frowning and asked, "What was a baby doing as part of this type of operation?"

"I thought the same thing, and I have some further news to share," Emma murmured. Before Dora could follow up, she opened the next telegram. "It's from Jeremy. He got back to the Pinkerton's base and started taking down the areas where the children were kept before moving them to the safe-houses. Looks like a very successful operation." *I wonder if he got to see the baby?*

"Good," said Dora. "These people are like bugs; they keep coming back."

"Yes. Clair has some ideas about that. Community centers like the ones we did here. More important is communication with the parents, especially the poorer ones who don't have anyone to watch their kids. We are also talking to the kids and telling them to stay in groups and watch out for one another."

"Will Clair and Thomas be gone long? That sound like a large project."

"The setup will take a while," Emma admitted. "Her people are in place at the houses and hopefully the identifications won't take long." She looked over at Dora with sudden tears in her eyes. "Do you know who helped set up the houses and take care of the kids?" she asked.

"No, who?" Dora asked, wondering why Emma was crying.

"The women we've helped at Clair's house. She just had to ask and they came. All of the safe-houses are being looked after by them. They're helping get the kids home safely."

Dora wiped her tears. "That's a good thing. Passing on the healing."

Emma dried her face on her sleeve and opened the final telegram. It was from Cole.

Dora noticed the telegram she was opening. "That one came just this morning."

Emma unfolded it. "There's a lot of information in this one," she said as she read. "John Harden was released!"

Dora gasped. She was aware of who and what he was.

"And," continued Emma, "Jacob Smith, the man behind the entire operation and John's man on the inside, was found hanging in his cell."

"Could John have been involved?"

"Yes, I think so." She looked up from the telegram and said, "Dora, that baby was John's granddaughter." Dora gasped in shock and Emma continued to ponder the timing of John's release and the death. She tapped the telegram on her hand.

"Well," said Dora, "good riddance. He was a horrible person!"

"Agreed," her sister said and grinned a slightly evil grin at Dora. "You know, if Cole and Jeremy were here, they'd say the process should have included a judge and jury to find him guilty and punish him."

"Blackmail with a baby. He deserved nothing less," Dora said matter-of-factly.

"Yes."

With that statement, Emma started to climb the stairs and Dora called out in frustration, "You can't leave me with no more explanation than that."

"After my bath," her sister said, not turning around. "Then I'll tell all."

Dora watched her go up and shook her head. *I'll corner her this evening.*

Emma hurriedly undressed and prepared her bath. All she could think of was getting clean. The water was hot and she reclined in the tub with her eyes closed. Time passed quickly and the water started to get cold. She grimaced and admitted to herself that it was time to get out. The towels were fluffy and warm, and she wrapped one around her hair and another around her body before pulling on her robe.

Emma moved slowly to her room and onto her bed. Once there, she took her time to towel dry her hair and brush it. Her energy had drained with each stroke and, when she finished, she laid down. She only meant to take a light nap, but when she woke up, she saw hours had passed.

Time for lunch, she thought. After pulling on a dress and petticoat, she pulled a brush through her hair and braided it, tying it with a red ribbon. Lastly, she pulled on her stockings and boots and headed downstairs.

Dora heard her coming down the stairs and went to wait for her at the bottom. "I have lunch ready; come into the kitchen."

"I wanted to send a telegram," Emma said, looking distracted as she headed toward the door.

"No." Her sister stopped her with a hand on her arm. "Eat first."

Emma looked at Dora's hand and then her face. She could see the beginnings of a slight frown and tightening lips. She wanted to pull away, but then her stomach growled. "There's your answer. Food first," Emma acknowledged as she followed Dora into the kitchen.

Ethyl, a kitchen helper, was wiping down the counters. "Hi, Ethyl," Emma greeted her. "Where's Amy?"

"She's upstairs changing sheets and putting clean towels in the bathrooms."

Emma sat at the table and Dora brought her a thick sandwich and an apple. While she ate, Dora asked, "What happened that made you believe John's related to that baby?"

"It's the only thing that makes sense. John told Jacob to shut the operation down and kill his sister. It should have ended there."

"But?"

"But it continued and John didn't want it to."

"But he was forced to accept it."

"I think so. It was obvious, when we caught Jacob, that it was his operation and not John's."

"And you think the baby was being used to keep John in line?"

"Yes. But I wonder why not kill Jacob sooner? The baby must have kept him in their control."

"And once the baby was safe?"

"He got rid of Jacob."

"How did he find out that she had been rescued in the raid?" her sister asked.

"It could have been anyone; John has a far reach," Emma said simply.

"And you think he used the vacation for you and Jeremy to keep you from realizing what was happening?"

"Yes."

"Did you know it when you went on vacation?"

"I suspected something," Emma admitted.

"Then why go?"

"Jeremy and I needed the time away. The entire operation was weighing on us."

Dora nodded. "Why kill Jacob now if they had him in custody?" she asked.

"John doesn't like loose ends."

CHAPTER 11

Jeremy stepped down the steps and off the train. Looking around, he saw Thomas walking toward him.

"Thank you for picking me up," he called.

Thomas smiled. "We received Emma's telegram. It's good to see you. How was the vacation?"

"Good."

"Ready to go to the house?" he asked.

"Yes."

"Want help with your bag?"

"No, I got it."

Thomas had a carriage waiting for them. He was driving, as they wanted to keep people from knowing what the house was being used for. They kept the conversation light as they made their way there. He pulled in and they made their way to the front door. It opened, revealing Clair.

"Jeremy! How good to see you!" He leaned in and kissed her on the cheek. She smiled softly and stepped back to let them in.

The house was significantly quieter than the last time he'd

visited. "How many kids are still here?" he asked, looking around.

"Once we got the pictures, the kids were identified quickly. Almost all were picked up," she said.

Jeremy was afraid to ask but forced himself to say, "And the baby?"

Thomas looked at Clair. She answered, "Why don't we go into the sitting room." Jeremy and Thomas followed her and they sat. Tea and cakes were set up on the small table.

Jeremy didn't want food; he wanted to know if the baby girl was alive. "Did she not survive? I thought she was stable when we left."

"Jeremy, no!" Clair said as she moved to sit by him. "We just wanted you to relax before we told you." His eyes went wide and she blurted out, "She's been picked up by her parents."

"Picked up," he said. He was set on the idea of adoption but felt a sense of relief that she'd gone home to her family. A smile returned to his face and he inquired, "Could I have some tea?"

"Of course," Clair said as she took a cup and saucer and poured it for him.

They watched him drink. Thomas asked, "You're all right with the news? You had wanted to see her?"

"I did, but I'm happier that she's with her family. How were they able to prove who they were?"

"We were nervous about that," admitted Thomas, and Clair nodded. "Per Emma's direction, we checked the baby for any identifying marks."

"She had a birthmark, almost perfectly round, located on her upper right leg," supplied Thomas.

"The people that took her were able to identify it?" Jeremy asked.

"Yes, and other things like hair and eye color," Clair added.

"And the baby's reaction to the mother, she laughed when she took her into her arms," Thomas reminded her.

Jeremy felt a weight lift off his shoulders. "So, tell me who's left to be picked up?"

Clair said, "Two little boys. The Pinkertons found their parents and they're on their way to pick them up. They should be here in a few days."

"What will you do then?" asked Jeremy.

"Close the house and head home," Thomas replied.

"You've done an amazing job here."

"Thank you."

"Will you be staying with us long?" Clair asked.

Jeremy looked contemplative. "No, just a few days, and then I think I'll go to the other houses and see if anything else is needed. I'll also check in with Cole and the other Pinkerton operatives."

"We love having you," said Clair, and Thomas nodded his agreement.

"Would you like to meet the boys?" Thomas asked and stood up.

"Yes," Jeremy said and followed his lead.

Thomas took him outside to where the boys were playing in the yard.

The days passed quickly and, as Jeremy was in his room packing to leave, Thomas entered.

"We just got a telegram from Emma."

Jeremy looked up curiously. "Is it from Chicago?" He hoped she had made it back home safely.

"No," said Thomas. "It looks like it's from New York."

"Here? Why wouldn't she tell me she was coming here before going home?" Jeremy asked. "May I read it?"

"I don't think Clair would mind," he said.

"Mind what?" Clair asked, walking the baby Mary Elizabeth in with her.

"A telegram from Emma," explained Thomas.

"No, go ahead and read it," she said as she moved to sit in the chair nearest the bed.

"Emma says the baby girl is John's granddaughter!" Jeremy read aloud.

Clair felt faint. "The mother is his daughter?"

"It appears so."

Clair asked, "Did we do the wrong thing, giving the girl to her?"

"No," said Thomas. "It's her baby. Who her father is shouldn't matter."

"I think it might," mused Jeremy. "She may be the reason the operation was allowed to go on as long as it did. John didn't like it and wanted it shut down. He would have known what was happening in his business. It must have been blackmail."

"It was a good thing we found her and got her back to her mom?" Clair asked.

"Yes, I think the abductions will finally be shut down."

CHAPTER 12

Jeremy got to the next safe house and found a similar situation; they were getting ready to close it up. The children had successfully returned to their homes. It was at the third house that he found Cole.

"Jeremy, finally! I've been trying to locate you for the last week."

They hugged. "It's good to see you, Pops. Is there news? Something I missed?"

His father communicated the information he had sent to Emma, that John Harden had been released and Jacob had hung himself in the prison.

"That's a lot of information," Jeremy acknowledged. "Emma sent me a telegram; she indicates the baby girl was probably John Harden's granddaughter."

"Hmm," said Cole contemplatively. "I hope that truly shuts down this type of operation."

"Me too."

What does this mean for John? Cole thought. *Will he start up somewhere else now? I think he may be a focus in the future.*

CHAPTER 13

$\mathcal{A}$ few weeks later, while Jeremy and Cole were busy closing out the case, Emma was settling back into her work and family life.

Breakfast that morning was ongoing and noisy; Jake was talking about his latest photography project, and everyone else was talking about their day. A knock sounded at the door. Emma wiped her mouth and stood, "I'll go get it." She hoped it was news that Jeremy and Cole were headed home. A knock sounded again and she quickly opened the door, finding the very thing she had hoped for: a telegram. She took it and tipped the courier and, once the door was closed, tore it open and quickly read it.

"Please come. Hugo took mine and Evelyn's youngest daughters and will not say where they are. Don't contact me, just come. Please afternoon only, will have a bike on the porch if he is gone. Signed Mrs. Banks." Emma had expected this communication at some point. The offer had been made a couple of years ago during another case. She wanted to give her a way out of her situation if it was needed.

And here it is, she thought. *He shouldn't have involved the children.*

She walked back into the dining room to finish her breakfast. Dora and baby Lottie were the only ones still at the table. "Who was it from? Jeremy?" she asked.

"No," Emma murmured, thinking about the telegram. "It's from the woman I visited in Ohio a while back; the bigamy case."

"I remember. You didn't expose the husband at that time?"

"No, we got what we wanted: a divorce for our client. At that time, the arrangement with the other two wives seemed to be working for them."

"Didn't only one of them know that?"

"Yes, and she's the one I gave the card to, in case something changed."

"Did you think she might change her mind?"

"Yes," Emma said, thinking about that time and the woman's reluctance to take her card. "Hugo Banks seemed too volatile to keep something like this a secret."

"Did she mention anything else?"

"Not much, but he has taken the two youngest girls. My theory? A new wife."

"A third?" Dora said, astounded at this man.

"No, I think an *only*. Mrs. Banks wants me to go there as soon as possible." Something just occurred to her. "The other wife must also know what's going on."

"When will you leave?" Dora asked, knowing that her sister would help anyone who needed her. *Another case involving children,* Dora thought. Will *this be too much for her after the previous case?*

"As soon as I can get a train ticket," Emma said absently. "And I'll have to notify Mr. Pennington that I've been called out of town."

"Do you have anything pressing?" Dora asked, wondering if Tim would need to fill Emma's position temporarily.

The lawyer's office where she worked as an investigator was involved in a divorce case. Emma had completed her background checks and wouldn't be needed until they went to trial. "I should have a few weeks to spare. You might ask Tim to check if clerical work is needed while I'm gone."

"I'll do that," Dora said. Tim was out meeting with new clients for their business. "When is Jeremy due back?"

"Not for another week or two, depending on travel."

"Did you want to take Savannah with you this time?" Savannah had been involved in this case previously.

Emma shook her head. "No, there's no need. I will go by Clair's office on the way to pick up my train ticket."

Dora reached out her hand to Emma and asked, "Is there something dangerous going on?"

Emma pressed her lips into a thin line. "Maybe, but I need to keep this quiet for now. Mrs. Banks said no contact, so whatever the situation, her mail might be monitored."

Dora slowly dropped her hand. "Will you contact the local police in case you need help?"

"I will," Emma promised and headed upstairs. Once there, she changed into her split skirt and descended the stairs. She went through the kitchen where baking was ongoing. Amy and Ethyl were busy with dinner preparations. Dora was keeping baby Lottie busy with some dough.

She kissed Dora on the cheek and grabbed an apple on her way out. Her bike was stored in a small building near the back door. Walking it around to the front, she climbed on and headed to the telegraph office. A hotel room would be needed as well as a train ticket.

The sun was bright and it warmed her face as she rode. It was early spring, the snow had finally melted, and the roads were fairly easy to navigate. She could see the trees were starting to get their leaves back. The sky was blue and the air clear. It was still early afternoon and it was a wonderful day to be out.

As she rode, the case details ran through her head. The two wives involved were in their thirties and each had two girls each of about the same age. One thing she'd learned about the husband, Hugo Banks, was that he liked things to stay the same. Same types of wives, same layouts on houses, same everything.

Her errands completed, she headed to Mr. Pennington's office. She entered quickly and waved to Ethan. He was reviewing files on his desk and didn't look up to greet her.

"Is Mr. Pennington in his office?" she asked, stopping in front of his desk.

"He is," he commented, and when she headed that way, he stopped her. "He has someone in there with him."

She nodded and moved back to put her bike in the closet. Reaching for the handle on her office door, she heard Mr. Pennington's door open. She glanced over quickly and saw who the client was. *Well, what a coincidence.*

The gentleman noticed her and walked over. "Emma, it's good to see you."

She looked over at the client. "Mr. Gilmore, how are you and your family?" Mr. Gilmore's wife was the first wife to Mr. Banks and the one who had started it all.

He smiled broadly. "We're doing well."

"Please send Mrs. Gilmore my regards."

"I will, goodbye." Mr. Pennington walked him to the office door.

She waited until he had closed it and approached him. "Mr. Pennington, do you have time to meet with me?"

"Yes, of course, follow me."

"I will get my files and join you."

She retrieved the files and, once they were in his office, she closed the door behind them. He sat at the round table in his office, and she joined him there.

"Do you have an update on my case?" he asked.

"Yes, I have the background with me." She pulled out the reports and handed them to him.

He looked through the information. "This looks complete. We'll be doing voir dire in another month."

She marked the date in her notebook. When she didn't leave, he looked over and asked, "Is there something else you want to discuss?"

"Yes, sir. The Hugo Banks case we were involved in." The case had been settled by Mr. Pennington, where he had used the threat of exposing Banks' other two families to get him to sign the annulment papers for their client, Mrs. Gilmore.

"Involving Mr. and Mrs. Gilmore?" he asked. When she nodded, he continued. "We didn't disclose the bigamy to the police or his current wives. Has there been a development that could affect the Gilmores?"

"Not directly," she said. She took a deep breath and started again. "This is about one of the other wives. I gave one of them my card if she wanted out."

"Did she?" he asked.

"Not at that time," she admitted. "But this morning I received a telegram asking for my help."

"May I see it?" he asked, holding out his hand.

"Yes, of course." She pulled it out of her pocket and handed it to him.

He read it silently, then he looked up at her and said, "Mr. Banks is not a nice man."

"No, and sadly, both women seemed happy with him."

"What do you think is happening?"

"New start, new wife," she said simply.

He nodded and sat back. "Are you concerned I'll try to stop you?"

"No, sir, but I wanted to let you know my plans. And the Gilmores shouldn't come up in this case. It should be specific to the current wives."

"Yes, that divorce is final. Once she married Mr. Gilmore officially, society gave a pass for any indiscretion. Go get those kids and women out of that situation. You let me know if there are any legal concerns that need to be resolved."

"I'm not sure there'll be any divorces, but I think the property settlement will require some assistance."

"Give me both ladies' names and addresses. I'll be waiting for you to contact me once they have Banks in custody. Oh, and you might need these," he said and walked over to his desk to retrieve a file from his drawer.

"Thank you, Mr. Pennington," she said, taking the papers. She opened the file and saw it was the marriage licenses they had obtained in the first case. *This will come in handy.* She reached out her hand to him.

He took it and said warmly, "Be safe. Keep us up to date as you can."

"I will." She was going anyway, regardless of his wishes, but she was glad he agreed with her plan.

She went out to the lobby and was surprised to see Savannah with Ethan. They had met on a case at Christmas and had been inseparable ever since.

"Savannah, hi!" Emma greeted the woman. "Are you out during the day?" she teased.

"Yes, we vampires have to get out occasionally." Savannah worked at a theatre as technical staff. While a show was going on, she would sleep until late into the day.

Emma smiled slightly and moved back to her office.

"Emma," Savannah called, "I'm actually here to see you."

"You are? I thought..." Emma started.

She smiled at Ethan and said, "Him? No, he's just a bonus."

Ethan's face flushed but he looked happy.

"Come into my office," Emma directed. Savannah followed her in and sat down on the corner of her desk.

"Dora told me where you're going," she said, no expression showing on her face.

Emma frowned and Savannah added hastily, "She told only me since I was involved last time. She thought I might want to know. I want to go with you. I know I can help."

Emma thought about that and admitted, "It would be nice to have someone along; you were invaluable last time. But I also don't want you to have to leave your show mid-run." She knew Savannah was running a rather large show at this time.

"Yeah, there is that. Are you sure it's okay to go alone?"

"Yes," she said firmly.

"But if something changes, you'll let me know?"

"Of course." Emma was drumming her fingers on her lips and said, "You know, I could use some support. If we need to take the older kids or need to hide them, having wigs would help. Change them into boys when everyone is looking for girls."

"How old are they?" Savannah asked, thinking about her wigs. She had seen the girls at the time but didn't remember much about them.

"Ten and eleven, petite," Emma replied, trying to remember what they looked like.

"That'll work. If they're a little loose that's okay. I'll include pins to help keep them on. When will you be leaving?"

"I was hoping today, but if needed I can get a ticket for the morning."

"Tomorrow would be easier for me and, with the extra time, I can provide pants and shirts from our costume department."

Emma thought about that. "Okay. I want to get there fast, but I need to be prepared." She reached down and picked up her bag. "I'll walk out with you."

They exited her office and Emma went to retrieve her bike.

Ethan watched. "Leaving early?" he asked.

"I have some work out of town. Mr. Pennington knows where I'll be," she confirmed.

He looked at her and then at Savannah but didn't ask any questions. "Safe travels," he commented.

"I have to go also," Savannah said. "I have to go get some things organized for Emma." Ethan knew she was one of Emma's specialists.

"See you tonight after the show?" he asked.

"Yes," she said, walking over to him. "Meet me backstage." She leaned over and kissed him quickly.

Emma and Savannah left together and as they walked downstairs. Savannah asked, "Do you think the other wife knows now?"

Emma nodded. "Yes, I think so. He's taken the youngest girls from both families and hasn't told the mothers where they are. I'll find out more when I get there. The Mrs. Banks who contacted me doesn't trust their telegraph office."

"What are you thinking? What's going on?"

"He took the little ones and is starting a new life."

"Any evidence so far?"

"Not yet, just a feeling at this time. It does sound like a restart."

"Why now, I wonder? Did something happen?"

"I don't know," Emma said. Once they reached the bottom of the stoop, she set down the bike and walked it as they continued to talk.

"I'm going to get the items you asked for and then head home," said Savannah.

"I'll see you there. I need to go to the telegraph office to secure the hotel and the train station."

Savannah waved and headed to the right, Emma directed her bike to the left and rode the few blocks to the telegraph station. She parked it outside and entered.

"May I help you?" the clerk asked.

"Yes. I have to send a telegram to a hotel in Cleveland, Ohio. The Weddell House at Bank and Superior."

"Got it. What's the message?" he asked, pencil ready.

"Arriving tomorrow night. Stop. Will need a room for three days. Stop."

"Is that all?" he asked.

"Just my name. Emma Evans."

She had stayed at the hotel before this and knew they wouldn't share her information.

Next was the train station. The clerk confirmed a ticket was available for the next morning. There would be no return ticket, as she wasn't sure how long the case would take. He told her the amount, and she paid it. The cashier thanked her, and she pocketed her train ticket. *I'm all set for tomorrow.*

At home, Emma went into the house through the kitchen. Ethyl and Amy sat at the table, taking a break before dinner. "Hi," they greeted her.

"Savannah got home a few minutes ago; she said to tell you she is in the attic sewing room," Amy told her.

"Thank you!" She went quickly into the foyer and up the stairs to the fourth floor.

Savannah looked up from the wig she was holding. "I've fashioned the wigs so we can put the hair up in them." She showed Emma the netting on the inside.

Emma went over to examine what she had added, "These are perfect. You won't get into trouble for loaning me these?"

"No, of course not, I'll put the things back when you return." She checked the time. "I have just enough time to finish these. Why don't you take a look at the clothes over there on the bed?"

Emma went over to them and evaluated the sizes. "I think these are just about right."

"Great, I'll put these in a bag as soon as I am done."

"Thank you for helping out. I'll go get my items organized."

She headed down to her room to pack. A variety of clothes would be needed for this case; the situation could require pants, skirts, or a business jacket.

A knock sounded at the door. "Come in," Emma called.

"Getting organized?" Dora asked as she entered. "Will you leave tonight?"

"No, I'll leave on the early train tomorrow. That way I can get in after Hugo has gone to work."

"How will you make sure he isn't there?"

"If a bicycle is on the porch, that means Hugo isn't home."

"Be careful."

"I will be and I won't make a move without data. There are kids involved and the wives need to be protected."

Savannah dropped the bag off on her way to the theatre. "Did you get enough sleep?" Emma asked her friend, watching her closely.

"Yes, plenty. Don't worry about me. Let me know if I need to make a quick trip to see you."

"I'll let you know," she promised.

Dinner was still an hour away and Emma finished getting organized for her trip. She looked around her room, at hers and Jeremy's things. The bookcase separating their rooms was just in place to protect their privacy from anyone who might get curious. She laughed and thought, *Anyone who knows us would know this room is shared.* Jeremy didn't keep his clothes on her side, but the table on his side of the bed contained all of his current reading —novels, case studies into criminal minds. *We do have a lot in common*, she thought.

On the dresser were pictures of Mama, Abbey, and Papa. And one of Papa and Cole. She missed Jeremy so much. Separation was hard, especially after they had finally had a long break together. She'd never expected to want to be with someone every night, but he was her family now.

The evening went by quietly and Emma read and went to

bed early. The next morning, she dressed in a dark skirt and a pink blouse with lace at the cuffs, then shrugged on a longish pink jacket. She sat on the bed and pulled on her black boots. Her knives were in place in her leg scabbard and the larger one was hidden in her hat. She had replaced her bowler with a more feminine basic black one. The key feature was that it could be outfitted so the knife could be stowed in the side and easily accessed.

Her bowler hat, made for her by Miss May and Miss Marjorie, was a treasured item and when it had started to show wear, she had retired it. It sat on the table across from her bed. She would forever be in debt to the two ladies who'd taught her how to throw knives and get out of tight situations.

Her bag was ready and by the door. She grabbed it and made her way downstairs. Once in the foyer, she set it by the door and headed to the kitchen.

In the early morning hours, Ethyl and Amy were already busy baking pastry for breakfast and getting organized for the day. Amy heard her come in, "Emma, good morning." Ethyl nodded from the stove. Her attention was taken by the frying bacon.

"Would you like some breakfast?" Amy asked.

"I should," she said. "I have a train to catch this morning."

"Sit down, sit down," Amy said and brought her bread, butter, and fruit to eat. They were Emma's favorite breakfast. "Dora left a note to make you lunch for the train. It's in that bag on the table," she said, nodding to it.

Emma looked over at it. "Thank you, I'll take it with me."

She finished her breakfast, took the bag, and headed toward the dining room. She called over her shoulder, "Tell Dora I left."

"You can tell her yourself," her sister called from the dining room doorway.

Emma ran over and hugged her. "I didn't want to wake you," she said.

"I didn't want to miss you," Dora countered, smoothing Emma's hair back. "You're sure you want to go on your own?"

"I am," Emma assured her. "Savannah helped me with disguises for the girls, in case I need them." She glanced at her watch and said, with a bit of worry in her tone, "The situation may require me to transport them to Chicago."

"You think it'll be necessary to bring them back here?" Dora asked. She was surprised that the girls wouldn't be taken home to their mothers.

"Not here," Emma qualified, "but close. I want them to have access to Mr. Pennington. I think the best place will be the safe house. I'll need to check there and make sure I don't surprise them with visitors."

Dora nodded. "Yes, you're right." She glanced at her time-piece and said with a frown, "But the time. If you go there, you won't have time to make the train. Would you like me to go for you?"

"I'd appreciate that," she said, glad to have that off her list.

"Who should they expect?" Dora asked.

"Right now, I'm not sure. I am hoping that we get all the girls and their mothers out of Cleveland safety. We need to get them away from Banks."

"Then that's what I'll tell them," she said firmly.

Emma kissed her sister on the cheek and walked quickly to the foyer. She put on her hat and picked up the bag and headed down to the stoop. Her bike would be faster, but she had nowhere to leave it at the station. Regretfully, she left it behind and walked the few blocks to access the trolley to take her to the train station. Jumping off at her stop, she checked her pocket for her ticket.

She didn't have a cabin assigned for this short-day trip and moved to settle into the seats in the third-class section. On the way to Ohio, she made notes of what she wanted to ask the two Mrs. Banks in her notebook.

The train arrived and she disembarked dressed in her female clothes. *Hotel first,* she thought. She wanted to settle in and wash up before heading over to the second wife's house. The telegram had specified she should arrive before the afternoon.

Hugo must come home for lunch, she thought.

The hotel she'd chosen was large and she could blend in with the crowds. It would provide the anonymity she needed. They had her room ready and would send lunch up. She took her bag and went to the room. There she washed, ate, and took a cab over to Mrs. Banks' house.

As she approached the neighborhood, she remembered the house clearly. It was the same. *The man likes things the same,* she thought again as she looked at the perfect yard and the bright colors on the house. *I bet the other house has also stayed similar.*

The main difference from her last visit was the children weren't in the yard. It gave a more solemn look to the home. *The bike is there,* she thought and moved toward the stairs to the front door. She knocked a few times and waited.

It opened suddenly, revealing the second Mrs. Banks. "You came!" she exclaimed and pulled her into the foyer.

"Of course, I told you I would," Emma said and allowed herself to be guided.

"Yes, you did." She hugged her tightly. "I'm so happy you're here."

Emma stayed where she was for a moment and then pulled back. "We have a limited time. Talk to me."

"We'll be more comfortable in the sitting room," the other woman said, leading Emma into the room.

They sat on the couch. Emma pulled out her notebook and laughed suddenly. "I don't know your first name. You were Mrs. Banks on my last visit."

The circumstances of their visit were serious, but this comment also made Mrs. Banks laugh. "Yes, that's true. We didn't have to get to know each other. I'm Isabella or Izzy."

"Okay, Izzy, let's get started. What's going on that changed your mind so suddenly?"

Izzy sat back and began to explain. "I was so settled, even with having to share him. I could get used to the limits on our relationship and NO changes to the house. I kept telling myself that the kids are happy, so I'm happy."

"So, what changed?"

"It was little things at first: out-of-town trips, money being tighter than we were used to. And. . ." She paused and her eyes filled with tears.

Emma gave her a moment to gather herself and then prompted, "Go on."

"The mail. We started getting mail from an unknown woman."

"Did you ask him about it?"

"I did, but he said it was just a mix-up. He brushed me and my questions aside."

"Was it a mix up?" Emma asked. It was doubtful from what she knew of the man.

"No, I don't think so. And it went on for a few months."

"Do you have any of the letters that were sent here?"

"No, that's another thing. Hugo took them immediately and I couldn't locate them later."

"Couldn't you have looked at one when it was delivered?" she asked, thinking he would be at work.

"No, he started coming home at the time the mail was delivered."

"What was his excuse for being here during a work day?"

She sighed and said, "The mail is delivered at lunchtime."

"Giving him the perfect excuse. What names were on the letters?"

"Catherine Banks."

"Hmm," she said. *Another clue about a new wife.*

Izzy had seen the same thing and started to cry again. "I think he's starting over with another family."

"Why?" Emma asked, even though she'd thought the same thing.

Izzy sniffed and put her tissue to her eyes. "Our relationship has changed; he makes time for the kids but not for me."

Emma asked the hard question, "Why not just let him go?"

"That's what I called you here for. It's time."

"What about his other wife? Is she aware of you and your family?" Emma asked. The other Mrs. Banks would need to have input if she was going to help with both children.

"Evelyn!" Izzy called, rather than answering.

The other Mrs. Banks walked out of the kitchen, wiping her hands.

"You!" Emma said. "You do know?"

"Yes," Evelyn said quietly as she sat down across from them on a powder blue chair.

"How did this happen?" Emma asked, waving her hands at both of them.

They looked at each other and back at her. "We've known for a while. It was our older daughters; they became friends at school and started to visit with us. The similarities are striking between the two."

"The houses! Did they notice?"

"Yes. They immediately saw the houses were the same and mentioned it to us," explained Evelyn. Izzy nodded.

"How did you keep this fact away from your husband?" Emma asked incredulously.

"He travels," Evelyn said, her mouth dipping downward. "It was easy. Once our daughters told us how similar our houses were and I saw the girls together. I called Izzy and asked her out to tea."

"It just came out," Izzy said. "I was tired of being the only person who knew what was going on."

"Did you know Izzy knew before you?" Emma asked Evelyn. *Had she been angry?*

"No. I found out that day," she confirmed.

"Did you have any anger about being the only adult not to know?" Emma asked.

Evelyn held out her hand to Izzy, and Izzy took it. She clasped it tightly. "No, it's hard enough for women today and we don't want to fight each other."

"How long ago was this?"

"About a year," Evelyn admitted and Izzy nodded in agreement.

"We agreed to try to make it work for the sake of the kids," Izzy said.

"Still keeping everything separate?"

"Yes, but now we could track his movements," Izzy said.

Emma raised her brows in question.

Evelyn explained. "We started keeping schedules of when he was with one family or another."

"Did you find anything out of the ordinary?" Emma asked, wondering how they were willing to live this very different kind of life.

Evelyn replied, "At first, the traveling could be confirmed as being at each of our homes."

"Then, what happened?"

"We started to notice longer trips, ones that included neither home," Izzy said.

"How long was this going on?"

"We worked it out about four months ago," Evelyn said.

"And why now? Why call me at this moment?"

"Hugo's taken our younger daughters," Izzy and Evelyn said at the same time.

"Both of them?" she confirmed.

"Yes," Evelyn answered, her tears starting to fall.

Emma mulled that over. "Legally, he can take them

anywhere. He *is* the father of both girls."

"Yes," Izzy said.

Emma continued. "And the police will say that as well." She stood and walked to the mantel and turned back to them. "When was this? When did he take them?"

"It was a few weeks ago. He said he wanted to take my daughter on a trip to New York. She was so excited and wanted time alone with her dad," Evelyn said.

"Did you know he was taking both girls at that time?" Emma asked Evelyn.

"No! I had no idea."

"Has he ever done this before, taken the girls together?" she asked, looking at them both.

"No, he always kept the families separate," Izzy said.

"Did you talk at that time? Were you aware that both girls were leaving with him?"

"We didn't know both were going; we had drifted back to our own homes and lives. We didn't keep regular contact at that time."

Emma understood and asked, "What happened then?"

"Then he came back without my daughter," said Evelyn.

"And mine," Izzy said.

"Who did he say he left them with?" Emma asked.

"He didn't," Izzy muttered.

"What?" asked Emma, surprised.

"He said he just left them with a relative," Evelyn clarified.

"He wouldn't say who it was?"

"No, he wouldn't. Only that she was happy there. And that he wouldn't bring her back," Izzy said.

"When he refused to bring my daughter back, I went to see Izzy," said Evelyn.

"And you confirmed that both daughters were gone?" They nodded, and Emma continued. "What about your other daughters? Where are they now?"

"They're away at school, the same school," said Izzy, answering for both of them. "I'm happy they're not here."

"That won't stop him," muttered Emma. She looked at them. "You will need to notify the school that they're not to be removed without your permission."

"I'm not sure that will work," Evelyn responded.

"Why?"

"Because they won't stop my husband from picking them up. As you said, he is their father."

Emma drummed her fingers on her lips, planning. "Then we need to get them before he can."

"You're going to get them?" they asked at the same time.

"Yes, it's the only way; if Hugo is starting a new family, he'll also want those two."

"Will there be concerns with the law on this? Even with our permission?" asked Izzy.

"I wouldn't think so, not if the school recognizes your authority." She checked her timepiece. "You mentioned we have limited time today?"

"Yes," Izzy answered, looking at the watch pinned to her dress. "He'll be here at noon, right on the dot."

"Then I'll leave now. Can you give me the address and each of you write a letter so I can pick the girls up from the school?"

Both women agreed and Izzy went to get writing paper for her and Evelyn.

"Be sure to use Molly Cooper as my name," Emma directed.

They both wrote quickly and handed her the letters.

"Where will you take them?" Izzy asked, suddenly worried.

"It's probably best I don't tell you now. I will keep them safe."

"What should we do in the meantime?" asked Evelyn, worrying the handkerchief in her hands.

"Act like nothing is wrong, be as normal as possible," Emma directed.

"That will be hard," Izzy said.

"Just remember who you're protecting," Emma suggested.

"Yes, you're right. Will you be, okay?" Izzy asked Evelyn.

"Yes, I am, knowing you're with me," Evelyn said, taking Izzy's hand. They had bonded over their circumstance and had become friends.

Emma took the notes and placed them in her pocket. "I'm cutting it tight on time."

"Me too," Evelyn said.

"Too close, I think," Emma said as she looked out the window. Hugo was walking up to the house with a smile on his face. He stopped by the mailbox and seemed to be waiting for someone. It wasn't long until a postman showed up. Emma kept watching. The postman walked up and handed over his mail. Hugo flipped through the pile quickly and removed a letter. Placing it in his pocket, he grinned and continued talking to the man.

"Go," whispered Izzy.

Emma walked quickly out of the back of the house and pulled her hat low over her face. Evelyn exited with her, took Emma's hand, and pulled her along through the back of several houses. She seemed to know her way around. Once they slowed, Emma turned to her. "Have you done this before?"

"More than a few times," she admitted. Emma followed her closely.

"How did you know he wouldn't go to your house?" she asked.

"It isn't my day. He has all of that special mail delivered to Izzy's place, so I don't see him much during the day."

They made it a few blocks and were able to move to the main streets as they got closer to her house. Emma said, "You're brave, the both of you."

"No, I'm not," the other woman said, "but Izzy is. And smart. She figured this all out first."

They made it to her house. Emma stood studying it. Again, it surprised her that Evelyn's house looked identical to Izzy's.

"Weird right?" Evelyn asked.

"A little," she admitted as they entered the house. Green! The inside of the house had a different color from the other one! She was shocked and looked toward Evelyn. "Green?" she asked.

"Yes, a lovely shade, don't you think?" Evelyn looked around with a rather evil smile.

"When did you do it?" Emma asked. The light green color was in the foyer and went up the stairs and into the sitting room.

"Back when I found out about Izzy"

Rotating, she looked at everything. "I love it! What did Hugo say?"

"What do you think he said?" she asked wryly.

"He didn't like it," she guessed.

"No, he wanted it fixed immediately."

"But it's still green."

"It is and it will remain so," Evelyn said, showing backbone.

"Even when the children are returned?" Emma asked, wondering about the upcoming changes.

Evelyn turned to face her. "Change will take place and the biggest change will be the removal of my husband!"

Emma didn't say anything. Instead, she checked her pocket. "I need to find a place to rent a wagon."

"Why not a carriage? It would be faster."

Emma didn't answer, not wanting to share more details. When she didn't answer, Evelyn walked over to her writing table and scribbled out an address, and handed it to her.

Evelyn hugged Emma. "Be careful," she said.

Emma hugged her back. "I'll be in touch once the girls are safely away."

"Once you get the older girls, what will you do next?"

"I'm not sure," she admitted. The older girls were her priority now.

CHAPTER 14

$\mathcal{B}$ack at Izzy's house

Hugo Banks entered and went to the kitchen, where Izzy worked on lunch. There were no changes in his menu; he would want a thick ham sandwich with fresh fruit on the side and a glass of milk.

He didn't say anything as he sat at the table and waited for her to serve him. It took all of her energy to restrain herself from dumping it in his lap.

He wasn't aware of the tension; he took a bite of his sandwich and casually said, "I'm taking a long trip this weekend. I'll be leaving on Friday."

She did what Emma said not to do and tearfully asked, "How long will you be away? Will you see Marcy? Can you bring her back?" She hadn't meant to say that last statement and, when she saw the anger build on his face, she tried to backtrack quickly. "I, uh, I just miss her, and I'll miss you." She walked over to him and touched his cheek.

The motion of her hand seemed to distract him. He even smiled when he told her, "I'll be back, but Marcy is having a nice time, so I'm going to leave her where she is."

"Whatever you say, dear," Izzy murmured and kissed him. She would do whatever she had to do to protect her and Evelyn's daughters. *Emma, please get them before he does.*

CHAPTER 15

First the hotel, Emma thought as she left Evelyn's home. *I'll need to check out and get my luggage. And food. I'll have to take some things that will last through tomorrow. Growing girls could be hungry.* With that thought in mind, she approached the desk at her hotel. A clerk stood behind the counter in a crisp white shirt, red vest, and jacket. He looked up as she approached. "Yes, how can I help you?" he asked.

"I'll be checking out," Emma said.

"Your name?"

"Emma Evans," she supplied.

He found her information in his card file. He frowned at her. "You were going to be with us for a few days. Are you cutting your visit short?"

"I am," she confirmed. "I may be back soon."

"Please try to let us know so that we have a room available," he said professionally.

"I will, thank you."

"Will you be gathering your things now?"

"Yes, and I have a list of food items I'd like to order from the restaurant. Could you have them prepared for me? And I'll need it packed for a trip."

He held out his hand for the list, which she supplied, and he glanced at it. "We can have this organized in about an hour. Is that enough time for you?"

"Yes, I'll go up to my room. Can you deliver it there?"

"That should work. Please drop off your key here on your way out."

The elevator was to the left of the desk and she headed toward it. She and two others watched the numbers tick down to their floor. The doors opened and the operator waved them in. Emma stepped into the back and waited as other people filed into the small space. The elevator moved slowly up to her floor. When it reached her floor and the door opened, she said, "Excuse me." The people shuffled around to let her off.

Her room was a few doors down from the elevator. She opened the door and went in. Looking around, she didn't see anything out of place. Her bag was by the door. She picked it up and started to fill it. When she got to her boy's clothes, she thought, *No, I'll need to be dressed as a lady to pick up the girls.*

She pulled out the letters from the moms and reviewed what they wrote.

Molly Cooper will be picking up my daughter Evie. She is needed at home. She has my permission and will act as her guardian.

She opened the other letter and saw it was similar. *Good,* she thought, *keep it simple.*

The hour passed quickly and a knock sounded at the door. Snapping her bag closed, she went to open it. It was her food delivery.

"Your lunch," the young bellman said and handed it to her. She looked at the basket and her bag. "Can you help me downstairs with that and my bag?"

"I can," he said. She did a final sweep through the room and walked to the door with her bag. "Let me take that," he said, indicating the bag she carried.

She smiled and handed it to him. Walking to the bed, she pulled on her light coat and picked up her hat. Turning back to the door, she said, "After you."

The bellman walked toward the elevator with her following closely behind. They stayed together on the ride down and to the front entrance. She handed him his tip and the key to her room.

"Will you need anything else?" he asked.

"No, thank you." The blacksmith was only a few blocks away. She picked up the bag and basket and headed that way. She patted her pocket and headed to find a wagon. She assumed that, if Hugo had the two little girls, he'd want to move the older two as soon as possible. The only thing on her side was surprise; she had to get to them first. She looked at the notes again. The girls were located at the Montgomery School for Girls.

Based on the instructions the moms had provided, she calculated the wagon trip would take ten hours. She could make it in one day, but she'd have to stop and rest herself and the horse. By tonight, she would be close and would be able to go to the school first thing tomorrow. She would have time to move the girls out of Hugo's reach.

The blacksmith sign was visible from her location. She'd have to be careful; she didn't know him and didn't know if she could trust him. The office was located beside the open areas where men were working. The sign indicated they shod horses and provided wagon rentals.

As she walked into the office, it didn't appear to be manned. She wandered out to the area where large open pits were set up and two men were working on projects. They were putting iron items into the fire and pulling them out. She waited, not wanting to disturb the dangerous work.

One of the men finished his work and stepped toward her. "Do you have a wagon and horse for rent?" she asked.

He looked over at her, rubbing his hair and then his large chest. "I might. Where do you want to go? And who's it for?"

"I need it for myself," she said firmly. "And I can't tell you where I'll be taking it."

This isn't the first time someone wouldn't give me a straight answer on what the wagon was needed for, he thought. Mulling that over, he asked, "How long will you have it?"

She thought quickly. "Four days maximum. I'll let you know where to pick it up."

"Hmm," he said, and finally added, "Come with me." They went back into the small office. "How do I know you'll let me know where it is?"

"You'll have to trust me on that," she said, her voice flat.

He sat on his stool. "Tell me what you really want this wagon for."

At that moment, two little girls ran into the room. He hugged them tightly to him. "Why aren't you in school?" he asked, his face transforming with his wide smile.

"Short day," the smaller one answered. "Ma said we could visit." He talked to them animatedly. Both girls shared their news and he sent them home to their mother.

Those girls are about the same age as the ones I am trying to protect. The truth, she thought, *I'll have to take a chance on him.* She made a decision and got up and closed the door to his office. They needed privacy for what she was planning to share. He raised his eyebrows as she took her seat again.

She started. "There are two little girls who need to be picked up before someone takes them."

He sat still at her pronouncement. Thoughts crossed his mind, but all he could say was, "What are you going to do with them?"

"Put them somewhere safe until their mothers can get to them."

"By yourself?" he scoffed.

"It's better if this operation is small. I can get them out and to a safe place."

His thoughts went to his girls and he nodded. "I'll help you, but I want the wagon back and it's gonna cost extra. I won't have it available while you're gone and I'll lose money on rentals from it."

"You'll get it back," she assured him, "and I can pay upfront."

He headed out to the back where the wagon and horses were kept. He turned slowly toward her. "Why don't you accompany me?"

Nodding, she followed him. As they neared the stable, she could tell it was kept in good condition, but a stable always had a certain smell. Her nose crinkled but she didn't comment. He walked the horse out.

Emma studied the horse. "Will she be able to make a long trip?"

"How long?"

"Nine to ten hours," she replied.

"Yes," he said as he patted the horse on the flanks. "Just stop for a break every hour or so. Watch her, you don't want to push her too much. She's solid and will make the trip. I will add her feed to the back and you need to make sure she has plenty of water."

"I'll keep that in mind," she promised him.

They exited the stable with the horse and he connected her to the wagon. Emma pulled money from her wallet and handed it to him. He shook his head. "No, I'll do this for you and those girls."

"But you said—"

"And now I'm changing my mind," he interrupted.

Once the wagon was ready, she asked, "Do you have any blankets?"

"Yes, we have some here." He didn't ask why but knew it was to cover the girls. The blankets were put in the back.

She climbed up, took the reins, and looked over at him. "Thank you." As she started to pull away, she warned, "You might have someone come by and ask if anyone took a wagon."

"I'll make sure they don't know it was you," he promised. "One thing, could you let me know when it's safe and that the girls are okay?"

"I will and I'll let you know where to pick up your wagon." She clicked her tongue at the horse and moved the wagon out.

She watched the horse as she rode away; breaks would be necessary. Once she was out of town, she slowed the wagon and pulled out the map she had picked up at the hotel. Even with additional breaks to rest, she was going to be at the school in the morning.

With late afternoon approaching, she pulled the wagon over into a meadow. There was a stream nearby and she pull down the bag of feed. The horse was unhooked from the wagon and tied loosely to a tree so she could get to fresh water and her feed. The area was covered with grass. The break refreshed both of them and she hooked the horse back up to continue her trip.

The weather was nice and the horse was easygoing. The day flowed into night and she found a wooded area to pull off into for them to rest. There was a stream nearby. She moved the horse's feed from the wagon and then tied the horse near the water. A fire wasn't needed; she didn't want any extra attention. She settled down in the back of the wagon and watched the night sky. *Jeremy, where are you tonight? Are we seeing the same sky?* she thought as she drifted off to sleep.

The next morning, she jerked awake. The morning mist had settled on her face. She wiped it off and sat up, looking around. This should be her last stop. They were just outside of the town where the school was located. The horse was well rested, but she'd need to work harder with the addition of two more passengers.

Her timepiece showed 8:00am. It was early and the school was probably just starting to open. She got up and stretched, her body stiff from sleeping in the wagon. Her baskets of food was nearby, she sat and pulled out a hard roll and some fruit. She grimaced when looking down at her wrinkled clothes. Thankfully, the area she had picked was blocked from the road by trees.

Her bag was in the back of the wagon; she opened it and took out a long black walking skirt, a white lace high-necked shirt, and her papa's jacket. It was oversized on her but would create a more polished image that the school would favor.

Her hair was taken out of a ponytail and pulled into a bun. *There*, she thought, *that should do it.* She checked the time, it was 8:15. The horse was rested and she led the easygoing mare back to her position on the wagon and hooked her up. The letters from the moms were in her side pocket. She patted them absently as she climbed into the driver's seat and then clicked to get the horse moving toward the school.

As it came into view, she saw there was a large area to park the wagon with a tie post to secure her horse. *It's certainly nice here,* she thought, looking around. It was all red brick with white sashes on the windows. The building looked inviting. The gardens looked well-tended and reached around the building. *Their day must have started,* she thought, not seeing any children outside.

The large stoop led into a long hallway. It gleamed, the wood polished and no dust to be found. Pictures of former deans hung on the wall and she glanced at them as she walked by. *A very austere bunch*, she thought. The office was ahead of her. She took a breath before opening the door, ready to be the person she was pretending to be.

Going straight to the desk, she stopped and the man there looked up. "Welcome to the Montgomery School for Girls. Is there something I can help you with?"

"Thank you. I'd like to speak to the director. Please."

The man frowned. "Our director is out and our assistant director is in charge. Do you have an appointment?"

"I do not," Emma admitted, "but it is very important that I speak to him."

"I'll have to see if he has time for you."

"Thank you, I'll wait."

"You may sit there," he said, motioning to the hardwood chairs across from his desk.

Emma walked over to them and sat down to wait. The man frowned at her but went through a door located directly behind his desk. He came out a few minutes later. "He has made time for you, but be aware he is a very busy man."

"I understand," Emma murmured and followed him into the office. Her expression was blank as she entered and got a view of the assistant director. The tall, thin man stood looking at the bookcases located behind his desk.

He turned toward her and smiled easily. "I'm assistant director Lee Baxter, and you are?"

This was not the austere man she had expected. She answered him easily. "Molly Cooper," she supplied, the name they had agreed to and had used in their letters.

He sat and waved her to the chair. "What is this about?"

"I need to pick up two of your students. Their families would like them back for a personal matter."

"Do you have something to show me to prove you have the proper approvals for this?"

She nodded and handed the letters to him from her jacket pocket.

He took his time opening the envelopes and read through each one. "Both families are involved in this personal issue?"

"Yes, their mothers are quite close and share a lot of their lives." *That's putting it lightly*, she thought.

"These seem to be in order," he acknowledged. "I'll need to check their files. Will you wait here?"

"Yes." She watched him exit.

He returned quickly. "There was nothing in their file to prevent them from leaving. Will you be taking them straight to their homes?"

"Yes, I will," she said, trying not to show her relief.

He studied her and then stood. "Follow me, please."

Emma followed him out. They stopped at the desk and he requested the office clerk. "Bring both girls up."

"Yes, sir." The clerk left the area immediately to retrieve the two girls.

They were brought in and Emma blinked when she saw them, trying to hide her surprise. The girls were almost identical: same hair and eye color. No one commented and Emma said, "Hi, I'm here to pick you up. Your mothers would like you to come home." They looked at one another and the assistant director.

The assistant director spoke directly to them. "Evie and Mabel, you'll need to go home at your mother's request. I'm sure you will be able to come back soon."

"Do we have time to get our things?" Evie asked.

"Yes, of course," Emma told her. "I'll be waiting down here." She glanced at her watch. "Try not to take too long."

The two girls nodded and walked back; the sound of their shoes ascending the tall staircase to the dorms could be heard in the office. As Emma waited, she wanted to get them out of here soon. It had almost been too easy.

CHAPTER 16

William Darnton, director of the Montgomery School for Girls, arrived back at the school later and entered his office, reading his mail.

The desk secretary entered the office. "Sir, two girls were picked up this morning."

"What did you say?" Darnton asked, still distracted by his mail.

"Two girls went home for a family concern this morning," the secretary repeated.

He frowned, then asked, "Which two?"

"Evie and Mabel Banks."

"Who took them? Was it their father?" Darnton asked in agitation.

This time, the secretary frowned. *Father? Singular?* he thought. "No sir, the mothers of both girls sent a representative to pick them up. A family matter, she said."

"She! Who approved this?" Darnton shouted.

"Well, I didn't. It was Assistant Director Baxter," the other man replied in a huffy voice.

"Tell Baxter to come to my office." His voice was curt.

When the secretary didn't move quickly, Darnton yelled, "NOW!"

The secretary jumped up and ran to the assistant director's office. He was out of breath when he entered the other man's office. He asked, "Sir?"

"Yes," Baxter said, smiling broadly and looking up. When he saw the other man's tense expression, he grew concerned. "Matthew, what's wrong?"

"Director Darnton is back," Matthew said, foreboding in his voice.

"That's nice. Will that be all?" Baxter smiled again. He was a happy, easygoing man who wasn't easily upset.

"No, sir, he wants you in his office to talk about the two girls you discharged earlier."

"Why is that?" he asked curiously. "There was nothing out of the ordinary. Except maybe it was two girls from two different families that left."

Were they from different families? Matthew thought, remembering the director's singular use of father and the girls' nearly identical appearances. "You should hurry, sir," he said quietly.

Baxter didn't understand the urgency, but if the director wanted him, it must have been important. Heading directly to the director's office, he knocked a few times and entered. Matthew sat back down at his desk and turned to stare at the door the assistant director had entered.

The director saw him at the door. "Lee, come in and close the door."

"Sure. You wanted to discuss something with me? Everything was in order with the release of the two girls. They had the permission of their mothers."

"Can I see the letters provided?" Darnton asked.

"Of course, I brought them with me," Baxter said and reached into his pocket. He handed them over and the director read each one.

"These are from the mothers. What about the father?" the director asked.

Father? Baxter thought. He heard the same thing from Matthew, a singular reference when he had been expecting a plural. "No, just the mothers. Miss Cooper picked them up at a little after eight this morning and took them home."

The director shook his head. "The one day I decide to take some personal time and what happens?"

The assistant director didn't answer. The question didn't appear to be directed at him.

"These girls were not allowed to be picked up by anyone other than their father!" Darnton yelled.

"I don't understand. There was no instruction in the file."

"No, no, there wouldn't have been," he said in a low voice. The director thought, *I will miss that money.*

"Money?" Baxter asked, perplexed at the turn of the conversation.

The director hadn't realized he had said that out loud. "The father had an understanding with me," he said smoothly. "He would fund the new library acquisitions, but only if we restricted access to the girls."

Baxter just sat in thought. Finally, he asked, "Father? Are the girls related?"

"Yes, he is the father of both children." There was no reason to hide it now.

"But they're in the same grade and both mothers are alive. I haven't heard of a divorce," Baxter stated, perplexed.

"Hmm. That was of no consequence to me. It's their private lives," Darnton said, trying to get himself extricated from the conversation.

Bigamy, thought Baxter. *The director was helping Mr. Banks hide his dual marriages.*

Well, it's too late now, Darnton thought. *I'll need to contact Banks.* "Matthew!" he yelled.

"Yes, sir," Matthew said as he ran in.

"Send a telegram to Mr. Banks and let him know both of his girls have been picked up. Tell him who was here and when this occurred," he directed.

"Yes, sir," Matthew said and exited to follow his instructions.

As volatile as Mr. Banks is, I hope he doesn't come to the school, thought Darnton as he sat heavily in his chair.

CHAPTER 17

The girls followed Emma's instructions and climbed into the wagon. She told them, "I have some fruit if you get hungry," and gestured to the basket at the back of the wagon.

"We're okay," Evie answered, "we had breakfast earlier."

Before they started out, Mabel stood up. "Where are we going?" she asked.

She is so much like Evelyn, thought Emma. She looked over at the girl and said, "I really don't have time to explain right now. Can you cooperate until we get far away from the school?"

The girls looked at one another and Mabel asked one question. "Did our moms really send you?"

"They did," Emma responded.

"We'll trust you and hold our questions until we're farther away," the girl confirmed and sat down next to Evie.

Emma was relieved. She turned back to the horse and said, "Okay, girl, let's go." They made their way to a fork in the road and drove into it. She pulled up, stopped, and got out to retrieve a large branch with leaves on it. The girls watched without comment as she swept their tracks. She dragged it behind her and jumped back into the wagon and moved them along. Turning around, she told them, "Girls, I need you to use the brush and let it drag behind us to hide our tracks. Can you do that?"

They nodded quickly and took turns holding the branch off the back. After a while, Emma said, "You can stop now." They were on a path that ran through a wooded area and would hide them from the main road.

Chicago was days away and they would be on the road for a long time. Train travel would have been easier but, they needed to stay hidden. They had driven at a steady pace for more than an hour. Rest was needed for both the horse and Emma.

The girls had been quiet as Emma lifted them out of the wagon. "I'll set up lunch if you would change into the clothes in those bags," Emma said.

They followed the direction and looked in the bag. "But these are boy's clothes," Evie said.

"That's right." Emma reached into her bag to pull out her own set. "It'll be safer for us to be traveling as a man and two boys."

"What are these?" Mabel asked as she pulled out the wigs. "It's hair!"

"Yes, those are wigs. Your hair is going to make it obvious who you are. Get dressed and I'll help you with the wigs and hats."

One sister held up a blanket so that the other could have some privacy. Emma changed and was placing her skirt and top back in the bag. "We're ready," Evie called.

She turned and saw the clothes were not a perfect fit, but the baggy trousers and shirts would be comfortable for the long trip. "One at a time," she said and lifted the girls onto the back of the wagon. She got out her wig and pulled it over her hair. The hair color was dark and completely changed her appearance. She felt her head. "I think just one pin will be necessary."

The two girls watched her and started to laugh at her appearance. "Now, none of that," she scolded lightly. "It's your turn now."

With their wigs in place, Emma got her revenge by laughing at them. They took the teasing kindly.

"Lunch?" she asked them.

"Yes, please," Mabel said, and Evie nodded.

They ate the hard rolls and cheese. She tossed them apples when they finished.

"Does Father know you have us?" Mabel asked, again assuming the lead for both girls.

"Father?" Emma asked carefully. She didn't want to tell them something that should come from their mothers.

"Yes," Mabel said.

"You know that you share one father?" Emma clarified.

They laughed. "How could we not?" Evie said. "It's like looking in a mirror."

She looked closely at them again; the resemblance had struck her from the start. "Did you know immediately?"

"No. It took some time to work out. Papa was our only visitor. He tried to keep us separated, but we figured it out," said Mabel.

"I followed him and saw him with Mabel," Evie said.

"I did the same," her sister said.

Smart girls! Emma thought.

"Now, where are we really going?" Mabel asked.

It was time to share the truth. She took a deep breath and told them, "Your mothers are concerned that your father may be running away and taking you and your younger sisters with him."

This time, it was Evie who spoke. "Why do they think that?"

"Both of your sisters went on a trip with their father two weeks ago and he returned without them."

Mabel frowned. "We've never been on trips together before."

Evie confirmed that with, "We're always kept separate, even at home."

"That's why your mothers are concerned. They don't want you taken from them."

"What about our sisters?" Mabel asked, holding out her hand to Evie. She took it and held it tight.

"Once we get you to a safe place, I'm going to find them and keep your mothers safe."

"By yourself?" asked Evie incredulously.

"If I have to," Emma said quietly, "but I have a team that will help. I'll need your cooperation and your promise that you'll follow my directions. I need to know you're in a safe place while we find your sisters."

Mabel looked at Evie and then back to Emma. "We'll do as you ask. We don't want to be taken from our moms."

Emma packed up their lunch, got the girls in the wagon, and headed down the road. "Do you have any questions?" she asked over her shoulder at the silent girls.

"Did you know about Dad before this?" asked Evie as she watched the scenery go by.

"I found out a couple of years ago," she admitted.

"You didn't turn him in? Isn't it wrong to have two families?"

"I didn't think there was cause at the time. Both of your mothers seemed happy. I didn't want to tear the families apart. I did leave my contact information with your mother in case something changed in your lives and you needed help."

"Why only her mother?" asked Mabel.

That is a hard one, thought Emma. "I had planned to help both families if something came up."

"Mom knew, didn't she?" guessed Evie.

Smart, thought Emma again. "Yes, she figured it out."

"And she stayed."

"She loved your father and your family. It seemed to be

working out. I think she was scared of what might happen if she left."

"Scared of Dad?" Evie asked.

"I didn't think so at the time but scared of the courts finding out about the situation. Bigamy is hard to cover up and harder to recover from. I wanted to make sure the families had options if you needed them."

When Emma said the word bigamy, both girls reacted with a shudder. She saw that and didn't say anything more.

After a few hours and another break, Mabel asked while stretching her arms, "Wouldn't a train have been easier? The wagon isn't built for a long trip."

"I agree, but that would be more traceable. I don't want your father to know where we're going."

"*Where* are we going?" Mabel asked.

"Chicago."

"But Father is from there. Won't people know him or us?"

"Not where I am taking you," Emma promised. They went quiet again.

A few hours later, after their trip had started again, Evie spoke up. "Will we be stopping for dinner soon?"

"I have some houses around here where people know me," Emma said. She and Clair had set up contacts on the various trips when they were moving the ladies from safe houses to their families.

"Will they tell our father where we are?" Mabel asked, her voice shaking.

"No. They'll help protect you," Emma said firmly.

The first house was another few hours away. The time went by and Emma wasn't pushing the horse more than she should. She finally pulled into a long driveway in the country. They got out of the wagon and a woman walked out and greeted Emma and the girls without questions. She walked with them into the house and began setting food on the table. "Go wash up now, through there," the woman directed them down the hall. The girls did as they were told.

"Betty, thank you for taking us in," Emma said, helping to carry food to the table.

"You know we'd do anything for you. Clair was by a few days ago," Betty said.

"How is she?"

"They placed the last child and were headed home. I think this one wore her out."

"Thomas will take care of her, and I hope we don't have any more cases like it in the future." *If Clair is headed home,* she thought, *Jeremy might be on his way also.* She might get to see him in Chicago when she dropped off the girls.

"Would you like to rest your horse a bit before continuing on your trip?" asked Betty.

"We should. It has been a long trip." They didn't talk about her plans, sharing only what was necessary.

After everyone ate, Betty looked at the girls. "Why don't you go lie down?" she suggested. "I have two beds you can stretch out on."

They looked at Emma. She nodded. "Go ahead, get some rest."

Betty took them to the bedroom and after a few minutes came out. "They are out."

"Already?" She hadn't realized how tired they were.

Betty nodded.

"You mentioned Clair and Thomas came by here on their way home?"

"Yes, they had a special request."

"What was it?" Emma asked curiously.

"She wanted to know if I would take in one of the older kids, a boy."

"The family wouldn't take him back?" Emma asked incredulously.

"No," she said, frowning, "I don't understand people like that."

"Where is he?" asked Emma.

"He and Ben went out to work the cattle while you were here. He's skittish around new people."

"How old is he?" inquired Emma.

"Nine, his name is Paul."

"Was he hurt?" Emma asked, not wanting the answer.

Tears formed in Betty's eyes and she brushed them away. "He was, but he'll be safe with us out here. It'll give him time to heal."

"Can I meet him? Do you think that would be okay?"

Betty looked at Emma and said, "I think so. He's shy around anyone but Ben."

"Taken to him, has he?"

She smiled widely. "Yes. He's from the city but seems to fit right into the country." They walked out to the barn and she called, "Ben! Emma wanted to say hello."

Ben walked out. He was a smallish man with dark brown hair; he wore pants and a loose white shirt. He also had a hat pushed back on his head. "Emma! It's so good to see you!"

"I'm glad you were on my path today, Ben," she said and stepped up to hug him. She backed away and said, "I heard you have a new family member?"

"Yes," he said proudly. "He's brushing the horses down. City kid but he has a knack for the horses."

"Will it be okay if I meet him?"

He glanced at his wife and she nodded. "Let's head in slow," he suggested. They walked in talking about family and when they got close to the stall, they heard Paul moving around.

"Son, would you like to come out and say hello to our friend?"

There was a long moment and he slowly walked out and ran quickly to Ben. He hid his face in the man's side.

Emma knelt down to be at eye level with the small boy. "Hello, Paul, how are you?"

He peered toward her and mumbled an answer.

"Louder, boy," Ben said.

Paul took Ben's hand and stepped out. "I'm good."

"My name is Emma, and I wanted you to know that if you ever need anything, you or your parents can contact me."

Ben bent down also and said, "Emma is an investigator. She's one of the ones who saved the kids."

"You helped with that?" he asked incredulously.

"I did," she confirmed.

Paul had used up all of his bravery and hid behind Ben again. Emma took out her notebook, wrote something on a piece of paper, and tore it out. She handed the piece of paper to Paul. "This is my address and my name. I also work closely with the Pinkerton Detectives if you need anything."

Paul put it in his pocket and patted it.

Ben said, "We're going to head back into the barn to see to the horses." Paul nodded his head. "Emma, it was good to see you."

The ladies walked back to the house together arm in arm. "Is he sleeping?" Emma asked.

"Not a lot," Betty admitted. "Ben and I pulled a pad into his room and if he needs us at night, we're there."

"That is wonderful," said Emma softly.

"That woman!" Betty suddenly spat out.

Emma stopped and turned toward her. The bitterness she heard was out of character. "What woman?" she asked.

"His so-called mother. They found her and she said she wouldn't take someone who had been damaged."

"It wasn't his choice!"

"No."

"He has you and Ben now."

"Yes, God brought him to us."

"Let me know if you need anything."

"I will," Betty promised.

Emma checked her timepiece. "We should probably get moving."

"Let me help you get the horse hooked back up. "

Emma thought, *One more stop and then I'll see about a train. It'll be far enough away so that they may not be identified.*

They walked over to the wagon and hooked the horse back up. The blankets were in the back.

Returning to the house, they each woke one of the girls and helped them put their wigs on. They grumbled a bit but understood the trip had just started.

"You finish with them and I will get you a basket of food ready," Betty said.

"Thanks, Betty."

The other woman smiled and went back to the kitchen. She came out a little while later with a basket. It must have been heavy, as she was using both hands to carry it. Emma took one side and helped her walk out to the wagon.

"Do you need anything else?" asked Betty.

"No, this is plenty. Let's get the girls; we should be on our way."

The girls were lifted into the wagon. She could see Ben and Paul at a distance. She lifted an arm and waved goodbye.

She climbed up into the driver's seat and clicked her tongue to get the horse moving. The girls were still sleepy and lay on the blanket, not saying much. The scenery rolled by at a leisurely rate. She pulled over a few hours later and said, "Break time." She could see a stream to water the horse. "Get out and stretch your legs." She unhooked the horse and took her to the stream for some water. She tied her loosely so she could reach water and grass.

"Can you get one of the blankets down, and we can have a snack?" asked Emma.

Once the blanket was set up, all three sat and Emma tossed each girl an apple. The crunching sound and birds were all that could be heard.

Mabel lay back on the grass and asked, "How much longer?"

"I was thinking about that," admitted Emma. "The horse will make it to Chicago, but I think we might try the train from here."

"I thought you said it was too dangerous," Evie said with a frown.

"I think we're far enough along, and I want to get back to your moms," she explained. They looked relieved that it was going to be train travel for the rest of the trip and no more wagons.

Things were organized and they caught a train about fifty miles from the school. They pulled into the station area and she parked the wagon. She turned to them. "Stay here. I need to get the tickets. Keep your voices down." She went quickly to the ticket office. As she paid for the tickets, she looked around and asked, "Is there anywhere I could stable my horse and wagon until they can be picked up?"

"Yes. A man named Caleb has a barn and, for a price, he'll board them until they're retrieved," the clerk said helpfully.

"Thank you. Also, is there a telegraph station in town?"

"There is," he said and pointed. "It's just down from Caleb's place."

Perfect, she thought. "What time does the train leave?"

"You have two hours, and we'll be leaving on time."

Emma turned and walked away from him and waved to the girls. Joining them at the wagon, they looked at her expectantly as she said, "We need to drop off the wagon first."

She drove the wagon and the girls to Caleb's place. The wagon stopped and she turned to them. "Keep your heads down," she cautioned, "and don't talk. Remember, you're boys. Keep silent and wear these." She tossed them cloth hats.

Jumping down, she headed into the office. A man wearing work pants and a loose shirt was writing something down in a book at the counter. "Sir," she said, deepening her voice some.

"Yes?" Caleb asked, looking up.

"I have a horse and wagon that will need to be boarded. The owner will retrieve them in a few days," she said.

"I can take them. I have room, but you'll have to pay upfront," he said gruffly.

"I can do that," she said calmly. He quoted his fee and she pulled the money out and handed it to him.

"Who'll be picking it up?" he asked.

"Floyd Bentley will be here. I'll send him a note now to confirm the location."

"Okay, I'll board them until he comes by," he said. Caleb walked out to help her move the horse and wagon into the barn.

"Boys, you'll need to get down," Emma said. They understood that they shouldn't ask for help and jumped down. Emma climbed up and retrieved their bags and the basket of food.

The girls helped with the bags while Emma carried the basket. The next stop was the telegraph office. She sent the message to Floyd to retrieve his horse and wagon. She started to leave and thought, they would need to be picked up at the station. "One more, please," she told the clerk.

He pulled out another piece of paper. "When you're ready."

She kept it simple. "This will go to Clair Flannigan at 221 Moffet Street. The message is: Please pick us up at the train station in a few hours."

They exited and headed to the station. She'd considered sending one to the safe house but decided it was best if there was no record of her or their location. The train had not arrived yet and they sat and waited for it. It came in on time and they boarded. Their tickets were third class; they didn't want to call attention to themselves. It wasn't as comfortable as first class but they felt safe. Emma gave each girl one of her books to keep them busy.

Less than a few hours later, they pulled into Chicago. "Keep your heads down," Emma murmured. "I have someone meeting us." They wandered out to where the wagons were picking up passengers. Emma saw Thomas waiting. He waved them over. He jumped down and helped with their bags, and he didn't say anything until they were moving. "The house?" he asked.

"Yes," she said in a low voice. As they drove into an alley, Emma looked at the girls. "Lie down," she instructed. They followed her direction and she climbed in beside them. Thomas got them covered up and pulled out, heading to the safe house Clair and Thomas managed. He pulled into the back and helped them quickly to the door.

Once inside, they found Clair and Katie the housekeeper sitting at the table. "You made good time," Clair said, standing up and going over to kiss Emma on the cheek.

"We did," Emma said.

"Tell me who we have here?" Clair directed. "Sisters?" she asked, taking in their appearances.

"Yes and no. Same father and different mothers. This is Evie and Mabel."

"I'm Clair and this is Katie. Welcome. Come this way," Clair said. "We have rooms for you." They followed the lovely lady quietly; the trip had worn them down. She called back, "Katie, will you bring up a snack to their rooms?"

Katie nodded and gave a quick wink to Emma. "Follow me back to the kitchen."

They got organized with tea and cakes. Emma swiped a few and got her hand swatted. She grinned and helped her carry the trays to the girls' rooms. Once they were settled, they closed the door and headed back downstairs.

"Emma, come sit with me," Clair requested. She hugged Emma's arm tightly.

"How are you?" asked Emma.

"We're better," Clair replied. "The operations lasted longer than expected, and then it turned out some parents didn't want damaged children back."

"Yes, I stopped by Ben and Betty's and met Paul," Emma said.

Clair teared up. "He's a lovely little boy. I'm so glad we found a home for him." They sat down and she noticed Emma grimace. "Are you okay? Would you like me to rub your shoulders?"

"I'd like that," she admitted. "My shoulders are tired from driving the wagon."

"Turn around."

Emma turned and groaned when Clair started to rub them. "Did Jeremy come back with you?" she asked.

"No, he stayed to process some of the paperwork we found and close down a large number of children holding locations."

"But you didn't find all of them," Emma said, disappointment sounding in her voice.

"Emma," Clair said and turned her friend around. "We will never find all of them. We'll just do the best we can."

"What did you find out about the baby?"

"Jeremy stayed with us a few days. He wanted to find the couple that took her. He found the father. Turns out he was paid to be there with the girl."

"What about the mother? Did he find out anything on her?"

"No word yet. Jeremy was concerned he might draw too much attention to her if he kept pursuing the topic."

"What persuaded you to give the baby to her?" Emma asked curiously.

"It was hers," Clair said simply. "The baby responded to her immediately. We also did as you asked and looked for identifying marks on the baby."

"What type?" she asked.

"A birthmark, almost perfectly round."

"So, John's daughter got her baby back and John is out of prison."

"Yes, and probably setting up new operations."

"Will he come back to Chicago?"

"I don't think he will right away. It'll be hard to trace him. He's good at new beginnings." Clair moved to another subject. "These older girls, what are the next steps in this operation?"

"We need to find their sisters."

"The two here, Evie and Mabel look about the same age."

"Yes, and the younger two are also extremely close in age." Emma went on to explain about the two families' houses and how similar they were.

"What an odd man," Clair commented.

"Yes, very odd."

"What about the mothers, will they be at risk if he finds out what's happening?"

"He hasn't been abusive before this, but I do need to figure out what he has planned for the other two wives once he's gone."

"Where he took the little ones, do you think there's another wife?"

"I do. He'll need a new mother for them. I'm also concerned about how he's funding all of this. He makes good money, but a third family is going to cost more and I'd assume he doesn't plan to leave his assets with the other two."

"Losing an asset like a home could harm the wives. They might never recover from that."

"Yes, these two ladies will fight for their homes and their children."

"So, we need to come up with a way to get the girls back and keep them in their homes?"

"Yes," Emma said, thinking. She yawned. "I need to get home and get organized. Who will stay with the girls?"

"I will," Lily said from the door. "I moved my things in today."

She looked over at Lily. The woman had come into their lives in an unconventional way. She had been robbing homes and was caught hiding out at the safe house. As Clair's assistant, she had turned her life around. "Thank you, Lily."

"Anything I could do to help."

"Thomas," Clair called, "we're ready to head home."

Thomas came into the room carrying a cup of coffee. "I'm ready when you are."

"Finish your coffee," Emma said. "How did the baby handle the travel?"

"She's a trooper." Thomas beamed.

"Where is she?" she asked, looking around.

"She's home with her nanny," Clair responded.

Thomas set down his empty cup and saucer on the table. He turned to Emma. "I moved your bags back into the wagon."

Clair, Thomas, and Emma headed out through the kitchen and got into the wagon. Emma lay low in the back until they reached the boarding house. Thomas uncovered her and touched her arm. "Emma."

She woke suddenly and realized she'd fallen asleep. "What?" She looked around. "Oh, yes, home."

Clair was concerned and asked her friend, "Do you want Thomas to help you into the house?"

"No," she said, yawning. "I can make it." Thomas helped her down and handed her the bag and basket. She slowly made her way up to the door and heard the wagon move past as she entered. The foyer was dark and she headed up to her bedroom. As she finally settled into bed, there was a light knock on the door. Dora's voice could be heard through it.

"Can I come in?"

"Yes," Emma called back. She didn't get out of bed.

Dora walked quickly over and climbed into bed with her. "Did you get the girls to Clair?" she asked.

"Yes." Emma settled down with her head on Dora's shoulder. "They're almost identical and they knew they were related through their father."

"Who told them?" her sister asked curiously.

"No one had to. They figured it out when they met each other."

"Hmm. What next?"

When Emma didn't respond, Dora looked over and saw she was asleep.

She slipped out of the bed. "Sleep well. We'll talk in the morning." She pulled Emma's covers up and quietly left the room.

CHAPTER 18

The next morning, Emma was up and trying to determine what she should do next. *Team,* she thought. *I need to run things by my team.*

She dressed and headed down to the kitchen. Tim had returned from his trip and sat at the dining room table. When she walked into the room, he looked up from his books.

"How was your trip? Did you have any problems?"

"No, not really. I'm thinking of next steps."

At that moment, Ethyl and Amy came in from the kitchen and put the platters of food on the table. Lottie ran in with Dora close behind. "Talk after breakfast," he suggested.

"Yes," she said, her mouth already full of a biscuit.

Ethyl called to Jake, "You need to come into the dining room." He came in from the kitchen and sat down. Savannah took a seat and Emma stayed where she was.

"Can you all wait after breakfast? I want to discuss a few things with you," she said.

"Of course," Savannah answered and the others nodded.

The conversation moved on to other topics. Emma turned to

Dora. "Have you heard from Jeremy?" she asked. He knew she was traveling and any updates would have been sent to the house.

Dora looked surprised. "Oh, yes! I forgot about that. Would you like it now?" She made a move to get up.

Emma stopped her. "After breakfast is fine."

The group continued to share their plans for the day, and when they finished the meal, they helped clear the table. Once they had moved all of the platters and dishes, they sat back down at the dining table for the meeting.

Dora was the last to join them. She had retrieved the telegram and handed it to Emma. She took it and said, "I'll read this after." She put it into her pocket and looked at her team.

She updated them with what had happened so far and when she finished, she stated, "I either go after the little girls or I keep an eye on the wives."

"Is Banks dangerous?" Tim asked.

"He can be about some things, but I'm not sure if he knows the wives are involved with the girls being moved," Emma admitted.

"Will he know the kids have been removed from the school?" Dora asked.

"That I'm unsure of," Emma admitted. "It was relatively easy to get them. The director was out and the assistant didn't give me any problems, but the clerk looked nervous about not getting the director's approval."

Savannah looked at her and said, "I want to go with you. I've been there and know both women. I wouldn't mind keeping an eye on them, that way you could see about the other two girls."

Emma looked at her. "I could use your help. Are you sure you can take the time?"

"I can." Savannah was ready to help. "Do you know where he took them?"

"No, but I have an idea of where to start. His place of business. If he's keeping his job, then a notice would be with his current company."

"When would you like to leave?"

"Soon."

"Okay, I just have a few things to do before we leave. I'll need to notify the theatre that a replacement will have to step in for the show."

"Will you notify Ethan?" Dora asked in an innocent voice. The two had been spending all of their time together since Christmas.

Savannah turned red at that. "Yes, I'll tell him I'll be out of town with Emma."

"Make sure you don't tell him why; we need to keep this private," Emma cautioned.

"Ethan will understand," Savannah said. Their team had helped him find out how his father died. He had seen how they worked.

They heard a bang of a door and running feet. Emma put her hand to her lips and her team nodded. Mark Sutherland ran into the room.

"Emma!" he exclaimed. "I hoped to catch you here. When did you get back?" Mark and Emma had met years before in New York City when she stopped his new career as a pickpocket when he was nine. He was thirteen now and his family members were on and off again team members.

"Just last night. Is everything okay?" she asked, suddenly worried.

"Yes, I just wanted to share some news!" he said excitedly. "My uncle is planning a visit!"

"Uncle," she mulled. "Have I heard about him?"

"I don't think so. We don't see him much. He is mom's brother. They were really close."

"Where does he live?" she asked.

"Upper New York State, at least, that is where his mail goes," Mark said as he shrugged.

"Mark, what do you mean? Does he travel for his job?" Emma asked.

"Uh-huh. He goes over the United States and sometimes Europe."

"What does he do?" Dora asked curiously.

"Don't know. Ma says business."

"Was the visit a surprise?" Emma asked.

Mark squirmed and finally answered, "I sent him a telegram and asked him to visit. Mom has been a bit down and this will be perfect for her."

"Is your father looking forward to the visit?"

Mark looked hesitant. "I'm not so sure. I don't think Dad likes him to visit as much as Mom does."

"Do they fight?" Emma asked.

"No. My uncle just takes most of the attention and I think Dad feels a little left out when he's here."

She thought about that and thought she would need to keep an eye on them. "When is he coming?"

"He said a few weeks," Mark replied.

"Be sure to bring him over for us to meet him," Emma said.

He grinned and added, "You'll love him, Emma. I just know it."

Will I? she wondered.

"I have to get back to school," he said.

"Can't miss that," she teased him.

He grinned and ran off.

The group didn't say anything until after they heard the door slam behind Mark. Tim spoke first. "The little girls. I'm concerned about your plan. I don't think it would be legal to remove them from their current location."

Emma frowned and asked, "What would be different from what I did at the school? I'll get the same letters to take them."

Tim explained, "In that case, you went in the front door and I think here you plan something more covert?"

"Yes," she murmured. "The girls are with a new wife who'll probably want to talk to her 'husband' before they're moved. We have to prevent that."

"That could be thought of as kidnapping, even with the mother's permission. You know the authority for the family still rests with the fathers," Tim stated.

She frowned and said slowly, "You're right. The other was different."

"What will you do?" Dora asked. She was concerned that this could get complicated.

Emma looked at her "I'll try to locate the address first at his business."

"Banks has gotten a new wife and a new life?" asked Dora. "Why would he do that?"

"A new start, a new life," Emma confirmed. "I don't know what caused him to want to start again, but my goal is to find out. I'll observe and then approach her when he's not there. If she's like the other two wives, she'll probably listen to reason."

"What if she knows and doesn't care?" Savannah asked.

"That's a chance I'll have to take, but I think she might care. This is getting complicated. I'm not even sure either of the two marriages is legal. He married numbers one and two when he was still married to Mrs. Gilmore."

They mulled that over. Tim spoke up. "The courts will have to straighten that out after the girls are safe."

"Yes." Emma looked over at Savannah and asked her, "Do you still want to go with me?"

Savannah said firmly, "I'm ready to help. When will we leave?"

"In the morning. Will that give you enough time to get things organized?"

"It should. I'll be ready." Savannah thought of the two women and the strain they must be under to get their children back.

"I'll get the train tickets and meet you back here," Emma said, standing.

"I can drive you," Tim offered.

"Will I need to pack wigs and makeup?" Savannah asked, thinking ahead.

Emma nodded. "Yes, and pack pants and dresses for yourself. We'll go first dressed as women, but we'll want the option to change if needed. I also have the girl's clothes and wigs you sent with me. They are in my room."

"I will take them to the theatre with me."

The team started leaving the table. Emma began walking out of the room, pulling the telegram out of her pocket as she went.

Before she could read it, Savannah's voice stopped her. "And Emma?"

She turned back to her. "Do you have more questions?"

"This time, I'd like to ride the train the whole way there," Savannah commented with a straight face.

Emma grinned wickedly. "What, you didn't enjoy the side trip of a train and rolling down a hill?" Savannah had been involved in the case the first time they met Hugo Banks. On the way home, they had been forced to jump off a train or be shot by assailants. They had gotten away, but they had lost two dresses and two pairs of boots rolling down the hill. She assured her friend, "I plan for us to make it to and from without any incident."

Savannah had only been half teasing and replied, "Good. I'll meet you here." She went up to get the borrowed clothes and headed back downstairs and out the door. *Ethan first*, she thought. *Then the theatre.*

The telegram from Jeremy was full of news about the captures and closing of the houses. He would be returning soon. Emma clasped it tightly in her hands and thought, *Soon. We'll be together soon.*

CHAPTER 19

That evening, when all their errands were completed and dinner eaten, the group settled into the sitting room for a quiet evening. A knock sounded at the door. "I'll get it," Emma said. She answered the door and walked back into the sitting room, reading a telegram. She looked over at Savannah. "Good thing we're going in the morning."

"Why?"

"Hugo knows about Evie and Mabel. He's gone to the school."

"What else does it say?" Tim asked.

"Nothing else," Emma said, looking up from the telegram.

"Should we be worried about the girls here?" Dora asked.

"There's no connection to us. I don't think he'll think to look for them here. The safe house is a secret."

Tim stood. "I'll stop by Clair and Thomas' house and tell them that Hugo knows the girls aren't in school anymore." He looked down at the floor where Patrick was playing with Lottie. "Would you like to go with me?" he asked his son. The boy nodded eagerly and got to his feet to follow his papa.

"Thank you, Tim," Emma called to him.

"It's not a problem," Tim said as he and Patrick headed out into the night.

CHAPTER 20

*E*arly the next morning, they headed to the station. Savannah and Emma were dressed in dark skirts and white blouses and their hair was pulled into buns. Savannah carried her case of wigs and makeup with her. The station was quiet that morning and their train stood waiting. They would only need a day and would share a cabin. They stayed there and enjoyed the day trip to Cleveland.

As they got closer to their destination, Emma said, "I think we should put on the wigs here in case we're spotted."

"Okay," Savannah agreed. She opened her bag and pulled out an auburn wig for Emma. "Your makeup will have to be a bit darker to wear this one." She showed her friend how to apply it so it looked natural.

They prepared for their roles and were ready by the time the train came to a stop. This time, their hotel room would be under aliases. The trip to the hotel was accomplished quickly and they dropped their bags off and headed over to Evelyn's house. The carriage took them close to their destination; they were cautious, not counting on Hugo being away.

"We'll have to keep an eye out as we approach," said Savannah and she pulled a book out of her bag.

"A Bible?" Emma asked.

"Yes, I thought we could use it as an excuse to be at their door if he is still around."

"Good thinking." At that moment, the carriage slowed down and indicated it was their stop. Emma paid the driver and they started toward Evelyn's house.

"It's quiet," Savanna observed as she looked around.

"It is," Emma said.

"How will we be able to tell that he isn't there?" Savannah asked as she bit her bottom lip and held the Bible closer to her.

"A bike will be on the porch if things are safe."

They continued their stroll. They were close but didn't want to rush and bring any attention to their activities.

"The bike's there," Emma murmured.

Savannah looked and saw her friend was right. *Just the same,* she thought and started to move more quickly toward the house.

Emma stopped her. "Slowly," she cautioned.

Savannah nodded and slowed her pace. They strolled together arm and arm toward the home and up the stairs to the porch. Emma raised a hand to knock at the door. They heard slow steps approaching. It opened revealing half of Izzy's face. "Yes, what do you want?" she asked, her voice muffled.

"We would like to share the word of God with you," Emma said.

Izzy's eyes widened when she heard the familiar voice. "Emma!" she whispered, hoping it was her.

Emma nodded.

"Hugo's gone. Come in. Hurry before someone sees you," the woman said and pulled them inside.

Once they were in the foyer, Emma and Savannah saw both sides of her face. The right side was mottled with bruises

"What happened?" Emma asked, concerned. She went over to her and cupped Izzy's face in her hands.

"Hugo is what happened to her and me," came a voice out of the kitchen.

It was Evelyn. She walked over to Izzy with a cloth wrapped around an ice pack. "You need to keep this on your face." She took her friend's arm and walked with her to the sitting room to sit down. She held the ice to Izzy's face.

Emma and Savannah followed and Emma said, "Tell us." She and Savannah sat across from them.

Evelyn started with, "Director Darnton sent a telegram yesterday and informed our husband that Evie and Mabel had been picked up. And that it had been approved by their mothers."

"Hmm," said Emma, "the assistant director was there when I picked them up and didn't give me much trouble."

"Darnton's probably in Hugo's pocket," Izzy said.

"What happened then?" Savannah asked.

Izzy spoke up as she lowered the ice from her face. "Hugo confronted me first and asked where the girls were. I told him if he brought our other girls home, I would bring Evie and Mabel home as well."

"His response?" Emma asked.

"You're looking at it," she said bitterly.

Emma observed Evelyn's appearance as the woman took a seat beside Izzy. "You look relatively unscathed."

She nodded. "That's thanks to her. After he hit her, he went upstairs and she ran all the way to my house and helped me hide."

"Do you think he would have done the same to you?"

"Oh, yes. We watched him storm out of my home. When he left, we went back inside. He had taken the picture of us on the mantel and twisted it and thrown it on the floor."

"I saw a similar reaction when he didn't get his way previously," commented Emma. Hugo's first marriage had been to solely get back at his friend. He felt he was slighted and had stayed married to the woman Mr. Gilmore was in love with.

Izzy couldn't wait and ask, "How are our girls?"

Emma smiled. "They're fine. You know, they already knew that they had the same father."

"But how? I just found out myself," Izzy said, her eyes going wide.

"The girls are nearly identical, so there's that. Plus, they saw their father when he visited. He would meet with each girl separately," she explained.

"They weren't upset?" Izzy asked, worried about what her daughter thought.

"No, just matter of fact about it. They seem very close."

Both of the mothers were frowning and Evelyn spoke for them. "We would like to go to them."

"I think it's best that you stay here," Emma stressed. "They're fine as of now and they're protected until we can work this out."

"How much time do we have?" Savannah asked.

"Not much," Emma replied. "His trip to the school will probably be faster than mine, especially if he pushes his horse and doesn't rest."

Evelyn asked hesitantly, "Will he be able to trace the girls?"

"I told Baxter I was bringing them home, so I don't think Hugo will be anywhere near where they are."

They looked relieved, then Izzy exclaimed, "He'll come back here!"

"He probably will," Emma acknowledged. "We need to make a plan for the younger girls before he returns. Do you know where he has them?"

"We don't," Izzy said.

Emma stood and walked to the mantel. She looked over at them. "I've been thinking about that. If he's changing jobs or transferring, then his work will know. I need to talk to someone in his office." She held up her bag and asked, "Would you mind if I changed here? I'd like to go straight over."

Izzy said, "Of course. Upstairs first room on the right."

Emma went up and found the bedroom right away. She looked around and thought, *This is the first time I've been up here. I wonder if both houses are the same?* She dressed quickly in the boys' clothes and placed her dress and wig into her bag. Going back downstairs quickly, she twisted her braided hair and pulled her hat over to anchor it down.

Savannah put her teacup and saucer down when she saw Emma on the stairs. "Ready to go?" Emma asked.

"Yes," she said and went over to both ladies and took their hands in hers. "I will find out where the little girls are," she promised. "We'll be in contact today. Be ready to go just in case." They nodded and watched them leave.

They headed out and found a carriage to take them to Hugo's business office. Once they were dropped off, Emma asked Savannah to wait outside on a bench. She pulled her hat down. "I'll be back in a moment."

She entered the building and went to the same person who had given her Hugo's address on the previous case. He had inadvertently given her the two addresses that led to the man's bigamy being uncovered. "Excuse me, I have a question for you."

His head swung toward her. "You!" he exclaimed. "Why are you back? Do you know what happened last time you were here?"

"What do you mean? I just got an address," she said innocently.

"No, you tricked me into giving you confidential information," he said in a loud voice.

"Really?" she asked, her tone dry. "Confidential information? Since when?"

"Well, not at that time," he admitted. "But it is now."

She looked at him consideringly and decided to tell him the truth. "Did you know what the two addresses meant?"

"Not at the time," he admitted in a calmer voice. "But after Mr. Banks' reaction, I went to both locations. They were eerily the same."

"Did you meet the wives?" she asked curiously.

"No! I didn't want to. I didn't want to be involved any more than I was then," he said. "Why are you here now?" he asked.

"It's bigger than last time."

"How so? What, did he get more wives?" he asked, laughing.

She looked around to make sure they were alone, then leaned in and said, "Yes, I think so. I think that's exactly it. Another family. I also think he's moving his children to that new wife."

He went white at that statement. "There are children involved?"

"Yes. Hugo has four currently, two with each wife."

He pushed his chair back and stood. "What can I do to help?"

"Is he transferring to one of your other locations? Or quitting to move to another job?"

He pulled his files and consulted them. "He's transferring to the New York Office."

She jotted down the information, looked over at him, and asked, "Any idea of his new address?"

"Yes, I have that also." He handed it to her. "A third family?" he asked, bewildered.

"Yes. Please don't tell anyone I was here."

"No worries, I don't plan to tell anyone," he reassured her.

She turned as he called out, "Let me know if I can help with anything else."

"I will," she promised.

She walked outside and went to sit next to Savannah on the bench. "Not only did I get the town he's moving to, but also his new address. Now to see If I can beat him to the little girls." She looked around and commented, "Let's walk some. I don't want to be seen here."

Savannah nodded and, once they started walking, she asked, "Where?"

"New York City."

"Will we go there?"

"Yes. And now that I know where the girls are located, we need to get moving."

When they returned to Izzy's house, they found the ladies in the dining room eating lunch.

"We saved some for you both," Evelyn said, getting up. She brought their plates back; Savannah and Emma quickly ate.

"Thank you," said Emma. Savannah nodded in agreement.

"Did you get his new address?" Izzy asked.

"I did," Emma confirmed.

"Thank goodness! But what if he moves them? Can you get to them in time?" Evelyn asked.

Emma frowned and looked down at the address. "My team at home pointed out that if I take the girls, I could be accused of kidnapping."

"Even if it's for us? Their mothers?" Izzy asked.

"This is still a patriarchy we live in. Though I think Hugo is more scared of being caught for bigamy; it is probably why he hasn't notified the police of the other girls being taken." She turned her gaze to Izzy and Evelyn, "I'm also concerned about something else."

"What are you thinking?" Evelyn asked.

"Hugo may have told the girls that you died and that the move was to start a new family," she said boldly.

Both women's faces lost color; Emma was glad they were sitting. She couldn't have caught both of them.

"Would he do that?" Evelyn asked faintly. "Would he just erase us like that?"

Emma took a deep breath before replying, "Yes, I think he wants a new start."

"Yes, since his first wife, Elle, and her husband announced her pregnancy," Izzy muttered. "He seemed to lose interest in me, in us."

"That's when the trips started," Evelyn confirmed. "I was a naive fool," she said bitterly. "I didn't know any of this was going on."

Izzy took her hand. "No, you shouldn't have to question if your husband has more than one wife."

"You figured it out first."

"Yes, and more the fool. I stayed knowing I was only sharing someone else's husband. And our daughters will suffer because I didn't want things to change."

Emma watched them clean up the lunch. She looked at Savannah and asked, "Do you have time to accompany me on the next part of this trip?"

"You couldn't stop me," she said.

"Good." Emma looked over at the two wives. "I've been thinking about the kidnapping issue. I think what you can do is accompany me and Savannah to retrieve your girls. That way, I know you two are safe and you can take the girls as their mothers."

"Us?" asked Evelyn in a high voice. "You want us to go along on the case?"

"Yes," Emma said. "Definitely. We'll need you to pack. Savannah, go with Evelyn to her house and meet us back here. I'll go get the train tickets. I'd like to leave this evening."

"We can do it," Izzy said to Evelyn bracingly.

"We can," confirmed Evelyn with a deep breath.

They started out and Izzy asked, "Where are we going?"

"The address I have is for New York City," said Emma.

"Will we beat him there?" Savannah asked.

"If Hugo comes back here first, I think we will."

Everyone headed to complete their assigned task. Izzy went upstairs and pulled out her bag and got organized.

Savannah went to Evelyn's house with her, telling her, "Go up and get packed. I'll wait here."

Evelyn nodded and went to her room. She got her clothes packed in a bag and, lastly, she pulled out a gun from the bottom of her dresser, examining it. *He will pay*, she promised herself and slid it under her clothes. Her bag closed with a snap and she carried it downstairs; they left for Izzy's house immediately.

There, Izzy and Emma were waiting on the porch. "Everyone ready to go?" Emma asked.

Everyone confirmed they were ready. They walked down the stairs to a waiting carriage and climbed in.

"Where to?" the driver asked.

"Train station, please," directed Emma. The group was quiet and, as they entered their two cabins, not a word was said.

"We can sit together for a while," Emma suggested.

The two Mrs. Banks put their bags in their cabin and then walked back to Emma and Savannah's cabin to sit together. There were so many plans and questions, but the group didn't talk; instead, one could hear the sound of fingers drumming on the book Evelyn held. Izzy's foot tapped on the floor, Evelyn's skirt rustled as she struggled to get comfortable, and Savannah's finger squeaked as she drew on the window.

When Emma finally spoke, it startled everyone. "Are you ready to go get your girls?"

The two women nodded.

"Then, now, we plan." She bent her head towards them. They leaned forward, listening intently.

CHAPTER 21

The train pulled into Buffalo and they moved to the day train to be transported to New Jersey. Once there, they disembarked and walked with purpose toward the carriages that stood by for rental purposes at the New Jersey station. Emma gave the address she had gotten from Hugo's work, and the group climbed on board. There was no talking; they had their plan and were concentrating on their individual parts.

The carriage pulled up in front of the house and both women looked on with shock. It was the same house.

"Oh, for God's sake! Couldn't that damn man do something original?" Izzy muttered angrily.

Emma paid the driver, and the women started walking towards the front door. They stopped suddenly when a young girl's laughter reached them. "Bess!" shouted Evelyn.

Emma caught her arm and cautioned the woman, "Remember our plan. We want to approach this logically. We don't want your girls to get hurt." That calmed Evelyn down. They formed a line and continued toward the door.

As they went up the steps, Emma waved them back behind

her. She knocked and waited patiently for the door to be answered. It swung open, revealing a younger version of the two ladies standing behind her. Emma could see past her into the house and realized that it was indeed identical to the two Hugo had with his other families. *The man finds a type and doesn't make a change.*

"Hello, can I help you?" the woman asked politely, blocking the doorway.

"I believe so. I'm Emma Evans and these two ladies..." She wasn't able to finish the thought.

The woman stared at Evelyn and Izzy and said faintly, "You're dead. He told me you were dead."

As she started to fall, Emma said, "Great. Another fainter. Quick, grab her!" As the others rushed to catch the woman, she continued. "Let's get her inside before we start attracting attention."

The others helped get the woman's limp body into the sitting room. They laid her on the sofa, and Izzy looked at the others. "How did she know us?" she asked.

Savannah was fanning the woman and said, "Check out the mantel."

The two wives walked over to see pictures of themselves. "Wow, he's mourning us already," Izzy said faintly.

"The girls," the woman muttered as she woke up. "They're out back playing."

"I'll go see to them," Evelyn stated.

"Thank you," mouthed Izzy.

Her footsteps could be heard going through the house and the back door opening. Screams followed.

The new Mrs. Banks kept saying over and over, "He told me you were dead, both of you. He brought the girls here after we married. He said you were dead!"

At the word married, Emma and Izzy glanced at each other.

The woman caught the glance. "We are married, aren't we?" she asked worriedly.

"Well…" Emma began. "You might be the only one truly married to him."

Izzy looked nonplussed and said, "Explain yourself."

"I believe yours and Evelyn's marriages happened while he was married to his first wife. I'm not sure those are valid. We can work that out with a lawyer."

"Well, I don't want to be married to him! I'm the fourth wife?" the current Mrs. Banks asked, looking faint again. She glanced at Izzy. "I'm so very sorry. I had no idea."

"Can I bring the girls in?" Evelyn called from the back of the house.

"Yes!" answered Izzy.

Her daughter, Bess, ran in and jumped into her arms. "Mama! Papa said you had gone to heaven."

"No, baby," Izzy said, pulling her daughter in for a tight hug. She looked over and saw Evelyn carrying her daughter, Rebecca.

The fainting woman sat up and said, "I think we should introduce ourselves. My name is Catherine. And you are?"

"Izzy Banks."

"Evelyn Banks."

"Emma Evans."

"Savannah Woods."

When Emma and Savannah didn't say Banks, Catherine looked relieved. But she had to ask. "You two aren't married to Hugo, too, are you?"

Emma laughed. "No. No, we're not."

"Oh, thank God," she said, relieved. She looked at Emma and asked, "Where do we go from here?"

"*We*," said Emma, looking at the ladies around her, "have some ideas about that."

CHAPTER 22

The three wives waited together. Catherine looked over at Izzy and Evelyn. "What made you realize your husband had two wives?" She couldn't bring herself to say 'our' concerning Hugo.

"It took a lot," Izzy admitted as she looked over at her new best friend.

Evelyn returned the look. "I didn't believe what Izzy was saying at first. I even threatened her with the police."

"How did you get her to see the truth?" Catherine asked curiously. It was a story she didn't want to believe either.

"I kidnapped her," Izzy admitted.

"Kidnapped?" Catherine asked, fascinated by her fellow wives.

"Essentially. I dragged her to a carriage and made her come to my house."

"Why would that make a difference?"

The other two wives laughed. "Our houses are identical to one another."

"Our?" Catherine asked.

"Yes, *ours*. Your house is identical to mine and Evelyn's."

"Wow," Catherine said. "Hugo had definite ideas on where we were to live and the decorating. Now I know why."

The other two wives nodded.

CHAPTER 23

*E*mma waited patiently, alone in the sitting room. It could be hours before Hugo turned up. A delay would have meant he'd gone to Chicago before coming here. She sat back with a book, looking forward to the confrontation that would take place.

Bang!

The front door crashed inward. Glass fragments clinked as they rained down on the tile floor. Again, she waited. She wouldn't rush this.

Hugo Banks yelled out, running by the sitting room. "*Catherine!* Where are you!" When he didn't get a response, he softened his voice and called out, "Girls? Daddy's home!" He ran back to the foyer and saw Emma in the sitting room. She wore pants and a shirt; her blonde hair was in a high ponytail. She wiggled her fingers as a greeting.

He looked surprised, then he frowned when he recognized her. "You! What are you doing here? You've caused me enough trouble!"

"Yes, I've heard I have that effect on people. Hugo, it's time for us to talk."

"How *dare* you enter my home and interfere with my family! I don't want to talk! Not to you! I want to know where they are!"

"Not just yet," Emma replied calmly. "I have something to discuss with you first."

He seemed at a loss about how to react to her calm demeanor. He moved to a blue side chair and sat, then stood and sat again; putting his hands in his hair, he pulled at it.

The time it had taken Hugo to arrive had allowed Emma to communicate with Mr. Pennington. The lawyer confirmed something she feared, and it was time to ask Hugo about the information. She shifted in her seat, her hat still in her lap, covering her knife.

"Hugo," she began, "I received a telegram today; it mentioned confirmation of burial plots in Cleveland. Who were those for?"

"Why do you want to know?" His voice went up an octave. "It's none of your business," he muttered. He jumped up and shouted, "*Where is my family*? If you won't tell me, I'll beat it out of you." He stalked toward her and, before Emma could pull her knife, Evelyn's voice rang out.

"Which family are you referring to Hugo?" Shoes clicked, and he whipped around to see who it was. He screamed when he saw her. Emma had told her to keep her distance. *This is starting to get out of hand, she* thought.

"Tsk tsk, you left a mess on the floor. I know how much you hate that," Evelyn scolded him.

"You! What are you doing here?" Hugo demanded.

"You didn't answer her question, Which family are you referring to?" Izzy said as she joined Evelyn in the doorway.

He looked from one wife to another and again seemed to be at a loss of what to say. "You're here also? *Where are my daugh-ters?*" he roared as he finally found his voice.

"They're safe," commented Emma again in a calm tone. They had all agreed to let him be the one out of control.

Hugo's rage took over and he swung his gaze from Emma to his wives as he tried to decide who to go after first. He made a quick decision and charged at Emma, his hands outstretched, She didn't stop him as he landed a fist on her face. Her head went back and she reached for her knife. Before she could pull it, there was the sound of a gun being cocked that caused everyone to freeze. Emma saw the gun and then Evelyn. "Evelyn," she said. "Wait, don't shoot."

Evelyn didn't respond. She kept the gun pointed at Hugo.

"Turn around, Hugo. Slowly."

"I'd do as she says," Emma advised. *This is not part of the plan.*

Hugo turned toward Evelyn and Izzy.

"Now, Evelyn," he said, trying to placate her.

"You don't sound like yourself, why is that?" Evelyn chided.

He gave up trying to reason with her and ordered, *"Put the gun down!"*

"There it is. That's the man I know," she said mockingly.

"We have some questions we would like answered," Izzy said.

Hugo didn't say anything. He just watched them. *I can still control them.*

Evelyn waved her gun at him again. "You were so talkative before. You have something to say?"

Emma decided to let this play out. She got a good look at the gun and didn't think it was loaded. But she couldn't take the chance that Izzy and Evelyn would end up with murder charges.

"I don't want to interrupt, but we should secure him. Do you mind?" she asked the wives.

Evelyn looked like she wanted to say no, but Izzy said, "I think that's a good idea."

"Savannah," Emma called. Her friend came into the room. "Come over here and help me with Hugo," she directed.

Both women took an arm and moved him to the couch. They secured his arms behind him with rope.

Once he was settled, he started with his demands to Emma.

"You bring my older girls to me. I want them with me and Catherine."

"Hugo, you're not in charge here. We are. Ladies, why don't you take a seat?" asked Emma.

Izzy and Evelyn stepped further into the room, revealing Catherine behind them.

Hugo was startled when he saw her but remained silent.

Once they settled, Emma sat down across from Hugo. "You are aware that you're supposed to divorce before taking additional wives."

Hugo looked at her, his mouth turned down and a heavy frown on his forehead. "You said you wouldn't interfere in my life. Once I let Elle free." He was referencing his interference in Mr. and Mrs. Gilmore's lives.

Emma responded, "No, the agreement was for that case only. You went too far when you took the children. They should be with their mothers."

"Bah," he said and looked at his first two wives. "I had plans for them."

Emma decided to play along and asked, "What were your plans?"

"My children would be taken care of by their new mother." His wives didn't say anything; they watched him closely

"I won't be here for that role," Catherine said. "I want out."

"You'll have to divorce me and I will not allow that," he said triumphantly.

"Why me? You had two other wives," she asked, looking at the man who was now a stranger to her.

"Yes," he said, "but my annulment occurred after those marriages. You're the only one I'm legally married to."

"No, that can't be right!" Catherine said in horror. "I'm the only one married to you?"

They looked at Emma. She responded, "We'll have to discuss that with a lawyer." *Though,* she thought, *he's probably right.*

Catherine charged at him, grabbing a lamp on her way. Savannah intercepted her before she could reach him. "Let me go!" the woman raged. "He deserves this."

Emma nodded and said, "I agree, and we'll be turning him over to the police for the pain he's inflicted. But I have one thing I still need to know, Hugo. What was the next step in your plans?"

He seemed eager to share. "Oh, after I get rid of both of you," he said, nodding at Evelyn and Izzy, "I'm selling the houses."

"You would just abandon us? With no home or children?" Izzy asked, her greatest fears coming true.

"No," he said, admitting to the entire plan, "I'll kill you both and that will reduce my wifely count."

Izzy and Evelyn looked at him in horror. He said it so confidently, so sure that he was right, that he would have his children with his true wife.

Hugo sat back and looked at Catherine. *She will see this is the best thing. She is just upset now. I will convince her that this is for the best.*

"Is that your whole plan?" asked Emma. The man was sick. She looked at the wives to see how they felt about his plans.

"Yes, all neat and tidy. The girls would forget you both over time. I'll see to that."

That must have been the final straw for Evelyn and she pulled the trigger. Emma was watching the woman's face and, when it changed, she knew it was time to act. She ran and dove at Evelyn as she pointed the gun at Hugo. There was at least one bullet in it, but her aim was off; the bullet went through the top of the mantel. Emma tugged the gun out of Evelyn's hands. "I think I'll keep custody of this," she said.

Catherine walked over to the mantel to survey the damage. "Well, it looks like you got your target," she said wryly. She held up the picture. Evelyn had blown a hole through Hugo's head.

Evelyn started laughing. The other women soon joined in.

"What is everyone laughing at?" Hugo asked belligerently.

This statement just made them laugh harder.

After a minute, Savannah spoke up. "You mostly." She then handed Emma a scarf. Emma took it and fitted it quickly over his mouth and tied it at the back of his head. "Are you okay?" Savanna asked, motioning to her friend's bruised face.

"I am. Don't worry. Ladies, it's time to take your husband to the police station," Emma announced to the group.

"I'll go see about a wagon," said Catherine. Her part of the plan was to provide transportation. Catherine's neighbor, Ian, had access to one and she knew he could be trusted.

"Oh, before you go, Catherine we will need to secure him," Emma said.

"What do you need?" Catherine asked.

"A couple of blankets, please," Emma said, thinking of the best way to keep him quiet.

Catherine ran up the stairs and looked around. "Found them," she called and ran back down. Izzy, Savannah, and Evelyn shook out the blankets and, with Emma's help, laid Hugo on the floor and wrapped them around him.

"Make sure he can breathe," Emma cautioned. She was watching how tightly they were binding him with the ropes around the outside of the blanket.

"Why?" Evelyn asked bitterly.

"Because we need him alive. He's going to prison this time—no deals—and that will be hard if he's dead."

Hugo's eyes widened. That was always his out; no one wanted to be known to be married to a bigamist. Are *they this strong? Could they testify against him?*

Catherine came back in with Ian. He was a large man who looked more suited to being a lumberjack than city life.

"I'll take it from here, ladies," he said and tossed the blanket-wrapped Hugo over his shoulder. He took him to the wagon he had stationed in front of Catherine's house, then placed him none too gently into the back. "Oops. Sorry about that," he said when Hugo bounced.

Emma smiled and said, "Everyone climb in." Evelyn and Izzy joined her and Savannah. Catherine sat beside Ian on the driver's seat.

On the way to the police station, Catherine turned to Ian. "Thank you for helping."

He stared straight ahead. "Not that it's any of my business, but what did he do?"

"He's married," she said simply.

"Well yeah," he said, "to you."

"Not just me," she murmured.

"What! Who else?" he asked, flabbergasted, stopping them abruptly.

"The ladies with us. Two of them are his wives," she said.

He got them moving faster. She gripped her seat and looked over at him with raised eyebrows. He said, "The sooner he's under arrest, the better."

When they arrived at the station, Ian hopped down and reached up to help Catherine to the ground. Walking around to the back of the wagon, he lowered the gate and assisted the other ladies. Hugo was rolled over and once again thrown onto his shoulder. They went into the station, ready for whatever they might need to face.

The desk officer looked around at the people in front of him; they were all talking at the same time. He called loudly, "Silence! Who's speaking for this group?"

Emma held up her hand. "We have a bigamist we'd like to turn in."

"He's married to all of you?" the office asked incredulously.

"Three of us are," Izzy stated. By agreement, they had chosen not to bring Hugo's first wife, Elle, into this mess.

"Who was married first?" the officer asked, looking at them in interest.

"I'm the first," stated Izzy.

"I'm the second," stated Evelyn.

"I'm the third," Catherine stated quietly.

"Are there any children involved?"

"Yes," Emma replied. "There are four girls. Two from Izzy and two from Evelyn."

He looked at Catherine. "None," she said. *Thank goodness.*

"Let me find someone to take this over and move you into another room."

"Excuse me, sir?" Ian asked.

"Yes?"

"I need to put this somewhere," he said, pointing to the carpet roll on his shoulder.

"What is it?"

"The bigamist, Hugo Banks," Emma answered for him.

He looked surprised and got up to find an officer to take them to a more private location. "Detective Daniels will take Emma and Mr. Banks into one room and the wives into another." He had Ian transfer his load to one of his fellow policemen and the others followed. Ian stayed with Catherine. She seemed grateful for his support and said to him, "Why don't you head home?"

"Are you sure?" He didn't want to leave her.

"I am." He nodded and turned to leave. The rest of their group went into their assigned rooms and Hugo was settled into a chair. Officer Daniels took one across from him and Emma stood in the small room.

The detective sat at the table and reviewed the other officer's notes. "The four children, where are they?"

"They're safe," Emma answered. Ian's mother had volunteered to watch the two little girls until they all returned.

Daniels looked almost regretful as he said, "I guess we'll have to untie him. Why is he wrapped in a blanket?"

"He got rather excited and we had to subdue him for the trip over here," Emma replied.

Daniels stood to untie and unwrap Hugo with a guard standing by. Once Hugo's arms were freed, he removed the binding covering his mouth. Immediately, the man started yelling, "They kidnapped me and held me prisoner! She... she..." he stuttered, aiming his fist at Emma. "She's interfering in my life again."

"Again?" Daniels asked.

"Never mind that," Hugo said, realizing what he had almost disclosed.

Emma smiled to herself. He had started to admit to a fourth marriage. Due to the confidential nature of the previous agreement, she couldn't share any details, but he could.

Daniels looked at her and she shook her head. *I'll have to follow up with her later,* he thought. He directed his gaze back to Hugo. "Now, why would this nice lady hold you hostage?"

"I don't know, but I'd just like to head home now," Hugo said, hoping this was the end of it.

"You won't be pressing charges?" Daniels asked idly.

"*NO!* I'd just like to go home."

"Well, now that that's all settled, there'll be no charges for the ladies here. Why don't we talk about yours?"

"Mine! What charges?"

"Bigamy," Daniels said simply.

Hugo's mouth opened and closed several times, but nothing came out.

"I see you'd like some time to continue gathering your thoughts," the detective said wryly. "We have three women out there who say they're married to you."

"Well, they're lying. I only have one wife." He thought, *I have them now. There's no proof of the marriages.*

"Oh, I forgot. Detective, I have these with me," Emma said as she pulled some folded papers out of her jacket and handed them to him.

Daniels took his time looking at them. Finally, he stood and went to the door.

Hugo watched him and thought, *He's going to tell me I can leave.* He sneered at Emma, *She thought she had me.*

Daniels stepped back into the room with two more officers. "Please take Mr. Banks to booking," he directed.

"*What? NO!*" Hugo started to run out the door. The two officers stopped him and placed cuffs on his wrist. "But you have no proof."

"Your wives are giving sworn statements now," Daniels commented.

"But they're lying!" Hugo screamed again.

"Are they?" the detective asked, feigning interest.

"Yes!"

"You see, Mr. Banks, I have these to back up their stories." He showed him the papers but didn't get close enough for Hugo to see what they were.

"What are they?" There was nothing that would calm him down.

"These are your wedding certificates for all three marriages. I'm afraid, Mr. Banks, that you will have to answer for this in court. You'll be going to prison."

"Prison for getting married?" Hugo asked, desperate for this nightmare to be over.

"Sir, you married more than your fair share," chided the detective.

Hugo seemed to have no answer to that and just stared at them.

"Take him away," Daniels told his officers.

Once he was out of the room, Emma looked at him and said, "You took me at my word."

"The Chicago Police Chief sent me a telegram this morning

and said that I should listen to what you have to say. He said you've worked investigations for him and the Pinkerton Detectives."

"We have him this time? Hugo won't get released?"

Daniels nodded. "We'll need to investigate some more but, for now, we'll keep him locked up." He looked at her face and asked, "Did he do that to you?"

She held up her hand to her cheek; it had started to throb. "Yes."

"I assume you'll file an assault charge as well."

"I will," Emma confirmed. She had let Hugo land that punch, knowing the assault charge would keep him locked up until the bigamy could be proven. She provided a statement so the charges could be filed.

"What will you do now?" he asked as he took the paper from her.

"That's a good question. I would like to reunite the families."

"Yes. Banks will be in custody for a while."

"I'll go to the women now. Thank you for your help in this matter."

Daniels nodded and Emma headed out of the room.

The young officer in the hallway asked, "Miss, are you looking for the wives?"

"Yes, do you know where they are?" she asked.

"I do. Would you like me to take you to them?" he offered.

"Yes, please." She accompanied the officer down the long hallway. It was lined with windows that looked into offices and conference rooms. As they turned a corner, the women came into view. Savannah stood looking out the window on the far side of their room. The wives sat together, alternately patting one another's arms.

Savannah turned and saw her first; she called over to the wives and gestured to Emma. They gave her all of their attention as she entered the room.

"We got him," Emma said quickly. "Hugo's in custody."

There was silence and they continued to stare at her.

Emma thought she was delivering good news.

"Izzy, what will we do?" Evelyn said. She looked distraught as she reached out and took the other woman's hand.

Izzy said bracingly, "Evelyn, we do what we planned before. We go forward together for us and our girls."

Catherine looked forlorn. Emma was stirred to ask, "What's wrong?"

"I'm not sure," she said, looking at the two wives and then at Emma. "This morning, I had a home, a husband, and two little girls. Now, I seem to have nothing."

"No!" the other two wives protested. "You have us."

"No. You're family. I think I need a fresh start."

"Will you need help with that? To start over?" Emma asked.

Catherine leaned back and laughed suddenly. "No, on that account, I have no problems. My family left me quite well off."

The other wives looked at each other and Evelyn asked, "Did Hugo know?"

"He knew," Catherine murmured. "I'm the daughter of one of his company's richest clients."

Izzy reached over to her. "We would like you to keep in touch and let us know how you are."

"First thing I am doing is selling that house!" Catherine said. "I never liked it, but he insisted."

The other two wives started laughing. Evelyn answered for Izzy. "We're thinking the same thing."

"What about the older girls, can we go get them?" Izzy asked Emma expectantly.

Emma hesitated. "I think we need them with you and in your custody."

"Will we have to go to Chicago for them?" asked Evelyn.

"I'm thinking you should come back to Chicago with me. I

work for an attorney there and he has experience with bigamy cases and, specifically, with Hugo."

"Oh," Izzy said, "I guess we do need someone to work out the legalities of this mess."

"Yes," Emma said.

"What about me?" asked Catherine.

Emma looked over at her. "You concern me the most."

"The fact that I might be the only one married to him?"

"Yes, the fact you were married after his previous annulment. I want to make sure you get the proper legal advice."

"Then," she said, "I'll also accompany you to Chicago."

"We should try to leave as soon as the police say it's okay," Emma told the group.

"What if we need to stay here?" Izzy asked. She was worried about finances for both Evelyn and herself.

"You can stay with me," Catherine said decisively. "I insist." She looked over at Emma and asked, "Can we head home now?"

"Yes," Emma said. "Detective Daniels will let us know when we may leave town." They headed downstairs and she hailed two carriages.

"Aren't you coming back to the house with us?" Catherine asked.

"No, I need to go to the telegraph office to let my boss know what's happened and let him know you'll be coming to Chicago. I'll meet you all at the house."

"Would you like me to go with you?" Savannah asked.

"No, I think we're just about done here."

"Good. I'm ready to return home," her friend said.

"I'll be back soon." Emma watched as they climbed into the carriage and headed to Catherine's. She wanted to notify Mr. Pennington to be ready for them. Lastly, she needed to get her and Savannah's bags and check out of the hotel.

Later, as she entered Catherine's house, she found everyone

settled in the sitting room. Without revealing herself to the other ladies, she motioned to Savannah to come into the foyer.

Savannah put down her book and went over to her to help her with the bags. As they got them settled, she said in a low voice, "The detective wants you to go back to the station."

"Did he say why?" Emma asked, her tone similar.

"I'm hoping it is so that we can go home."

"I'll head there now," she said. "Tell them I'll be back soon."

She went outside and hailed a carriage.

"Where to, miss?" the driver asked as he helped her into the carriage.

"Police station, please."

He nodded and climbed back on his seat. He clicked at the horses to get them moving. The trip to the station was short, and he helped her down. As she paid him, he asked, "Should I wait for you?"

"I'm not sure how long I will be. If you're in the area, check here in about an hour."

"I can do that," he promised.

He departed and she went into the station. The officer at the front desk recognized her. "No additional ladies with you this time?" he asked, grinning.

"No, they're at home resting. Can you ask Detective Daniels if he has time for me?"

"Yes, I believe he does." He called behind him and said, "Officer, please take Miss Evans to Daniels."

Emma followed the officer into the offices they had passed earlier that day. The officer knocked lightly on a door and announced, "Miss Evans is here."

Detective Daniels called her to come in. "Emma, I appreciate you returning so quickly."

"We'd like to get the wives out of town as soon as possible. I have an attorney ready to take their case and I'd like to reunite the mothers with their children."

"That is a good idea."

"What will happen now?"

"We have him on the assault charge. We can probably use that as a pressure point on the bigamy case."

"Can we head out of town tomorrow morning?"

He nodded. "It's probably for the best. Can you give me your contact information in Chicago?"

"Of course, let me know if anything changes. Especially if Hugo's released for any reason."

"I will," he promised.

She left and found the carriage outside. "You were able to come back," she said as he jumped down to help her into the carriage.

"Yes. Back to the same house?" he asked.

"Yes, please." They started and she called to him, "On second thought, I need train tickets. Could we go by the station first?"

"Of course." He took her to the train station and waited while she picked up the tickets.

When she returned, he asked, "Back now?"

"Yes, please."

They made it back to Catherine's house and Emma got out of the carriage. "Thank you," she said and waved as the carriage pulled away. She made her way back into the house, looking down at the tickets. *This will allow everyone to get safely out of town while the police build their case.*

She entered and found Izzy and the little girls sitting on the floor together playing.

Izzy saw her enter. "Emma, you're back."

"Yes, and I got permission for us to leave. I picked up the tickets for the morning." She showed her the tickets.

"Good! Evelyn, Catherine, come down. Emma has news!"

Catherine and Evelyn came down the stairs, and Savannah appeared from the kitchen.

"Get packed, we're leaving tomorrow." All of them looked relieved.

"Mama, are we going on another trip?" asked Rebecca.

Evelyn bent down and said, "Yes, baby, we are going to pick up your sister."

"Good. I missed her."

"I'm sure she missed you also."

"Us, too?" Bess asked, tugging on her mother's dress.

Izzy pulled her close. "Of course."

"We have dinner ready," Catherine said. "Why don't we go in, and then we can have an early night?"

"Yes, I think that's a good idea," Emma said, taking Savannah's arm and walking into the dining room. The food was good and the company was talkative. After dinner, she and Savannah were in the living room lying on bedrolls.

"I'm looking forward to the bed back at the boarding house," Savannah said.

"Me, too," said Emma. *And Jeremy,* she thought. She looked over at her friend and asked curiously, "How are you and Ethan?"

Savannah flushed. "Good. We're good."

"Do you think it's a long-term thing?" Savannah was currently working for a theater and traveled three to four times a year with various shows.

She turned to her. "I think it might be."

"But you have doubts?"

"I love Ethan. I want to be with him and marry him."

"Well then, what's the concern?" Emma asked. She didn't believe in marriage for herself, but she didn't force her views on other people.

"I'd like to keep working at the theater and traveling with shows."

"Have you mentioned this to Ethan?"

"No."

"Maybe you should. He might not find this a problem. Be honest and find out. The worst thing you can do is not to say anything."

"You're right," Savannah said as she thought about that.

"Has he asked you to marry him?"

"Not yet, but soon, I think. He's been very nervous as of late."

"He's easy for you to read?" It was like that for her and Jeremy.

"For me. Yes."

"Give him a chance," suggested Emma.

"I will," she promised. "Home tomorrow?"

"Yes, on our way tomorrow."

"Emma?" Savannah asked her friend.

"Hmmmm?"

"You let Hugo punch you, didn't you?"

"I did."

"Ha! I knew it!" Savannah exclaimed. "Why, though?"

"Just in case the bigamy charge didn't hold, I figured an assault charge on a 'poor, helpless' woman would hold him until we could get everyone out of town."

"Helpless? You?" Savannah scoffed.

"Oh, shut up and get some sleep." Emma smiled at her friend.

They woke early and had the girls eat before they left. Everyone was packed and dressed, and Ian had the wagon waiting to take them all to the train station.

"I appreciate you helping out again this morning," Emma said to Ian.

"I want to help." He looked behind her and saw Catherine carrying a bag. He walked over to her. "Are you going with them?"

"Yes. Emma recommended that we see the lawyer she works for to protect ourselves before Hugo goes to trial."

"Good idea," he said, but he didn't want her to leave. "When do you think you'll be back?"

"Soon," she said.

He saw his one chance to say something, and he grabbed her hand and pulled her to the side of the house.

She looked startled but accompanied him. She saw Emma's expression and said, "It's okay."

Emma nodded and watched in case she might need to intervene.

"Catherine, I couldn't let you go and not tell you something," Ian said desperately.

"What is it, Ian?" she asked softly. She had known this man her whole life; he had always been around. When she moved here with Hugo, he'd bought the house next to hers.

Now that Ian had her alone, he looked nervous.

"Ian?" she asked. "What did you want to tell me?"

"I love you," he said, looking down at their interlocked hands.

"What?"

"I love you!" he said loudly

"Love me? But you never said anything," Catherine said, shocked.

"I was finally getting up the nerve to talk to you and then Hugo showed up. He just took you over."

"Yes, I think he did that so I didn't have time to think or make a proper decision," she explained.

"I wanted to ask you to marry me."

"Is that why you moved here? To be near me."

"I wanted to be here, even if you couldn't be mine. I wanted to be able to see you each day."

She touched his face with her hands. "Ian, can you wait for me a little longer?"

"If I knew you felt the same way I do, I would wait forever," he said fervently.

"I'll be back soon and then we can make some plans," she said softly, gazing into his eyes.

He kept a tight grip on her hands.

She smiled softly and said, "We should be going now."

"Okay," he said, not able to take his eyes off her.

Emma walked up and said, "I think we're ready to go."

"Yes." Ian let Catherine go and said, "Let's go to the train station."

They made it to the station and he lifted Catherine out last. They watched each other and she told him, "I will see you soon," she told him.

"I will be here," Ian promised and watched until they board the train before heading home. *Waiting*, he thought. *I can do that. I will wait for her.*

CHAPTER 24

The trip took a week and, when they pulled into Chicago, the group was glad to be off the train.

"Emma!" a voice called out. She looked over and saw it was Thomas.

"Thomas, you got my telegraph!" She had sent it from the station the morning they departed.

"I did," he said as he rushed over. He snatched the hat off his head and said hello to the group. The women responded with grateful smiles.

"What happened to your face?" Bess asked loudly.

"Bess!" Izzy scolded.

"No, that's okay." Thomas bent down to the girl. "I got burned when I was younger. This happens if you get too close to a fire." Thomas had gotten caught in the 1871 Chicago fire.

"Does it hurt?" she asked, reaching out to touch his face.

"Not for a long time," he said. He let her touch the wrinkled skin. He stood and looked at the group. "Would you like to go to the house now?"

"We would," said Evelyn gratefully.

"Savannah!" a man's voice called. She looked over and saw it was Ethan. She ran to him.

Emma looked at Thomas. "Did you tell him we were coming?"

"I had to. He was at our office daily hoping for an update," Thomas explained.

Emma turned to Savannah and called, "Go with Ethan."

"Thank you, Emma!" they both called back, then ran off together laughing.

Thomas helped the wives and girls into his wagon and, when they were settled into the back, he moved back to the driver's seat. He clicked to move the horses. A few blocks from the safe house location, he pulled into an alley. He turned to them. "Ladies, we need you to lie down and be quiet. The house we're going to is special and we don't want people to see who's coming and going. Do you understand?" He looked at the wives first, then the girls. They all nodded. "I have blankets that I'll cover you with." Once they lay down, he pulled the blankets over them and exited the alley.

It was a few minutes later when they stopped and Thomas said in a low voice, "Wait here." He jumped down and tapped lightly on the door. It opened quickly. Katie came out with Clair and they went to the back of the wagon. They uncovered everyone and held a finger to their lips to remind the girls to stay quiet. They got out quickly and made their way inside. Once the door was closed behind them, Clair said, "I think there are people here who would like to see you." The two older girls ran into the room, each of them going to their mama.

"Oh, Mama! I've missed you so much," Evie said.

"Me, too, Mama," Mabel said to her mother.

"What about me?" Bess asked.

"Yes, I missed you also," her sister said.

Mabel had already moved to pick up Rebecca.

"Let's go in into the sitting room," Clair said. She turned to Katie and asked, "Tea and treats?"

"Of course."

The group moved into the other room and Clair walked over to Emma. "You look tired. Can you stay a little while until we get them settled?"

"Of course."

They sat down and introductions were made.

"What type of house is this?" Izzy asked, looking around.

"We call it a safe house. Somewhere we can house women and children who need to be hidden from things in their lives."

"I didn't know places like this existed," Evelyn said.

"We have to keep them hidden, otherwise it would defeat the purpose," Clair explained. "How long do you expect to stay?"

Emma answered for them. "I want to meet with Mr. Pennington. We need his advice on their situation."

"Of course." Emma had briefed her on the case. Clair hadn't expected a third wife, but she understood they needed to be together at this time.

Katie brought in the tea. Once everyone had their fill, Clair told the group, "I'll show you all to your bedrooms. You can tell Thomas which bags are yours."

Once they were settled, Clair came back downstairs. "Thomas," she called. He came in from the kitchen. "Can you take Emma home?"

"Of course."

"Come back for me after. Lily should be here soon to take over for the night," said Clair.

He kissed her and motioned for Emma to follow him out.

CHAPTER 25

*E*mma was yawning now and said, "Thomas, thank you. Tell the ladies I'll go by the office first thing tomorrow to see Mr. Pennington and then come by here."

"I'll do that," he promised.

She climbed into the back of the wagon and he covered her up for the trip home. When they arrived at the boarding house, he took the blanket off and found Emma sleeping. He nudged her shoulder. "We're here."

She sat up quickly and looked around. "I must have drifted off. This is becoming a habit."

He helped her down. "Do you need help with your bag?" he asked, holding it.

"No," she yawned and reached for it. "I can manage it."

He gave it to her and then watched until she was in the house before he left. It was an old habit he had of watching out for her.

She unlocked the door and as she started up the stairs. Dora met her halfway up with a hug. "Is everyone okay?"

"Yes, I just want to go to bed." Dora nodded and helped her sister with her bag.

Emma didn't turn up the gas lights, but grabbed her night clothes and went to the bathroom. Once there, she cleaned up. She would have liked a bath and to wash her hair, but the tiredness was overwhelming. She made it back to her room and climbed into the big bed, wishing Jeremy was back with her.

$\mathcal{E}$mma slept hard and awoke at her normal time. She made her way downstairs and grabbed some butter and bread as her breakfast. "Tell Dora I'll be back at lunch and will tell her everything then," she instructed Amy and Ethyl.

"I will," Amy said, watching her hurriedly eat her breakfast and leave out the back door.

Emma wanted to be in the office when Mr. Pennington arrived for the day. It was early and Ethan had not yet arrived when she pedaled her bike up to the office location. She got off and sat on the stoop waiting for him.

"You're early," Ethan said as he walked up. He had a smile on his face. Emma knew Savannah being back had put it there.

"Yes, lots to do."

"I do have several files for you to review."

"I'll pick them up after I store my bike," Emma said and followed him up the stairs. She got the files and started working on them, listening closely for Mr. Pennington to arrive for the day. When she heard the door open, she hurried to meet him.

He saw her and said, "Emma, you're back. Can you come into my office?"

"Yes, sir. I'll be right with you." She took the files she was reviewing back to her desk, holding back a yawn. She had slept hard but felt like she was still tired from the long trip. There was just no time to rest and the ladies would need some support.

She walked into his office and Mr. Pennington looked up. "Sit down. Tell me what happened."

She sat in the chair across from his desk. "Hugo was arrested for bigamy," she said simply.

"Finally got him," he said with a laugh.

"It's just as we thought," she said. "He has another wife, but this time the charges included kidnapping, possible attempted murder, and assault."

At that last part, he raised his eyebrow in question. "Who did he assault?" Pennington asked.

"Me."

"Your cheek?" The bruise had started to fade.

"Yes. When I was questioning him, Hugo hit me in the face."

"He hit you, or you allowed him to hit you?" Pennington knew Emma could take care of herself and also knew Hugo wouldn't have been able to hit her unless she'd planned it that way.

"Well..." Emma began.

"Say no more. The assault charge will stay."

Emma smiled and continued. "We believe he meant to get rid of the second and third wives." She told him about the stories Hugo had fed to the new wife about the prior wives' deaths, the funeral plots, and trying to sell their homes.

Pennington sat back, watching her speak.

"I have the wives and their daughters with me and they're safe. I could think of no one else who knows this case and this man's history as well as you do."

His eyes glinted and he rubbed his hands together gleefully. "Well, well, so we get another opportunity to go after him."

"Yes. The two wives just want out of their marriages and they want full custody of their girls. The current wife will probably need an annulment."

"It will be complicated with his criminal case. Will the women provide testimony?" he asked.

"They want him stopped so, yes, I believe they will testify."

"Can you bring the ladies here to the office?"

"I think it might be better if you went to them," she said, thinking of the children. "I'd rather not parade them around. We have them in a safe location."

"I'll do what I have to do," he said. "Can you set it up?"

"Yes, I can arrange that, as long as you keep the location confidential. No one can know where they are."

"I can do that. Can you arrange our visit for this afternoon?"

"That works," she confirmed and left his office.

She asked Ethan to send a note to Clair's office informing her of Pennington's visit. She waited for a response. Clair sent back a response and said that would be fine as long as it was just the one person.

She closed the note and went to Mr. Pennington's office. She knocked lightly and was asked to come in.

"The visit has been confirmed for after lunch," she said.

He nodded and she returned to her work. The morning went by and she told Mr. Pennington, "I'll meet you here and then we'll proceed to Clair's office to get the necessary transportation. Is 1:00pm okay with you?"

"I'll be here and ready."

She nodded, retrieved her bike, and carried it downstairs. Riding home, she enjoyed the air on her face; it kept her awake. She made it home, put the bike up, and headed to the back door. Ethyl saw her first. "Welcome back."

Amy saw her and said, "Welcome back. You left so fast this morning, we didn't get a chance to greet you."

"I had a meeting to plan for," she explained.

"Lunch is on the table. Go on in and get some food," Amy commanded.

"I will and thank you. You sound more like Dora every day," Emma teased.

Amy tossed a towel her way and Emma laughed as she entered the dining room. The family was all in place around the table, even Jake and Savannah.

"Jake, you came home for lunch?" she asked, surprised. He never changed his schedule if he could help it.

"Yes, I heard you were home and I didn't get to see you this morning," he explained.

"Well, thank you," she said and went to sit next to him.

"Papa and Abbey want to come to dinner tonight and catch up on the cases," Dora told her.

Emma thought about that. "That should be okay. I do want to keep it within our immediate team for now."

"Can you give us some details?" Tim asked.

She looked regretful. "I want to but I need to take Mr. Pennington to meet the ladies. We have to figure out where they stand in this mess."

"Okay, we can wait until this evening," he said.

Savannah was eating hurriedly. "Do you have someplace to be?" Dora asked.

"I thought I might go back with Emma and see Ethan," she admitted.

Emma smiled at her and said, "I'd love the company. We can take the trolley. I won't need my bike."

Savannah grinned over at her.

After lunch, they got their things and started toward the office. "Ethan, huh," Emma teased.

"Yeah. I think you're right. I need to tell him what I'm thinking about. He means too much to me to leave him out of any future decisions."

They hopped off the trolley and made it to the office. As they entered, Ethan didn't look up when he commented, "Mr. Pennington should be back soon. There are files on your desk for you to work on for now."

Emma grinned at Savannah. "Okay. Oh, Savannah, thanks for walking over with me."

At that, Ethan's head popped up. When he saw who was with Emma, he jumped to his feet and went around the desk to take Savannah into his arms. "It's good to see you," he murmured and buried his face in her neck.

Emma gave them their privacy and went into her office. She closed the door and sat at her desk. Like Ethan said, he had placed new files there.

A light knock on the door pulled her away from her reading. "Come in," she said.

Savannah stuck her head in. "I'm going to the park with Ethan. We should be back soon."

"Okay, is Mr. Pennington back?"

"He is," Pennington called out. "Please come to my office."

"On my way." She waved as she followed Savannah. Her friend ran over to Ethan and they exited the office together. Emma headed over to Mr. Pennington's office. "Are you ready to go?"

"I am," he replied. He walked her out and locked the door behind them. Ethan would open back up when he returned from the park.

"Where to, young lady?" he asked.

"We'll go to Clair's office on Moffit Street and Thomas will take us from there."

He hailed a carriage, as he didn't want to walk the multiple blocks necessary to get to the office building. Once the carriage arrived, he helped her in and they sat quietly enjoying the day. When they pulled up at Clair's office, he helped her down and paid the driver. Just as they prepared to go in, Emma heard a long whistle. She looked over and saw Thomas.

"Mr. Pennington, over there." She nodded to Thomas. They headed toward him and climbed into the back of the wagon. Once they got within a few blocks, Thomas pulled into an alley. Emma said, "Mr. Pennington, we'll need to hide under the blankets and lay flat."

"I understand." He did as he was asked.

They drove a while longer and stopped. She touched his shoulder and whispered, "We wait."

He nodded and stayed where he was.

Presently, Thomas said, "You can come out now." They lowered the blanket and Thomas helped her down and offered Mr. Pennington a hand as well. They entered through the kitchen. Katie was there cleaning up from lunch. "Well, hello," she said. "We have a new visitor?"

"Mr. Pennington, this is Katie. She keeps the food and the house."

"It's very nice to meet you, Katie. I am James," he said suavely. Emma peered at him; she hadn't seen him around anyone other than clients before.

Katie blushed prettily and said, "The ladies and girls are in the sitting room."

As they walked out to meet them, Emma told him, "They don't have any other guests right now. It's just the wives and their children."

"Hmm, we might need Katie to distract the children," he said.

"Wait here a moment," she stopped him outside the sitting room. "and I'll let her know." Emma walked back and reappeared with Katie.

"Just take them to the study," Emma suggested. "There are books they might want you to read to them."

"I can do that," Katie said, understanding the intention behind their request.

They enter the sitting room. The ladies were keeping busy with sewing and conversation. The kids sat together with dolls on the floor. "Girls," Katie said. "Would you like me to read you a book in the study?" The older girls looked at their mamas and they nodded. They stood and took the small girls by their hands and left the room.

"Ladies, I am James Pennington. Emma asked me here to go over the law and see what help you might need."

They looked relieved.

"Why don't we start with your names and addresses?" he asked.

They each gave their name and address. Emma jotted them down quickly for him. She handed him the paper.

He went over each of their marriages and the timing for each. "I'm assuming Hugo will be going to prison for a long time for the bigamy and the assault charges."

"Good," all three said together.

"I did want to bring up that there is a way to keep this quiet," he said.

"How would that work?" Evelyn asked.

"We could ask him to sign for the divorces and give you the houses as part of a deal."

"Would the deal mean no prison time for him?" asked Izzy.

"I am afraid so," he said regretfully.

"Then no deal. We've thoroughly discussed this and have decided that, whatever it takes, Hugo is not doing this to someone else," Izzy said.

Emma watched them and thought, *They are brave.*

"What about the girls?" asked Emma. She wanted Hugo in prison as much as they did, but she wanted to make sure they knew the children could be affected by all of this.

Evelyn spoke for them. "We talked about that also; we'd like to sell the houses and move far away to start over where no one's aware of our backgrounds."

"That would probably be for the best," allowed Mr. Pennington.

Emma drummed her fingers on her lips and said, "Our charity can probably help you with that."

Catherine spoke up at that time. "No, that won't be necessary. I'll help them. Whatever they need, I'll be here for them. Always."

The other two wives teared up and went to hug her. They were a family, a very different one from the norms of today, but a family nonetheless.

Pennington looked at all three. "So, our goal is to get you your homes and children, am I right?"

"Yes. Do whatever you have to, but keep Hugo in prison," stated Evelyn fiercely. The wives nodded their agreement.

"Can we go back to our homes until this is worked out?" Izzy asked.

"No, I think you should stay here. Emma, can we use your contacts to have officers patrol the homes until we get this finalized?" said Mr. Pennington.

Emma nodded and made a note to contact the Chicago Police Chief for a favor.

As they were leaving, she asked him, "Will you need to go to New York to talk to Hugo?"

"I'm hoping that, given the extenuating circumstances, we can get them to bring him here," he commented.

CHAPTER 27

Emma and Pennington confirmed that Hugo Banks would be brought to Chicago for the interview. They used the time he had to travel to strategize how to handle him.

Emma watched Hugo walk into Pennington's office. He looked self-assured and his lawyer had a smile on his face. An officer accompanied him and waited in Ethan's office area. "They think they have us, don't they?" she murmured to Mr. Pennington.

"They do," he said in a similar tone, "but this time I have the wives on our side." She smiled slowly. "Why don't we sit down?" Mr. Pennington said to Hugo and his lawyer,

Hugo's lawyer began, "The only evidence against my client is the testimony of my client's 'supposed' wives."

"You don't think they will follow through with testifying?" Pennington asked.

"Them? No, they won't go against me. They love me," Hugo stated confidently.

Mr. Pennington looked at the man and said, "Love? I don't think that's the emotion they're experiencing right now. Have you talked to them since you were charged?"

"No, but I know what they want." Hugo's voice didn't sound as positive as it did initially.

Pennington looked at him. "I'm afraid when you took the children you played your final card." He looked over at Emma and said, "It's time."

She nodded and stood. She left the room and entered her office. All three ladies were there. "Are you ready?" she asked them.

They looked at each and Izzy spoke for them. "Yes, we're ready."

"Please be aware, Hugo thinks you're on his side and has no doubt of his ability to get through this with no prison time."

"Does he? Well, we'll just have to dispel that notion," Catherine said.

"Catherine, you will wait outside the office."

She nodded and Emma opened her door and walked them to the other office. It was a very proud parade. His two wives stared at Hugo. They weren't demure, and they weren't going to let him have his way.

"Ladies!" Hugo said. He stood to go to them. His lawyer put a hand on his arm and pulled him back into his seat and began whispering furiously in his ear.

"What? No, they love me. NO! I want to talk!" Hugo looked at them, but this time he stayed seated. "Ladies, I was always going to make sure your girls stayed with you. This was just a short vacation for them."

"A vacation with a new wife?" Evelyn sneered.

He looked at the formally submissive woman. "Why, yes. I mean, it's worked out fine so far."

"Has it?" Izzy asked.

"Yes!" His lawyer pulled his arm again and continued to offer him directions. "Fine! Fine! My lawyer says I have to tell you I won't take the children," he muttered.

The lawyer leaned in again and whispered more advice.

Hugo said in a rush, "Or the houses."

The two women started to relax, but then Izzy asked, with a frown, "Are you going to put that in writing?"

"Yes, of course," said his lawyer, "but we would like you to drop the bigamy charges. Say that you were never married."

"Never married? We have marriage licenses and children who need their father's name," Evelyn said loudly.

Mr. Pennington knew it was time to speak up. "Mr. Banks, there will be no deal."

"But the other time…" Hugo started, he noticed the way his wives glared at him and stopped talking abruptly.

"We have found the information that you planned the sale of your wives' homes and you purchased burial plots for each of them."

"Oh, those," Hugo said nervously, "those are for the future. In case anything unfortunate should happen to them." He chose a different tack and nudged his lawyer to speak.

"My client would like to dissolve the first two marriages of Evelyn and Isabella Banks," his lawyer stated.

"What about the marriage to Catherine Banks?" Pennington asked. Catherine didn't want to stay married to Hugo either.

"Oh, I want to stay with that marriage," Hugo said confidently.

"You do?" asked Catherine. Emma had stepped to the door and waved her into the room. She heard his statement.

He looked at her in surprise. "Yes, of course. We've just begun our lives together."

"Well, it's ending here. Mr. Pennington is handling my divorce case also. Though I might get an annulment, given the amount of time we actually spent together."

Hugo hadn't known the meeting would go like this. He expected the ladies to go along with his plans; after all, they always had. They stood in a proud line, together and against him.

Mr. Pennington spoke. "Mr. Banks, we will be invalidating all of your marriages. Once your first one was declared annulled, the other two were not valid."

Hugo tried one last thing; he shook his hand at Izzy. "You knew. You should have to face charges also."

"Did I know?" Izzy asked. "There's no one to testify that I knew anything."

He looked at all three and saw there was no one on his side. His lawyer spoke low in his ear. He finally nodded.

Hugo's lawyer said, "Mr. Banks will sign off on the paperwork to divorce wives one and two and annul the third marriage."

"What about the houses?" Pennington prompted.

"They can have those also," the lawyer allowed. "Mr. Banks will remain in town until the paperwork is completed."

Hugo thought agreeing to the meeting would give him his freedom, but it had not. He was taken into custody and would be remanded to the Chicago jail until the paperwork was ready.

The ladies and Mr. Pennington went to lunch.

"How long do you think it will take?" Izzy asked.

"The paperwork to dissolve the marriages?" Pennington asked.

"Yes."

He looked thoughtful. "A few days. I'll draft them today and arrange for him to sign them tomorrow. I will come by here afterward and get you all to sign yours."

Izzy and Evelyn looked at one another and back at him. "We plan to sell our houses and move away from the area. The girls need a fresh start."

"Can I contact you when it's time for you to return for your testimony? You all must be here."

"We'll come back for that, and we'll give you our contact information."

Evelyn and Izzy walked out with Mr. Pennington. Emma

hung back to speak with Catherine. "Will you stay in your current home?"

"No, I'll sell also. We all need a fresh start."

"What about Ian? I noticed he'd like to see more of you."

"Yes, I want that also. I think it was always meant to be Ian."

"Then why Hugo if you felt that way about Ian?"

"You have seen how he is. When he wants something, nothing will stand in his way. I just got swept up. It was exciting," she admitted.

"Yes, I see." Though she didn't. Hugo Banks was all surface and any time spent with him showed what his true nature was.

They walked to the other ladies. They would take the train to Cleveland two days after the paperwork was signed. Catherine had promised to accompany them and set up a money manager to sell the houses and furniture. The packing would be completed and Catherine had set up a house for them to move to in another state.

"We got him," Emma said to Mr. Pennington as they watched them leave.

"Yes, we did. You did a very good job on this. Now, I need to draft that paperwork. Ethan, can you come into my office?"

"Yes, sir," Ethan said and followed him.

Mr. Pennington looked over at Emma. "Take a few days to rest. This whole thing has been trying."

"I would appreciate that. Let me know if any help is needed with the wives' paperwork," she said. She returned to her office to prepare to go home.

As she was leaving, Pennington stepped out. "You did a good thing here. You protected three families when society would have just abandoned them."

"And Hugo will finally get what's coming to him."

"That, too." He laughed.

Emma took her bike and went home.

Emma pulled her bike to a stop in front of the boarding house and heard a familiar voice calling her name. She turned toward the sound and saw Mark running over to her.

"Emma! I'm so glad you're home. My uncle arrived and Mom is smiling more now that he's here. You have to meet him!" he told her in a rush.

"I want to," she assured the boy.

"Emma!" called a voice from the stairs.

She looked up in surprise at Jeremy. "You're back!" she exclaimed happily. She got off the bike, laid it against the stoop, and ran up the stairs and into his arms. "When did you get back?"

"Today," he murmured, pulling her in close and lowering his head to kiss her. She sank into him, not willing to stop.

A loud "Hmmf" could be heard directly behind them on the street.

"What?" they said and looked around, their eyes glazed. She shook herself and saw who was there. "Papa! It's good to see you," she said as she accompanied Jeremy down the stoop to kiss him. Jeremy shook hands with Ellis and kissed his mom on the cheek.

"We were invited over for dinner," Papa said.

"Dinner," Jeremy murmured in her ear. "Too bad."

"Papa, I need to clean up. Can I meet you downstairs?" she asked, wanting to spend some time alone with Jeremy.

Mark called, "Emma, I'll bring over my uncle later for you to meet him."

"Thanks, Mark," she called back and waved to him.

Papa looked at her. "Sure, I'll meet you downstairs. Jeremy, will you be accompanying me to the sitting room?"

Abbey punched his arm in warning not to tease them. "Let them be."

He nodded when Jeremy said, "No, I think I'll get something from my room first."

"Fine," Papa said and, as he turned away from them, he smiled broadly and followed them into the house.

Emma and Jeremy continued upstairs. Once they got to her door, he said in a low voice, "Meet you inside."

"Yes," she said and opened the door. They walked purposely to their bedroom doors and went in. She leaned on the door and waited for Jeremy. It didn't take long and the bookcase slid to the side. He came through and strode over to her. "I think we have just enough time for a quick rest," he said, laughing, and threw her on the bed.

She laughed and pulled him to her. A short while later, they heard the dinner bell. It was clanging rather loudly. "I think they want us downstairs," she said, raising her head from his chest to look him in the eye.

"Yes," he groaned, pulling her to him.

"Now, don't start that again. We're wanted downstairs." She got up gracefully and looked over at him. "Come on," she said.

He moved over to the side of the bed, stood up, and headed to his room.

"Throw me my brush," she said.

"Catch," said Jeremy, throwing her hairbrush as he passed her dresser to enter his room.

She caught it and ran it through her hair, finally pulling it into a ponytail. The bell clanged again; she ran to the bathroom to wash up. She was tucking her red shirt into her black skirt when a knock sounded on her door. "On my way," she called. She grabbed her boots and tied them quickly

The knock repeated and Emma rushed over and opened it. "Dinner?" Jeremy asked with a slight smile and offered his elbow.

She returned the smile and took his arm. They walked down together and found everyone already at the dining table. No one mentioned their absence.

Prayers first, and then the trays started making their way around the table. Tim broke the silence and said in a light voice, "Mark's uncle has been over to visit a few times." Emma noticed Dora's face flushed at Tim's words.

Well, well, she thought, her interest tweaked. Mr. Pennington had kept her occupied that when she returned home in the evenings she would eat in her room and go straight to bed. She hadn't been listening to the events going on around her. Now though, she turned all of her attention to her sister and said, "Tell me about him."

Dora's face was still flushed and she said in a rushed tone, "He is very handsome and suave."

"He is that," acknowledged Tim. He wasn't threatened by the other man. He knew his Dora.

"Tell me more," Emma said.

"He's so worldly. He knows about everything, books, business, and clothes," Dora said.

"Clothes?" asked Jeremy.

"Yes. His clothes are tailored and from England," Tim said. He had noticed the cut and asked him about it.

"He sounds very dapper," murmured Jeremy, wondering where the man's money came from. Mark's family wasn't rich; they worked as teachers in the poor districts of Chicago. Jeremy had yet to meet the man since he had just gotten home by train that morning.

"Mark mentioned Elizabeth had been depressed. He was worried and hoped Joseph's presence would help," Emma said, remembering her conversation with the boy before her case started in Cleveland.

"She isn't any longer. Her face lights up when he's in the room," commented Tim.

"Enough of that," Dora said, trying to get them off of the topic of Mark's uncle. "Tell us about your cases."

Emma put the new visitor out of her mind and said, "The evidence is pretty clear for bigamy, and I did press charges to keep him in custody."

Jeremy frowned at her. "You did? What for?"

"He punched me in the face and left a decent bruise," she explained.

"Are you okay?" Papa asked, concerned.

"It has mostly healed," she assured them.

"How was he able to land the punch?" Jeremy asked. He wouldn't have expected someone soft like Hugo Banks to be able to hit her before she could stop him.

She looked down at her hands and then looked him in the eyes. "I let him," she admitted.

"Emma! He could have hurt you," said Abbey.

"It's fine. I rolled with the punch so it didn't hurt as much. Besides, we needed the assault charge to hold him. I didn't want him out where he might be able to threaten the wives or take the children again."

Jeremy nodded. "Good for you, but I'd prefer you chose another method next time."

"Me, too," she said, lightly touching her cheek. Most of the pain and color were gone.

"What about the children, are they sorted?" Tim asked Jeremy, moving on to the other case.

"For the ones we could find," he said. "As you know, some went to new homes."

"Yes," commented Dora. They had been told that some of the families wouldn't take the children back.

"That's just terrible," Abbey said. The rest of the people at the table agreed.

"We did get everyone to a safe location. Clare and Thomas set up a network of homes between here and New York City. Renting some and buying others where they could."

"And the children they haven't found?" Papa asked.

"We have some leads overseas. Officers have been assigned there to search." Jeremy didn't mention that he didn't think there was much hope at this point. The case had so many highs and lows. It still depressed him to think about those they couldn't save.

Emma saw his expression and wanted to help him. She changed the subject. "This is nice, being back home." Abbey and Dora saw what she was trying to do and changed the subject to more newsy topics.

Emma smiled and thought, *Family-they were always there when she needed them.*

After dinner, she headed upstairs for a bath and an early night. Jeremy chose to stay down with his mom and the family in the sitting room.

When her hair was washed, she climbed out of the tub and wrapped one towel around her hair and one around her body before pulling on a robe. She crossed the hall into her room and changed into a night dress. It was cool outside, so she opened the window and sat down to brush her hair. It took longer than expected, and she was still sitting there when Jeremy came into the room. He walked over to her and said, "Scoot over." He took the brush, helping her until her hair was dry. She climbed into bed and watched while he disrobed. After he climbed in with her, she laid her head on his chest.

"It's times like this I miss that beach house," he said softly into her hair.

"Me, too," she admitted. She propped her head up so that she could see his face. "I wanted to talk with you about that." She told him about how their vacation had come about.

Jeremy nodded. "I figured it must be something like that. Pops said he didn't arrange anything."

They let the silence settle around them.

"What are you thinking?" he asked, running his fingers through her hair.

"Having a place of our own, like the beach house, where we can be together."

"Our own place?" He liked the idea. "Are you thinking of the beach?"

"I did like it there." *Though probably not that actual location*, she thought.

"Maybe this summer we find some houses to look at purchasing," he said, mulling it over.

"It would just be ours," she said with a sigh.

"Yes, I think that would be perfect."

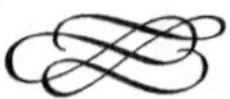

CHAPTER 29

The weekend was spent with Emma and Jeremy locked in their room, getting to know one another after their extended separation. They weren't looking forward to Monday and being apart again.

When Monday came around, Jeremy sat up reluctantly to begin his day and tried to nudge Emma awake. When she burrowed deeper into the covers, he called, "Hey!" and tried to wrestle them from her. She laughed and rolled, trapping the covers under her. Jeremy located the end of the cover and tugged it hard, sending Emma to the floor, laughing.

"Okay, okay, I'm up. Well, sort of," she said, sitting on the floor.

"What a picture, wish I had a camera to remember this moment," he teased, putting out his hand to help her up.

She took it and stood, trying to pull the sheets from around her. Her eyes found the clock. She looked at Jeremy and warned, "Time is slipping by this morning."

"I'll go get ready now. Meet you on the other side," he said and went into his room through the bookcase.

Emma walked over to her dresser and gathered a light blue

skirt and matching blue top that buttoned up the front. She thought about her schedule that day. It would be at Mr. Pennington's office. Work had piled up while they had been occupied with the bigamy case. *Time is speeding by.* Dropping her sheet, she pulled on her robe, tying the belt. She walked quickly out the door and to the restroom to clean up for her day.

When she came out, she found Jeremy there, tapping his timepiece. "I'll be quick!" she said, slamming the door open to her bedroom. Closing it, she dressed, yanked on her boots, and finally pulled the brush through her hair. She was slipping it into a low ponytail and bun as she exited. They made their way down just in time for the trays to be placed on the table. Breakfast was a fast affair, as Emma and Jeremy wanted an early start.

"See you later," Jeremy said, watching the trolley come toward them.

"Yes, I'll see you this evening," she said as he kissed her. She watched him run for the trolley, then climbed on her bike and headed to Pennington's office.

She rolled to a stop in front of the office and looked up. The lights were still off. Frowning, she got off the bike and stood there staring up at the door. *Well, I might as well wait,* she thought. Leaning the bike against the stoop, she sat and waited. It was highly unusual for Ethan to be late. *Where is he?* she wondered.

The sound of boots scraping on the sidewalk could be heard from her left. She turned toward the sound and saw it was Ethan, and he was in a rush.

"How did I beat you here?" asked Emma.

"Late night," he muttered, going up the stoop and opening the door. She watched him. Her friend seemed a bit out of sorts. She lifted her bike to her shoulder and followed him into the office. She took it to the closet, watching Ethan race around turning up the gas lamps and opening Mr. Pennington's office door.

"Do you need some help?" she offered.

"No, I have it. Your work for today is here," he said and held out a folder.

She nodded and took it from him. He was already out of sorts and she didn't want to add to it. *Though,* she thought with a smile, *I'll have to ask Savannah what may have delayed him this morning.*

The day was productive, though the time away had increased the work to be completed. Emma took her bike and headed home for lunch. She had several notes from clients that indicated her courier work was back on. At the house, she pulled the bike to a stop and climbed off. She started to roll it to the side of the house when she heard a voice say, "Well, hello. I don't think we have met."

She turned slowly toward the voice and thought, *This must be the infamous uncle that Mark mentioned. Dora was right. A nice-looking man.* She stared at him longer than she should have. She had guessed his identity but asked, "Can I help you?"

"You haven't heard about me?" the man asked, sounding disappointed.

"No, I don't think so," she murmured. She didn't know why she kept up the ruse except that he seemed to get what he wanted without much effort. This man had been given too much based on his looks.

He strolled close to her. "I'm Joseph Black, Mark's uncle, and you are?"

"Emma Evans," she supplied. Joseph seemed to be advancing at a steady pace toward her and, before she could stop herself, she had moved back a few steps and kept the bike between them.

"Emma," he said, "I believe I've heard that name before." He tilted his head as if trying to remember. "Ah, now I have it. You're Dora's sister. You work in a law office?"

"I do," Emma said cautiously. This man was too everything—too suave, too good-looking, and a little too interested in her work. The family didn't share her investigations with strangers. Mark and his parents also knew this and wouldn't volunteer the information without letting her know.

"I want to hear everything about you," Joseph said and, even though he hadn't moved, she fought the urge to back away again.

"I'm not sure that everything would be appropriate, Mr. Black."

Was that a frown? It was just a flash, she thought, but *of what? Annoyance. Did he expect her to just giggle and fawn over him like some schoolgirl?*

Instead of responding, he winked and said, "I'll see you at dinner."

"Dinner? Are you and the family coming over this evening?" This man was being deliberately baffling. She wanted some answers.

They were not forthcoming. Instead, he looked up the stoop and called out, "Hello, Dora." Emma turned and saw her sister had come out to sweep the steps. Dora raised a hand in greeting but kept at her task.

Emma watched Joseph go. She leaned her bike on the stoop and walked up to greet Dora. "That is a handsome man," Emma commented, looking at Dora.

"Hmmm. Yes," Dora said, yet her cheeks didn't flush this time.

What changed? thought Emma. "You're not sweet on him anymore?"

"Was it that obvious?" Dora asked, embarrassed.

"A little,"

Her sister paused in her sweeping and leaned on the broom handle. "I think I was taken in by his looks and charm."

"Did something happen to change that?"

"Well, there is Tim," Dora said dryly. "When Joseph came over this morning, he really wanted a dinner invitation and he seemed a little manipulative. I started to wonder why he wanted one so badly."

"What does he want with us that he had to wrangle an invitation to dinner?"

"I think it's you," Dora admitted.

"That's ridiculous. And how would he know about me? Hold it, he mentioned that he had heard about me when he walked up just now."

"Mark told him all about you, I would expect," Dora said, starting to sweep again.

"Well, Jeremy will be here tonight and that will be an end to that," Emma said decisively.

"You know," her sister said innocently, "if you were married, you wouldn't have these issues."

Emma looked back the way Joseph had gone and said, "No I don't think even that would have stopped him. He's after something."

Dora mulled that over. She didn't like the idea of someone having a hidden agenda that involved her family.

Emma walked back downstairs quickly and said, "I'm going to put my bike up. I'll go in through the kitchen."

"Careful, Ethyl and Amy are canning today. Fruit preserves," Dora called out in warning.

"Yum!" Emma said, hoping to steal some of the treats as she made her way through.

"Yes, but it's going to be hot. They'll be moving the pots around and filling the jars, so be careful."

"I will," Emma said, rolling her bike around to the side of the house.

Dora shook her head and finished sweeping the steps. With her task complete, she headed back in and saw Emma coming out of the kitchen licking a spoon. "Got a sample, did you?"

"I did," her sister said, the satisfaction clear in her voice. She walked toward her and held it out. "Taste?"

"Yes, please," Dora said and took it from her. "You're right, yum!"

"Got any for me?" Jeremy called from the stairs. She looked up, the pleasure evident in her voice as she said, "You're home early."

"Yeah, but not for long," he said, holding up his bag for her to see.

"What? Why?" She didn't mean to sound angry, but they had just gotten to see each other after a long separation.

Dora quietly left the foyer, giving them their privacy.

Emma folded her arms over her chest. He touched her shoulder and she pulled away. "I would prefer to stay here with you."

"I know," she said, her mouth turned down and eyes wet with tears.

"Pops sent me a telegram," Jeremy explained. "They have one more location to check for the missing children."

"Will Clair and Thomas be there also?" She knew they could also use a rest. Both of the cases had required them to be present.

"Only if we get confirmation of children being there. If needed, we can have them set it up and send personnel to help with management and counseling."

"Most of the other locations are closed now?"

"Yes."

"Where are you headed?"

"The location found is about halfway to New York. Everyone is on their way there. We'll be staging a raid."

"You said it's not confirmed?"

"Never a guarantee, but the rumors are pretty sound." Emma had her head down. "What is it, Emma?" he asked, using his finger to lift her chin.

"You just got home," she complained and wiped her eyes. "We haven't had enough time together."

"You could come with me," he suggested.

The excitement was tempting, but she replied sadly, "We finally move past the Hugo Banks case and our trial work will be starting soon. Mr. Pennington would come after me if I disappeared."

"So, you stay here and I go," he said simply. He leaned in and kissed her slowly. Her knees were weak when he pulled back.

She signed shakily. "You're sure you have to go?"

"Reluctantly, yes." He pressed his forehead to hers.

Tim came in the front door. "Jeremy, your carriage is here."

Jeremy pulled his gaze from Emma and responded, "Thank you." He looked back at her. "I'm going to have to run. I'll send you a telegram once we find out if more children were located."

"Okay," she said and watched him go. Dora came back into the foyer and slid her arm inside of hers. "Come on and help me with setting the table."

She nodded and followed Dora to the dining room. She retrieved the silverware while Dora set out the dishes.

"He'll be back," Dora said in a soft tone, watching her.

"I know. I am usually the one running around or leaving at a moment's notice. But I have missed him."

"You got to spend a week alone with him," Dora reminded her.

"I did, and I think we're going to try to make that a normal part of our lives."

"Vacations?" asked Dora.

"A home that would be just for the two of us, to get away."

"You know, that isn't a bad idea, and it's something Tim and I might also want to go in with you to purchase."

When Emma looked alarmed, Dora laughed. "Not to go with you but maybe to use or rent out when you aren't there."

Emma nodded slowly. "I guess you and Tim would also like some time alone occasionally."

"Yes, it would be nice," her sister agreed.

Emma reviewed the table. "Do I have to worry about unwanted attention from Joseph tonight?"

"I don't think so, not with all of us here," Dora said consideringly. "Give him a chance. It may just be a bad first impression. And it'll mean so much to Mark and his mother."

Ethyl called from the kitchen. "The trays are ready."

Dora called out to Tim and Patrick, "Lunch!" They came in with Tim carrying Lottie. Dora took her daughter and sat her down for lunch. The others helped retrieve the trays and the pitchers. After lunch was cleaned up, Emma was putting on her light coat and hat to go out again.

"Courier work today?" Tim asked.

"Yes, I'll be back later."

"Be safe."

"I will," she promised and headed out the door. Emma purposely delayed her deliveries; she wasn't in a hurry to get home that evening. She'd been counting on Jeremy to provide the buffer she might need between her and Joseph. The men in her life weren't normally so forward with their intentions.

What gives him the idea that I'm open to spending time with him? Did someone give him that impression? I'll have to watch him with the other ladies. Savannah will be there. Will he act the same way toward her? Am I overreacting?

Emma walked her bike slowly to the back of the boarding house. When she couldn't wait any longer, she took a deep breath and went to the kitchen door. Ethyl saw her first. "They're just now sitting down to dinner." Emma nodded, slipped off her coat, and laid it on a chair. She took a deep breath before she pushed open the door to the dining room.

The first thing she saw upon entering was that Joseph had taken the seat next to where she normally sat. *Who put him there?* She walked to her seat without comment and sat down. Her eyes darted around the table and she quickly noticed Savannah was not there.

She mouthed to Dora, "Where's Savannah?"

Dora mouthed back, "Rehearsals"

No help there, thought Emma with a grimace.

Joseph was attentive and his questions started immediately. "Emma, you have been tied up."

"Yes, just some business to take care of," she said noncommittally.

"What type of business?" he asked, curious about her comings and goings.

"Really nothing too interesting," she said, trying to steer him off the topic.

Dora saw she needed some help and looked to her husband. "Tim, I understand the church is looking for baked goods to be donated for a bazaar this week."

"Yes, I heard the same thing." He knew what Dora was doing and contributed to the conversation. "If you have them ready tomorrow, I can take them."

"Thank you," she responded. The conversation lulled and it moved to the weather and how good dinner was. Emma was relieved to be able to eat in peace.

As they were cleaning up, Joseph asked, "Emma, would you like to take a walk with me?"

The room grew silent, waiting for her response.

"Thank you, but I'm tired and I have to go to court tomorrow."

He didn't argue. Instead, he nodded and said, "Maybe another day?"

She nodded and didn't comment.

After he left, Dora looked at her sister. "He is persistent."

"I know, I didn't know how to turn him down."

"You know," her sister said, consideringly, looking at her hand. She held it up and pointed to her wedding ring. "One of these might help."

"Yeah, yeah, you mentioned that before. That isn't going to happen."

Dora was resolute. "Then *you* have to make it clear to him you *aren't* available."

"I know," Emma said. It wasn't like she could pull her knife and threaten him; this would have to be handled delicately. She would keep Mark's family on her mind as she dealt with him.

The next morning, she was pulling on her coat and Tim called to her, "Emma!"

"In the kitchen," she called back.

Tim came in and went directly to her. "This came earlier. I must have missed you." He handed her a note.

She opened it. "It's from Mr. Pennington. There's an important client he wants me to meet this morning. Thank you, Tim." Inserting it into her pocket, she headed out the back door. Her foot made contact with something other than the step, and she tripped and fell into Joseph's lap. "What?" she yelled in surprise. She struggled to get up, but he held on to her firmly.

"You don't have to leave so soon," he said smoothly.

"Yes, yes I do. I'm on my way to work." She pulled away forcefully and stood. "What did I trip on?" She looked up the stairs and saw a cane. She reached for it and swung it around to him. "Yours, I assume?"

"Mmmmm. Careless, I know," he said. "But I was hoping to see you."

She dropped the cane in his lap and walked over to get her bike from the shed. She looked over her shoulder at him. "Why did you want to see me?"

"You didn't have time for me last night, so I thought I'd walk you to work."

She checked the timepiece attached to her top. "I don't have time for that. I need to be in the office early." Without waiting for his response, she started walking the bike toward the street.

"Emma, are you avoiding me?" he asked, there was an edge to his voice.

His question startled her, not the content but his location. He was so close she could feel him behind her. She had no room to turn and looked ahead when she responded, "No, of course not." She took a deep breath and said, "I don't want to get into this now, but I am with Jeremy."

He walked around her and took her hand. "I don't see a ring," he said, looking at her fingers.

Dora was right, she thought. *Society allows for this type of behavior to unmarried women.* She yanked her hand out of his. "No, no ring. It isn't something I want. But I am committed to him."

He smiled suddenly and said lightly, "There's no reason for us not to be friends, though, is there?"

"No," she said slowly, watching him. His attitude seemed less menacing. *How did he change like that? One moment he's predatory, and the next he's a person you could see as a friend.*

"Well then, friend, I heard you have an interest in old books and I have some with me. Would you like to view them with me after dinner tomorrow?"

That didn't sound too bad, and she'd be with other people at the boarding house where he was staying. *And I can ask Mark to stay with us.* "I would like to see your books," she said politely, "but now I have to go to work."

Joseph walked with her to the gate and held it open for her.

"Thanks," she said, stepping onto the bike in the street. She arranged her satchel over her shoulder and climbed onto the bike and headed to work.

"Anytime," he said and watched her leave. *Bikes*, he thought, *another thing I'll have to get rid of. Why is it that the ones I pick always have to be changed? Why can't they be what I need in the beginning?* He pondered that. Initially, each one seemed to have only small flaws for him to correct. Though, eventually, these flaws turned into something he couldn't ignore. He thought about Emma. Will *she be able to change or will I need to do a final correction on her as well?*

He wandered back to the boarding house he was currently residing.

CHAPTER 30

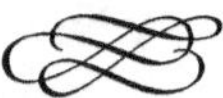

"How are you?" Ethan asked as Emma entered the office.

"Good," she replied, not sharing her concerns about her new acquaintance. She glanced over and saw her friend had a wide smile.

"What are you so happy about today?" she asked as she walked her bike to the storage closet.

"I have a lunch date," he said importantly.

"You do? Can I guess who with?" she teased.

"You may," he said, nodding his head.

"Savannah, perhaps?" she teased.

"It is," he admitted and moved around to the front of his desk.

"What are you planning?" she asked, interested.

"Picnic at the park. We have a late day in court and should have enough time."

"Yes, Mr. Pennington sent me a note and said he's going to review a new case with me today. When did it come in?"

"We were notified on Friday. Mr. Pennington worked this weekend to get things organized."

"What are the charges?"

"Murder," he stated simply. "The prosecutor says our new client killed her husband because he lied about his money."

"I would assume the fact he had so little of it?"

"Yes. After she was charged, the creditors started calling and they wouldn't leave her alone."

"Why her?"

"He signed her name over to the creditors and, with the marriage, there was little she could do."

"Did she admit to killing him?"

"No. The prosecutor is going to have to show evidence and there's no body."

"No body," Emma said thoughtfully, mulling that over. "Why do they think he's dead and not just missing?"

"Blood. They found it in their stateroom on the steamer."

"Were they traveling?"

"Extended honeymoon. They found the blood when the ship docked in New York."

"But why are we defending the case? Shouldn't it be someone in New York?"

"Mr. Pennington knows Mrs. Mercer. She's a personal friend."

"Hmm… What do you think? Did she kill him?"

"Mr. Pennington believes that the man is alive and waiting for her to take the fall." His phrasing was to be expected. Ethan didn't voice his opinion, he only voiced Mr. Pennington's.

How to find this man? "Do you think she'd sit down with a sketch artist? I could get Dora to do it for us."

"Mr. Pennington would like that. You could investigate the disappearance while Mr. Pennington's in court."

"Okay, could you let Mr. Pennington know I want to speak to the client?"

Mr. Pennington's door opened and he saw Emma and beckoned to her. "Emma, please come in."

She looked surprised. She hadn't known he was there. "Yes, of course," she said and started to follow him into his office.

"The client's already in his office," Ethan whispered.

She nodded and mouthed, "Thanks."

As Emma entered Pennington's office, she saw a lovely woman of about forty years old. She wore very stylish clothes and had perfectly coiffed hair, but the effect was spoiled by the woman's flushed face and swollen eyes.

"Ma'am," Emma greeted her.

The woman inclined her head but didn't say anything, using her handkerchief to wipe her eyes.

Emma looked toward Pennington and raised her eyebrows in question. He responded with, "Emma, have a seat. This is Mrs. Eloise Mercer. Eloise, Emma Evans is our investigator."

"You have one on staff, James?" Mrs. Mercer asked as Emma took a seat.

"I do," Pennington admitted. "Trials are expensive and are to be avoided. Emma might find us the evidence we need."

Mrs. Mercer nodded stiffly.

"Emma, I assume Ethan told you about the case. What are your initial thoughts?"

She pulled out her notebook and consulted it. "First," she said, looking at Mrs. Mercer, "we believe he is missing and not dead?"

"Yes," Pennington said definitely, answering for Mrs. Mercer.

"What about the blood, how do we account for that?" Emma asked bluntly.

"The blood won't matter—no body, no case," stated Mr. Pennington firmly.

"I think you're wrong there, Mr. Pennington. I think once we find the body alive, then that will make this no case," stated Emma.

He nodded. "You're right, that would be the best. That way, the creditors can go after the right person."

"I think we need to get a sketch unless you have pictures of your husband," Emma said to Mrs. Mercer.

"No, John refused to have his picture taken. I thought it was endearing," the woman said bitterly.

Emma nodded, taking notes. "I can have Dora come over to get the sketch."

Mrs. Mercer sent a worried glance to Mr. Pennington. "James, I would like to find John and talk to him."

Mr. Pennington looked at her. "I think we need to have Emma start investigating."

"I can accompany Ms. Evans to her residence to have the drawing made," suggested Mrs. Mercer.

"I don't think that will be necessary." He looked at Emma. "Can you bring Dora here this afternoon?"

Emma nodded. "I have a few more questions. I can follow up when I bring Dora back."

Mrs. Mercer sniffed. "Yes, I can do that."

"What attracted you to him initially?" Emma asked. Details like this would matter. She needed to know what kind of man she was looking for.

"He was charming, very suave. He said all the right things. He was thoughtful; he knew how to make me happy."

"Tall?"

"Taller than me." Emma looked at her; the woman was about 5'6", so he might be 5'8" or 5'9".

"Dark hair, light hair?"

"Light hair. He loved the sun."

"Was there anything that made you have second thoughts about marrying him? Did you see any money issues ahead of time?"

"No. He seemed to have an unlimited income. He paid for everything. At first."

"When did you realize, he was lying to you?"

"When he disappeared. Then the bills started coming in," Mrs. Mercer admitted.

"How long after the marriage was this? "Emma asked.

"Six months."

"Why didn't you find out about the bills earlier? I would have expected the creditors to come for the money once you married."

"He insisted on an extended honeymoon. We weren't in one place long enough to receive our mail."

"Who paid for the trip?"

"I did," Mrs. Mercer admitted. "I did it as a gift to him. I realize now that he was avoiding creditors."

Pennington said, "Men like this do not do this just one time. It's usually part of a pattern. Eloise, I think you're lucky."

"Lucky? Why do you say that?" she asked in disbelief. She could think of a lot of names for her situation, but lucky wasn't one of them.

Pennington sighed and sat back in his chair. "Sometimes, these men don't run off; sometimes, things happen to their brides."

Mrs. Mercer gave him a long look, almost like she wanted to argue, but she instead turned to Emma. "Will you be able to find him?" she asked.

"Where did you meet?" Emma asked, avoiding the woman's question. She didn't want to promise anything at this point.

"We met at a library auction. We both have an interest in rare books. He bought me a wonderful first edition," she said, lost in her memories.

Emma pulled her out by asking, "How long had you known each other before you were married?"

Mrs. Mercer turned red and looked down at her hands. Pennington prompted her, saying, "Eloise, please answer."

She looked back and mumbled, "One month."

"Who suggested the wedding should occur so soon?" Emma asked.

"I don't know," the woman said helplessly. "He was going on an extended trip and I didn't want to be without him. So, we married."

Emma didn't show her feelings but thought, *She should have been more cautious.* "Tell me about the last time you were with him."

"We were on the way home on a steamer. He said he had a headache and wanted to stay in the cabin. He insisted I go to dinner without him."

"How long were you gone?"

"Just through dinner. I returned as soon as it was over."

"What did you find when you got there?"

Mrs. Mercer shuddered and stood, pulling out her tissue. "There was blood, so much blood. I screamed and everything went black. I woke in the captain's cabin."

"Did they accuse you of killing him?"

"Not initially," she admitted, "though they made me move from my cabin and restricted my movements until we got to port. The local police in New York City took me into custody."

"I can take it from there," Pennington said. "They searched the cabin and found no body. They said the door was not tampered with and she was the only other person with a key."

"But doesn't the room steward also have a copy?" Emma asked, remembering her trips.

"I haven't traveled by steamship before this," he said. "That's a good question. I'll find out who the steward was."

"The blood could be from anything; it even could be animal. There's no way to tell," Emma remarked. "There's some talk that Karl Landsteiner in Vienna is working on the ability to tell the difference between the two, which would have helped here."

That's for the future, she thought. So much was coming up

that would help law enforcement. Now, though, it was time for the hard question. "Mrs. Mercer, did you kill him?"

"No," she said immediately. "I loved him. I would have helped him through this mess."

She would have stood by him? "What if we find him? Will you take him back?"

Even Mr. Pennington looked shocked at that question, but he watched Mrs. Mercer for her answer.

Mrs. Mercer stood and walked around not answering.

Mr. Pennington said, "Eloise, you know what kind of man he is now."

"Maybe he was just scared," she suggested.

"Scared enough that you would go to prison or possibly be hung for him?" Pennington asked. He needed to scare her straight. If his friend continued down this path, he didn't know if he could save her.

That statement penetrated and she asked, "Could that happen? I thought we would just find him and this would be over."

This is why I didn't promise to find the man, Emma thought. If he isn't found, the authorities can presume death. It'll be hard to convict her, but not impossible

"Yes, it can happen," he said," and you have to be prepared for it. Even if we find him, he's not good for you."

"You can do better," Emma said quietly.

Mrs. Mercer looked over at the much younger woman and said, the bitterness coming up again, "At my age? No, this is who I attract now. Or I should say, my money attracts."

Pennington decided to let that go. "I'd like to have the sketch done as soon as possible. Can it be done today?"

"Yes, of course. I have some business matters this afternoon to attend to here. Will you let me know?" Mrs. Mercer asked.

"Eloise, remember, you need to let me know where you'll be. That's the only way you can stay out of jail," he reminded her.

"Of course, James."

Emma noticed she didn't look him in the eye as she said that. "I'll check with Dora, but we should be able to be here at two o'clock this afternoon."

"Eloise, can you come back at that time?" Pennington asked.

She nodded. He looked over at Emma. "I need some time with Eloise." Walking to the door, she left the room. *The creditors,* she thought, *I need to find out who wants her husband to pay.*

Ethan sat at his desk and raised his eyebrows at her. She shook her head and mouthed, "Later."

He nodded and she headed back to her office. Before she could get to the door, raised voices could be heard from Mr. Pennington's office, then it suddenly went quiet. The door opened moments later and Mrs. Mercer exited, looking more frazzled than when Emma had seen her. She went directly to the door and before Ethan could stand, she had left the office.

They turned and looked back at Mr. Pennington. He just glared at the door, then stepped back into his office and slammed his own.

Wow! Emma thought. *Emotional case.* She went back to her office to organize her notes and look at the next steps. *Should I tell him about my suspicions that she might run off?*

When she left her office, she found his still closed. With her hand raised, ready to knock, Ethan said, "I wouldn't do that."

She was conflicted, but lowered her hand and backed away. *I'll tell him when I return this afternoon.*

Going back to her office, she sat and reviewed her notes from the interview. The description of Mrs. Mercer's husband was generic but why did it remind her of Joseph?

CHAPTER 31

"What time will we need to go over?" Dora asked at lunch. Tim was home. He and Amy could take care of the children while she was out.

"About two o'clock," Emma said.

Dora nodded. "That will work."

They were finishing up when a knock sounded on the front door.

Tim stood, wiping his mouth, and said, "I'll get it." He came back in quickly with a note and handed it to Emma. She opened it and said, "Dora, you don't have to make plans to be out today. Mrs. Mercer won't be available. She had to head home for business reasons."

"Let me know when we reschedule," Dora said.

"Can you tell us more about this case?" Tim asked.

Mr. Pennington knew when she needed to share certain information with her team. The discussion moved to how fast the couple had married, the blood that was found, and the creditors demanding payment.

"What are you thinking, Emma?" Dora asked, seeing that Emma was drumming her fingers on her lips.

"Did it strike you that her description of him was very similar to that of Joseph? Not just the physical, but in the way she described their relationship. How fast it developed?"

"You don't think he's the man involved in this?" Dora asked, alarmed.

"Not really," her sister admitted. "I just had a feeling."

Dora pondered that. "You know, you're right about him rushing you in the same way. Though he can't be after your money; there isn't any. Not the amounts she has, anyway."

"No, I probably had him on my mind when I went into the interview."

"Emma, be careful," Dora cautioned her sister.

"Like you said, Dora, I have no reason for him to want me," she said lightly. Inside, she thought this was the same kind of man Mrs. Mercer had married.

That evening, Emma was home, thinking about Mrs. Mercer. *What business could be more important than the murder trial?* She picked up her lacework while she thought about the woman's sudden disappearance.

There was a knock at the door. Patrick ran to answer it, and Tim followed behind. There were voices and then Patrick called, "Emma! You have guests!"

She walked out of the sitting room and saw Joseph and Mark.

"I am the bearer of a gift," Joseph called out, holding up a package.

"We have a book for you," Mark said, knowing Emma would love this gift.

"Book!" Emma said. "That is nice. Would you like to go into the study?" Tim had finished his work for the day and they had the room to themselves. Books were her favorite thing and she was curious about what he had brought her.

The gas lamps were turned up in the room and Emma

motioned to the desk. "You can place it there." Joseph took the book out of his bag and laid it on the table.

Emma picked it up and reviewed the spine, before opening it carefully. It was a first edition. "This is very nice," she said. *And expensive*, she thought. "Daisy Miller, A Comedy in Three Acts."

He told her, "I would like you to have this."

"No, it's yours. You don't have to give it to me," she protested. Though she would have liked to have the book, she didn't want to be indebted to this man.

"I insist," he said smoothly, pressing it into her hands.

She turned it over in her hands and said, "It is a lovely edition. I'll treasure it."

"Mom wants us back soon," Mark reminded his uncle.

"Yes, that's right, I don't want to disappoint her," Joseph said absently. All of his focus was on Emma.

Emma looked up from the book and blinked as she saw his intense interest. "I'll walk you to the door." As she pulled it open for him, she said, "Goodbye, and thank you again for the book."

They left and she shut the door and went back to the study. She picked up the book again and thought, *It is so lovely*. Flipping through the pages, she found an inscription that said, "To TC from LT with all my love".

How wonderful. Books that have a history are so interesting. Thinking about those people who had read and enjoyed the book before her, Emma clutched the book to her and went to her room to read it. The dinner bell distracted her and she saw that she had been reading for an hour. She put down the book reluctantly and got up to go downstairs to dinner.

Something occurred to her as she made her way downstairs. *Didn't Mrs. Mercer say that one of the things she and her husband had in common was rare books? Another connection or another coincidence?*

Mark and his family were already seated around the table.

She went over to Mark's mom and kissed her on the cheek. "I haven't had time to come by and see you."

"That's all right, I knew you were busy with work. I'm glad we can spend some time together tonight," Elizabeth said.

She turned to George. "It's good to see you also."

"You, too," he said.

She took her seat, prayers were said and the food was passed around. Dora had sat Emma closer to her so she could help if Joseph made her uncomfortable. Conversation flowed around the table. Savannah was there and talked about her latest show. Emma watched and noticed Joseph wasn't as forward with her.

When Joseph took over the conversation, she saw George's eyes narrow. *Hmm,* she thought, *what's happening there? Not such a loving family after all?*

The topic Joseph chose to discuss was the woman's place in the home. How important it was to the family structure. What he was saying was true, but it seemed to have a second meaning. "Like my sister here, she stays home to take care of Mark and his father. She's a shining beacon to women everywhere."

Emma sent a look to Dora and shook her head. They wouldn't mention Elizabeth's job; evidently, they kept that information from her brother. *He wouldn't approve?* After that statement, she saw George had bent his fork. She casually said, "I'm sorry we gave you a damaged fork. Here's another one." He didn't say anything but exchanged forks with her.

Dinner ended quietly and it wasn't until dessert was served in the sitting room that Joseph approached her. The others had gathered into small groups talking amongst themselves. It was just the two of them on the settee. "I love the book, especially the inscription," she said.

"Inscription?" Joseph questioned. His eyes narrowed almost imperceptibly.

She wondered at that reaction. "Yes, it's from LT to TC with all my love."

"I didn't know someone had done that. I can take it back and give you one that's not written in," he said smoothly.

She protested. "No, I want to keep it. That makes it more valuable to me."

"I would rather take it back," Joseph said, his voice starting to show his displeasure.

"No. I love it as it is," she insisted. *Why the intense reaction? Does this mean the book is connected to someone, maybe Mrs. Mercer?*

"If you're sure..." he said, his voice trailing off.

"I am," she assured him, not wanting to part with the book.

A knock sounded at the door. Emma excused herself to answer it. She stepped back into the room with a telegram.

"Who sent it?" Dora asked.

Joseph watched her open it.

Emma smiled widely. "Finally. Jeremy's on the way home. Business is complete and successful."

"That's great," said Tim. "How soon until we see him?"

"Should be about a week with travel and cleanup," Emma replied in a distracted voice.

"So, I get to finally meet the mysterious Jeremy," Joseph said, suddenly appearing behind her.

She didn't have to hide the note. Jeremy had kept any information about the missing children out of it. "Yes, you'll like him. He reads as much as I do."

"Then I'd say I can't wait to meet the gentleman."

The evening came to a close with Mark's family leaving for their boarding house. Emma couldn't wait to get upstairs to read her book.

Early the next morning, as she was getting ready, she looked at it with regret and thought, *I can't carry a first edition with me. I'll have to leave it here.* She placed it on her desk and grabbed her bag to head down to breakfast.

Her day was rather ordinary, just paperwork at the law office. Mrs. Mercer had not returned for them to get a sketch and Mr. Pennington had managed to get a trial delay. He did mention Emma would receive the creditor's information soon. After a quick lunch in the park, she finished her courier duties and went home and back to that book.

Once there, she barely stopped to say hello to Dora and the kids as she headed upstairs. Going directly to the desk, she didn't find it. The handkerchief she had laid on top of it was still there, but the book was missing. *Did it fall?* She knelt down and looked around the floor. It wasn't there. She stood and continued to her door, at the landing she called, "Dora!"

"Yes," Dora said and came out of the sitting room with Baby Lottie in her arms. "Do you need something?"

"Yes, have you seen my book? The one I got from Joseph?"

She frowned. "No, I haven't."

"It isn't here."

"Let me check with Ethyl; she did dust your room this morning."

Dora took the baby and went to the kitchen. "Ethyl, could we see you in the foyer for a moment?"

The woman looked surprised and glanced at Amy for permission. "You can go, just don't be long," Amy said.

As Ethyl approached Dora, she said over her shoulder, "Of course, I'll be right back."

They walked back to the foyer. Emma had come down the stairs and was waiting for them. "Ethyl, did you dust my room this morning?"

"I did," she said. "Wasn't that okay?" She pulled on her apron, worrying it with her hands.

"Of course, it was okay," Dora reassured her. "Emma just can't find a book that was on her desk."

"Oh!" Ethyl said in surprise.

"What is it?"

"I did leave your door open for a few moments," she admitted. "I had forgotten your sheets. I went down to get them. I wasn't gone long and I didn't see another person other than family in the house."

Emma thought that was enough time for Joseph to take the book. He didn't want her to have it after she told him what she had found. *I need that book back*, she thought.

"Did I do something wrong?" Ethyl loved her job and didn't want to lose it over something like this.

Dora assured her, "No, you're fine. You may go back to the kitchen."

Ethyl looked relieved and almost ran back to her workstation.

"I didn't mean to scare her," Emma said.

"She'll be fine. Who do you think took it?"

"Who else?"

"Joseph," Dora supplied.

"Yes, he didn't know that inscription was in there and it must lead to something or someone in his life."

"Something bad?"

"Something he wants to keep quiet."

"What will you do?"

"Get the book back," Emma said determinedly.

"Be careful, we don't know if he can be dangerous."

"I will," Emma murmured. *What is his schedule? I'll have to watch him to determine the best time to go into his room.*

Emma took off the next morning at her scheduled time and doubled back through the backyard. She left the bike hidden in a bush. The spot she picked to watch for Joseph allowed her to see the people coming and going on their street. Finally, he appeared. He looked in both directions and she stayed out of sight as he strolled down the street.

Should she chance it? *Yes.* She hurried in through the kitchen and was seen by Mrs. Spencer, the housekeeper.

"Emma, why the rush?" Mrs. Spencer asked, pulling her hands out of the dough she was kneading.

"Dora asked for some linens from the attic; we might need them for tonight."

Mrs. Spencer looked at Emma but didn't ask too many questions. If she was investigating something, then Mrs. Spencer would help however she could. One of those past investigations had helped her find out how her son died. "Let me know if you need anything."

"I will," Emma promised and took the stairs two at a time up to the third-floor room she knew Joseph was using.

Emma looked around and, when she confirmed it was clear, she used her lockpicks to open the door. Entering, she quickly scanned the room; the book was not on any surface. She went to the desk to check the drawers. Next, she went through the dresser and the closet. When the book could not be found, her gaze shifted to the bed. *Mattress*, she thought, and lifted it up. *Still nothing*, she thought in exasperation and she dropped it back into place.

The weather had been unseasonably warm. She cast a gaze toward the fireplace. *Could that be it?* She reviewed the outside of it and did not see any abnormalities. *Inside*, she thought, and crawled in. She stood carefully. Running her hands on the bricks, she found there were several protruding. Her fingers slid around and down the bricks until she found a crevasse; she pried the bricks out and felt inside. *Twine and paper!* She pulled on the item and saw it was a book. "Got it," she said triumphantly and carefully bent down to crawl back out.

She kept the package close to her as she made her way out and locked the door carefully behind her. The stairs creaked as she made her way downstairs. She stayed close to the wall and avoided the sitting room as she made her way into the kitchen. Mrs. Spencer gave her a nod as she went past her with a small wave. Emma walked quickly through the yard and into her home and up to her room. She opened the book quickly to confirm it was the one Joseph had given her. *Where can I put it? He knows all of the hiding places. But not Jeremy's room!*

Emma went through the bookcase into his room. There was a loose floorboard. She crawled under the bed and pulled the board out and placed the book inside. Once done, she crawled back out and looked down at herself. The dress was done for, not only ripped but also stained from the fireplace soot. She heard Dora's voice calling her.

"Emma, you received a note from Mr. Pennington's office. A package came with it," Dora called to her.

Emma glanced down again and thought, *There is nothing to be done now.* The note from Mr. Pennington could be important. She went down to the foyer and took the package from her sister.

She opened it and said, "Oh, this is the creditor information I have been expecting for Mrs. Mercer's missing husband."

"What do you expect to find?" Dora asked.

"His last known locations. The purchases should tell me where he's been. We have no job, no friends, and no family to follow, so we will follow the bills."

Dora noticed the state of her sister's clothes. "What in the world have you been doing? That dress may have to go into the rubbish bin or be torn to make rags."

"I hope it can be salvaged," Emma said, picking at the sleeve. Motioning to the package, she said, "I'll take this up with me while I change."

After she washed off the soot as best she could, she left the garment to dry in the bathroom. She changed into a skirt and top, then retrieved the package and went to the study where Tim and Patrick were working.

Are Mrs. Mercer's husband and Joseph the same person? she thought. *There are similarities.* She opened the packet and started documenting the locations where he had spent money.

She looked at the list thoughtfully. *Would Mark have an idea if these locations were where Joseph was located? It would be a new lead.* Answers were needed about the man who had shown up in their lives. *I need to check with Mark first.*

"I need to get something. I'll be back." Tim and Patrick waved as she left the room. School would be out soon and, if she wanted to see Mark before he left, she'd have to hurry. The ride over was an easy one and once there, she leaned the bike against the fence and waited for him.

The kids started coming out of the large building. When Mark didn't turn up, she locked the bike up to a wood post and headed inside. The school had long hallways that led to classrooms on either side. Each one had a few students working or talking to the teacher. About halfway down, she found him talking to the teacher. When he started back to his desk and glanced toward the door, he called out in surprise, "Emma!" He walked over and hugged her.

Their relationship had always been close. After their first meeting, they had kept in touch by letter, then again a couple of years later when the team had helped his family escape from kidnappers. Eventually, they moved into Emma's family's second boarding house and became part of their larger team. Mark's parents were occasional team members for her investigations. Both were teachers and could provide insight into the children if the case called for it.

"Well, I just couldn't wait to talk to you and I wanted to walk you home. Is everything all right here?" she asked, motioning to the teacher.

"Yeah, I just had some questions about my homework."

"Ready to go?"

Mark nodded and got his things. They walked out together. Emma retrieved her bike and asked him casually, "Do you remember the locations where your uncle has been or lived."

"Yes, of course! I want to travel like him, so I started keeping a journal about it. I want to go to all the places he told me about."

"A journal?" she asked, surprised.

"Yes, but," he said looking around, "don't tell him. He wouldn't like it."

"What makes you say that?"

"He just likes to keep to himself. He said writing these down is the wrong thing to do. It could be incriminating."

"Can you show it to me?" she asked in a whisper.

He looked at her; she was family now and he would do anything she asked of him. "Sure. When do you want to see it?"

"Is today too soon?"

"No, I don't think so. But I'm not sure where Uncle Joseph is today."

"Where do you keep it?" Emma asked, drumming her fingers on her lips.

"The basement at our boarding house," he answered.

"We shouldn't be seen together. How about you go first and I'll meet you?"

He nodded. "I'll see you there."

She stopped and he continued on. If anyone was watching, they wouldn't be seen together.

When she could no longer see Mark ahead of her, she walked her bike to his boarding house. She glanced around quickly and moved the bike to the side entrance. After putting it away, she made her way through the kitchen and waved to Mrs. Spencer. "I need to borrow a book," she mentioned.

Mrs. Spencer nodded, watching Emma from her position at the large pot. *Twice in one day,* she thought. *Who could she be investigating here?* The new addition was Joseph. She narrowed her eyes; she would help out if she could. Her assistant wasn't aware of any undercurrents and continued to roll out her bread dough on the table.

Emma passed through the dining room and into the foyer.

The study first, she thought. They had set it up so that the boarders had plenty of reading material. She went to the shelf and removed a book. After pretending to read a few pages, she glanced into the hallway; it appeared to be empty. She closed the book and walked to the basement door and opened it.

The lamps were turned up and she followed the stairs down. The noise of papers being shuffled caused her to pause and move more cautiously. On the last step, she saw Mark looking around frantically, pulling open drawers; things were scattered on the floor from his search.

She frowned. "What is that smell?" she asked. *Has something been burned? That could be dangerous in this small space.*

Mark didn't hear her question. He was frantically looking around. "Emma, I can't find it!"

"Well, it must be here," she reasoned, looking around the piles of paper on the floor. "Maybe you left it in some of the other furniture here." Emma and Dora had bought a little too much furniture when they were furnishing the second boarding house. Dora had kept the extras, thinking a third boarding house would require more furniture. *The dresser looks like it might be the place to start.*

"Take that end," Emma directed. She and Marked adjusted the dresser and the burning smell got worse. "It's here," she said and bent down to look at the floor. She felt around and found something warm and picked it up. "Well, I found what was burned," Emma said and held up what appeared to be the spine of a notebook. It was scorched and tattered; there were no pages left.

"My journal," the boy said, running over to take it from her.

"Careful, it's still a little warm. Did Joseph know about it?"

"He did," he admitted. "When he got here, I told him I was writing about his different trips."

"Did he know where it was?" She looked around at the area, trying to determine if anything else was out of place.

"I didn't think so. No one comes down here," Mark explained.

"Did you pull out all of this?" Papers and books were scattered and the furniture had been moved away from the walls.

"Some of it. I emptied the desk. It's where I kept it hidden." He reached down and started picking up the papers he had displaced.

"Have you always kept it down here?"

"I have since his first night here."

"How come?"

"After I told him about the book, I found him looking around my room. I didn't know what to think, but I knew he wanted it, so I hid it. I didn't write anything bad," he muttered.

She pondered this. "How about you go walking at the park with me and we'll try to put the details back together?"

"Do you think we can?" he asked, relieved. He had worked hard on that journal.

"We can try. Why don't we go now?" she suggested.

"Sure."

Emma stuffed the journal remnants into her bag. They headed upstairs together and into the hallway.

"Going somewhere?" Joseph asked, startling them. They looked toward him. He was leaning nonchalantly against the wall, just outside of the basement door.

"Emma wanted to take me to the park and maybe a bookstore," Mark said.

"Sounds like a plan. May I come with you?" Joseph said as he straightened from the wall.

Emma was finally learning how to handle this man. "No," she said firmly. "I think we want to do this on our own today. Don't we?" She looked at Mark for his agreement.

"Yes. We go all the time," he said eagerly.

"Okay then, if I'm not wanted," his uncle said.

Emma looked at him and couldn't read his tone. "We'll see

you tonight," she assured him. She turned to Mark. "Ready to go?"

"Yes."

Emma smiled indulgently and thought, *I will be spending some money in the bookstore today. Mark will be a well-paid source.*

They walked to the park, neither of them turning back to see if Joseph was behind them. They reached a bench in the shade and sat down. *Did he follow?* She looked and, when she didn't see him, she pulled out what was left of the leather journal.

Mark reached out and touched it. "Why burn it?" his voice trembled as he asked.

"Mark, do you think you could remember each destination?" she asked trying to distract him.

"I think so, but I wouldn't be as good with the dates."

"Could you guess?"

"I think so. But how do I work on it? If Uncle Joseph finds it, won't he just burn it again?" he said, his tone miserable. "He was my favorite person before this. I prayed for him to visit my mom to help cheer her up. And he does this!"

She hated to see his relationship tarnished. "Maybe he had a reason for the privacy?" she asked. *Were there things he didn't want others to know? What occurred in those places that he wanted to keep hidden?*

"Yeah, are you going to ask him what that reason is?" the boy asked.

"Maybe later, but not now. I'd like to look into the locations and dates that you remember."

"Do you think he did something bad?" Mark asked tentatively.

"I hope not, but I am concerned he went to this extreme to hide the information." She didn't mention her other suspicions about Mrs. Mercer's husband.

"I get that. You could meet me after school like you did today and I can give you the pages that I've put together. He shouldn't be able to search there."

"No, that's true. I'll also keep what you give me at the Pinkerton offices. When do you think you can start?"

"Tomorrow," he said decisively. "Can you be there after school?"

"I'll make time." Her courier duties allowed her some flexibility with her schedule.

"What if you can't always be here?" Mark asked, thinking ahead.

"Leave it on your desk and, if needed, I can get into the school at night," she said decisively.

Mark wanted to move on. "Can we go to the bookstore now?" He was ready for the heavy conversation to be over.

"I think that's a great idea," she said and stood up.

"Can I get two books in exchange for the information?" he negotiated.

She smiled and held out her hand to him. He grabbed it and they rushed to the bookstore.

On the way back, she kept her bag close to her. She still had the burned journal in her possession.

Mark picked out a varied selection but also showed interest in journals describing the 1849 California gold rush. Emma saw them and teased, "Do you have an interest in gold mining?"

"In adventure," he said and grinned at her. She grinned back, knowing they had that in common.

They separated at his boarding house; he carried his bag of books and journals into his home with him.

She watched him enter and started up her stoop; she wasn't watching where she was going and ran into Joseph. He placed himself in her path.

"We must stop meeting this way," he said.

"Yes, you do seem to be everywhere today." When he didn't move, she asked, "Is there something I can help you with?"

"No, no." He stepped to the side and, as she started to brush past, he placed a hand on the bag she held tight. "That's funny," he said, "I smell something burning. Should we check your bag?"

"No, there's nothing in my bag," she said, wrestling it from his grasp. "I have things in there I consider work-related, so I can't show them to anyone."

"You do? Well, now I want to see them even more." He reached for the bag again.

"Joseph, please let the bag go." Her voice was almost a growl. She was tired of his shenanigans and was ready to pull her knife if he didn't move out of her way.

He must have seen that he had pushed too much and let it go.

She didn't comment further and headed into the house, slamming the door behind her.

Dora was walking down the stairs when Emma came in. "Goodness, what is all the noise about?"

Emma looked at her sister and thought about what was in her bag. *All I have is a burned journal; that doesn't prove anything.* "It was nothing, the wind caught it."

"Wind? Do we have any?" The day was settled and the trees didn't seem to be moving with even a gentle breeze.

"Yes, the wind," Emma muttered and headed upstairs.

CHAPTER 32

Mark set to work on his new journal. Emma stopped by each day to gather the pages. She spent hours at the Pinkerton offices going through them. Jeremy was still away, so she was able to use his space. The dates and locations were more numerous than expected. Mark told her that he would be finished with the journal entries the next week.

The door to Jeremy's office was open and, when Cole walked by, he stopped and called to her, "Emma, are you here today?"

"Cole, do you have time to meet with me?" she asked, looking up from the paper she was reviewing.

"Sure, what's up?" he asked, walking into the office and laying his coat on the couch before sitting down in the guest chair at the desk. She handed him the new journal pages and the credit records. She had circled the ones that were identical in location.

"What are these?" he asked, looking at both sets of papers.

"Mark's uncle, Joseph, is visiting and something about him bothers me."

Cole listened intently; her instincts were rarely off.

"He's very similar to the man we're looking for in a murder case. You have heard about Mrs. Eloise Mercer?"

"Yes, they say she killed her husband. You think this Joseph is him?"

"I have no proof. There are no pictures or drawings of the man."

"Why do you think he is the same person?"

"Something happened. Mark was keeping a journal of all the locations his uncle had mentioned he had traveled to. His uncle found out about them and that journal was found burned soon after."

"Burned? Why do you think the uncle is responsible?"

"Because Mark found him looking through his room. Mark had moved the journal to the basement and that's where we found it burned."

"So, he was concerned someone would see his movements, the dates, and the locations. You're thinking there might be possible criminal activities on those dates and times?"

"The dates may not be perfect. Mark had to try to remember each of them and populate a new journal with the information."

"He did all of this from memory?" Cole asked, impressed. There must have been ten pages of dates and locations.

"He's a smart kid."

"That explains the first document. What's this one?" he asked, holding up the credit report.

"That's a credit report that says Mrs. Mercer owes money. It's her husband's bills from various creditors. That might be the first evidence linking Joseph to my murder case," she stated.

Cole studied it and said, "Tell me what these circles mean."

She came around the desk and took both documents and laid them side by side. "The circled ones match almost identically to the locations where Joseph was during the month before the wedding to Mrs. Mercer."

"It isn't enough to arrest him."

"No," she agreed, "but I was hoping we could investigate the dates and see if we have anything that may pop up."

"Like what?" he asked.

"More wives, unexplained disappearances or deaths."

He nodded. "Other wives are possible. I can do that. First, I'll send telegrams to the police precincts in each of these cities."

"Thank you so much! Let me know if you find anything," she said, relieved someone else was on the case.

"I will," he commented, looking at the data.

CHAPTER 33

$\mathcal{E}$mma spoke to Mr. Pennington. "Will Mrs. Mercer be returning soon?"

He shook his head. "I don't know. I can't contact her. "

"When was the last time you heard from her?"

"A few days ago. She said she would be back soon."

Emma nodded. She had feared Mrs. Mercer would flee.

"Will the case continue without her?"

"Yes They can try her in absentia. I'm asking for a delay. That should buy us another month."

CHAPTER 34

Things at home had calmed down and Joseph had stopped pressuring her for dates. He had also stopped showing up at inopportune moments. Does *he know the book is no longer in his fireplace?*

Mark was over early one morning, returning a book he had borrowed and Emma asked him, "Is Joseph still in town?"

"He had a trip a few days ago but was back by that evening."

"When was this?" she asked.

"Earlier this week."

"Where did he go?" Emma asked.

"No way am I asking that question," Mark said. He and his uncle were just starting to talk again.

"Hmm," Emma said.

"Thanks for the loan."

"Anytime," she said and watched the boy leave. Her thoughts turned to Jeremy. He was still away and she missed him more each day. To distract herself, she found Dora in the dining room "Where's my paper?" she asked.

"Patrick put it in your chair."

Emma had two papers delivered—one for her to scan for

possible cases and one for the family. When she picked her copy up, pieces fell out. "Who's been cutting up my paper?" she called loudly.

Dora smiled indulgently and said, "It may have been Patrick. He likes to cut the comics out."

She shifted through the pages and said, "No, I don't think so; the comics are here. It's other articles that are missing," she said. "Where's the other paper?"

"I'm not sure," her sister admitted. "I don't remember seeing a second one this morning. Check with the other boarding house; I know they get a paper."

Emma went straight over and into the kitchen door. Mrs. Spencer was sitting at the table making a list for the day. She greeted Emma. "Good morning. What can we do for you?"

"I was hoping you had a paper I could borrow this morning."

"I haven't seen it yet. Have you checked the front stoop? Mark normally gets it for me."

"I'll go check," Emma said, heading that way. She opened the door and didn't find the paper on the stoop. She closed it turned and saw Mark coming down the stairs.

"Good morning, have you seen the paper?" she asked.

"Not yet, I was just going out for it," he said, heading toward the door.

"It's not there," she said, stopping him.

"No? We may have gotten missed. It's happened before."

"Hmmm," she said, doubtful that two papers would be missed. She kept her tone light and said, "I'll check it later."

"Were you looking for anything in particular?"

"No, just reading through it. You know I like to read the news. Have a good day," she said and headed back home to get ready for her day.

On her way back in, she picked up her newspaper again and thought, *I can go down to the paper itself and get a copy.* She checked her timepiece and saw that she had an hour to spare that morning. She started to rush out, but Dora called out, "You need to eat! And get your lunch!"

Emma wanted to leave but knew Dora was right. "All right, I'll be right there." She went into the kitchen and quickly grabbed bread and butter and her lunch pail.

"That isn't enough!" Dora said.

"It's plenty and I have an errand this morning."

Dora shook her head and watched her sister leave.

Emma got her bike and, once she was on the street, she jumped on and headed to the paper. She got there and pulled up. Wagons that had been out in the early morning for deliveries had returned. Emma called to the boy on the loading dock handling the returns. "Hey, Toby, could you toss me one of those papers?"

"Sure, Emma, but don't you get a delivery at your house?" he asked and tossed her the rolled-up paper.

"Yes, but the only one I could find was cut up this morning," she said absently and opened the paper. She read over it and almost missed the small update about a murder in another state. She frowned and looked closer at it. It gave a location but no specific date. She needed to take it to Jeremy's office and compare it with the journal entries that Mark had provided. Glancing at her timepiece, she saw it was getting close to her start time at Pennington's office. She'd have to stop by Jeremy's office in the afternoon.

The court had approved the delay for Mrs. Mercer. They still had not heard from her. Once Emma arrived at the office, she placed her bike on her shoulder and made her way inside. She was shocked when she saw the office full of people. Mr. Pennington was already in. *It's too early for him to be here,* she thought. There were also multiple police officers and the prosecutor for Mrs. Mercer's case. Taking her bike to the closet, she went over to Ethan and asked in a low voice, "What's going on?"

"Mrs. Mercer is missing!" he said in the same tone.

"It has been confirmed?"

"Yes, the officers went to the house to escort her back and she wasn't there. Her bags were also missing."

"When did they think this was?" she asked.

"A few days ago."

Joseph was also gone during that time she thought. "Why do we think she ran off?"

"Mr. Pennington is sure she didn't go by herself."

"Do we think someone took her or did something to her?"

"That is a possibility," he admitted. "Though, if she is with her husband, I think she went willingly."

Pennington looked around and saw Emma in the room. "Emma, come over here. Officers, I'm sure you all know Emma Evans. She's our investigator."

"Hello, Emma," one of the officers said. "Have you spoken to Mrs. Mercer?"

"Hello, Pete. I planned to have another one, but she had to go home for personal business," Emma responded.

"Do you have any idea where she may have gone?" Pete asked.

I don't she thought but I can bet who she is with, she thought, *but with no evidence, now isn't the time to share.* "No, but I think her husband may still be alive. I've no way to trace him right now."

"What do you know?"

"We just know tall, light hair, slim build."

"That could be almost anyone," Pete muttered.

"You're right," she admitted.

Pete looked back at Mr. Pennington and said, "We'll let you know if we're able to locate her."

"I would appreciate that," Pennington said as he walked the officers to the door. On his way back, he said, "Emma, Ethan, my office please."

Emma looked at Ethan and he shrugged; they were surprised at the request but followed him into the office.

Mr. Pennington shut the door and they sat down at his round table.

Mr. Pennington started with, "We will have to delay the trial, again."

"Yes, until we find her," Ethan commented.

Mr. Pennington nodded. "There could be additional charges."

"Do we think she ran away?" Emma asked. "Or that she was taken?"

"A few days ago, she was still angry but seemed committed to taking this to court to prove her innocence."

"Then why disappear now? Wasn't her money locked up?"

"Yes, due to the creditor's claims, her investments and property were not under her control. All of her business decisions were run through the courts."

"Then how could she leave?" Emma asked.

"There are ways," he said.

When she looked at him questioningly, he said, "Jewels. She had managed to sew a large number into her dresses."

"Oh!" Emma exclaimed.

"Yes. I told her to do that, just in case, but I didn't think she'd use them to run away. Have you made any progress on the creditors and identifying the husband?" Mr. Pennington asked.

"I have some suspicions, but no real proof right now."

"Let me know when you feel there is something to go on," he said.

She nodded. She and Ethan left the office to start their day.

CHAPTER 35

She was home that evening, going over the information they had. They were still waiting for the information Cole had requested from the police officers. The night was cool and she wanted to take a walk and think about what they had in evidence.

She had walked about six blocks and started to turn around when someone grabbed her arm. She reacted and swung her leg around to trip him. The hit was successful and she glanced down at who had taken her by the arm. It was Joseph.

He didn't look hurt but he seemed shocked. He stood up quickly, but this time he didn't touch her. Instead, he leaned toward her and asked, "What do you think you're doing?"

"What do you mean?" she asked, feigning ignorance.

"You think a few articles, an inscription in a book, and my travel locations will add up to something?"

"I don't just think so, I know so, Joseph. Or should I say-Benjamin Mercer?"

His eyes narrowed. Then he changed his expression to say pleasantly, "Emma, we could be together. You, at home, and me..."

"While you do what? Run up credit and marry other women? I don't think so," she scoffed.

"I thought you could be like my sister," he said. "I had it all planned."

"What you need to do is turn yourself in so that Mrs. Mercer won't be charged with your death." When he didn't say anything, she said, "Unless you have her somewhere under your control. Did you take her?"

He looked around and said, "I like it here. I think I'll be putting down roots and have a family of my own."

"Not with me!" said Emma indignantly.

"We shall see," he said, walking off.

"We'll get you!" she called.

He stopped suddenly and turned to her. "Will you? I don't think so." He turned back and continued at a leisurely pace.

CHAPTER 36

At dinner that evening, the door slammed open in the foyer. Emma looked at Dora and she shrugged.

"I'll get it," Tim said as he stood.

He didn't make it out of the dining room as Jeremy strode in. Emma jumped up and jumped into his arms. "You're back!"

"I am," he said, kissing her and swinging her around.

"Successful trip?" she asked when he put her down.

"Yes, and a final one."

"Did you find everyone?"

"Everyone that's in the States. The Pinkertons have a line on the ones in Europe."

"I'm glad."

"Me too. I'll be here for a long time."

"Sit and eat," Dora said. "You must have come straight from the train station."

"I did, and I am hungry. I could also use a bath," he said in a low voice to Emma.

"Whew! You sure do!" She smiled back, happy he was here with them.

"Tell me," he said looking around, "how is everyone?"

They all talked and updated him on the activities. After dinner, he said, "I need to go get cleaned up."

"We'll have dessert waiting," Dora said with a smile as she watched Emma and Jeremy head upstairs.

"Meet you in your room," he said, bending his head to hers. She returned his kiss. He reluctantly lifted his head and went into his bedroom to retrieve his towel and a robe. He went back to the bath and ran the water. The bath was so nice, he soaked for a few extra minutes before he got out, dried off, and put on his robe. The towel was used to dry his hair as he entered his room. He looked over toward Emma's room and saw the bookcase door was open. *No need to change*, he thought and went to see her.

She was on the bed reading.

"Want some company?" he called.

She looked up and smiled slowly. "I think I would."

He ran over and leaped on the bed, bouncing her. She was giggling as he dropped down beside her. The giggling stopped as he pulled her into his arms. They stayed like that for some time. After, he sat up in bed. Emma pulled up her sheet and moved with him. He asked casually, "Is Mark's uncle still around?"

"Yes," she said and frowned.

Reading her face, he asked, "Did something happen?"

"Odd things," she muttered. "He just pops up when you least expect him." She told him of tripping over his cane at the back stairs. "He can be nice," she admitted. "It masks the creepy stuff."

"Is that all?" he asked. Now that he was back, he'd make it clear to Joseph that Emma wasn't available.

"No," she said, "I think there's much more." She reviewed the Mercer case with him, the credit comparison with Mark's list, the fact that the first list had been burnt, and the disappearance of Mrs. Mercer. While he mulled all of that over, she said, "I also told him I knew who he was—Benjamin Mercer."

Jeremy sat back. "When I asked if anything happened while I was gone, I meant this! Emma, he could have hurt you! Well, I'm here now, so that should quell his interest."

"I hope so. Dora said that one thing would have stopped him."

"And that is?" he asked.

"A ring," she muttered.

He caught her chin and tilted it and asked, "Is that something you would like?"

"You know it isn't," she said, looking him in the eye. "I don't need a piece of paper to tell everyone how I feel about you. It's just society's rules, but it may have been enough to keep him away."

The dinner bell clanged.

Emma smiled. "I think we're being called."

"Dessert," Jeremy said.

They cleaned up and headed downstairs. They were talking softly, holding hands.

Emma glanced down and said, "He's here."

Jeremy looked where she indicated and saw Joseph leaning against the sitting room entrance. He straightened as they approached. "Jeremy," he said and walked toward them. He waited at the base of the stairs.

"I am, and you're Joseph?" responded Jeremy.

"It's nice to meet you," Joseph said with that same charm that he could turn on and off at a whim.

Jeremy watched him and saw what Emma saw. This man was not what he seemed. "Come on, Emma, we're going for a walk." They had planned to have dessert, but he didn't like this man.

"I insist you stay for a toast," he said.

He insists! thought Jeremy.

Elizabeth came out of the sitting room. "Oh, please do stay. We'd like to enjoy the evening together."

Emma tugged Jeremy's hand and he told her, "Of course."

Joseph moved to the center of the room, taking his place and telling stories that made everyone laugh. Dora brought in desserts and he turned the conversation to morals.

"Oh, I also forgot to mention he has views on the woman's place," Emma told Jeremy in a low voice.

His tone had shifted from pleasant to no inflection at all. "Women are too free with their bodies, giving themselves outside of marriage. Society has rules for a reason."

"Surely you don't believe that?" asked his sister.

Joseph just shook his head. "Too much freedom. Soon we won't have brides, just working companions. Then what form will the family take?"

"Are you talking about something in particular?" Jeremy demanded.

"Why nothing, of course, just expressing my opinion," Joseph said smoothly.

Emma gripped Jeremy's hand and gave an almost imperceptible shake of her head.

Joseph strolled by Jeremy and leaned down and murmured, "I know about that bookcase in your room."

Jeremy had had enough! He jumped up and grabbed Joseph by the collar and pulled him through the foyer and into the study. He shoved him to the floor and pulled the doors shut violently.

Emma stopped everyone from going after them. "Let them talk."

George sat back in his chair and looked happier than he had in weeks.

"Have you been in Emma's room?" Jeremy demanded, watching as he stood and dusted off his clothes.

"That bookcase doesn't hide the dirty deeds the two of you are doing outside of marriage."

"It's time you left town! Now!" Jeremy said, grabbing him and slamming him into the wall again.

"Leave?" Joseph laughed. "No, I think I'm staying here. After all, my loving family lives here."

"Even with all the loose women?" Jeremy asked sarcastically.

"Oh, I can fix that."

"Is that a threat?"

"No, of course not."

"You *will* leave town and you *will* not threaten Emma or anyone else again. *Do we understand each other?*"

Joseph was silent for a moment. "I feel that I should make plans to leave."

"Good," Jeremy said. "I thought we could get on the same page."

"Can you release me now?"

Jeremy slowly let him go and they rejoined the family.

"Why don't I make a toast?" Joseph said, entering the sitting room as if nothing had occurred. "I will make this my final goodbye."

"What? Why would you leave?" asked his sister. "We've loved having you here. Please, can you reconsider?"

"You know if he has to leave it must be for business," George said. "He can come back some other time." Though he hoped it would be a long time before they saw his brother-in-law again. His wife was almost a different person when he was around.

Mark's mom and dad had privately talked about Joseph a few weeks after his arrival. "Why do you keep encouraging him to see Emma?" George asked.

"I'd love it if they were together; that way our family can stay together here in Chicago."

He shook his head. "What are you thinking? You know she's with Jeremy."

"I haven't seen a ring," she stated, sounding too much like her brother.

George frowned. "You get like this when he's here. You know Emma doesn't want to be the home and family type. The fact is, you hide your work when he's here and you seem to believe everything he's talking about. It just isn't right."

"I do that," Elizabeth admitted, collapsing on the bed. She stared at the ceiling. "I just don't want him to be disappointed in me."

"Would that be so bad?"

"You never have liked him," she accused, turning over on the bed to look at her husband.

"I did," he contradicted her, "in the beginning. I bought into his charm just like everyone else."

"What changed? He's always been the same," she asked, confused.

"That's it exactly! He's been saying the same things he said ten years ago. The same rhetoric."

"But that's because he wants things how they used to be," she tried to explain.

"Look around," he said, "we tell our students that the world is changing. The industrial complexes will allow more and more women to work and help their families. You're an example of this progress, except when your brother is here."

"You're right," she murmured, realizing she was hiding who she was from Joseph. "Do you think Emma will forgive me?"

"I wouldn't worry about Emma. It's Jeremy who might have the problem with your interference," he stated dryly.

CHAPTER 37

*B*ack to the present

The next morning at the Pinkerton office, Jeremy was still railing about Joseph's actions.

"He has to leave town. He's dangerous," he said.

"We still don't have enough proof. We need Mrs. Mercer for an identification," Emma said.

Cole nodded. "I was thinking we could take custody of him on the train when he leaves. Question him outside of town. I'll have agents on the train and, as soon as he boards, we can take him into custody."

"We'll need to escort him to the train," Jeremy said.

Emma nodded and hoped it would be that easy.

That evening, Emma and Jeremy went to the second boarding house to confirm Joseph's plans. He was sitting on the stoop enjoying the evening.

"We have your train tickets," Jeremy said. "You'll be leaving in the morning."

Joseph shrugged, seemingly indifferent to the plans they'd made for him. He looked at Emma. "Why don't you accompany me to the train tomorrow? Make sure I get off and out of your town."

"Now that, we will do," she confirmed.

"No. Only you," he said and looked at Jeremy.

Before Jeremy could disagree, Emma said, "I'll do that." She looked at Jeremy. "We can take separate carriages and meet you there."

"No," said Joseph. "I want to take the trolley one last time."

She frowned but said, "That should be fine." She just wanted him gone.

Back at their boarding house, Jeremy confronted her. "I don't like it."

"Me either, but you know I can protect myself if he tries anything."

He kissed her and said, "Yeah, I know you can. I'll meet you at the train station."

CHAPTER 38

The next morning progressed without drama. Joseph said a grand goodbye to his family and accompanied Emma to the trolley. They climbed on board and watched the city go by.

"You know," he started, "I had plans for you."

"Plans?" she asked, wanting to keep him talking.

"You appeared to be everything I wanted to help me build a strong family. Someone with a solid work ethic that could be used at home."

"There's just that persnickety issue that I don't want to stay home and be a 'housewife'. Oh, and the fact that I don't want to be with you."

He didn't react to that; he just continued on as if she hadn't said anything. "There were also other facts I could not overlook."

"And those would be?"

"Perhaps that you choose to live out of wedlock with Jeremy," he said calmly.

She stopped him abruptly and said, "Nothing I do is of any

concern of yours." She was glad the trolley was fairly empty at this hour.

"No, it's women like you that made me the man I am."

"I don't think you can make women as a whole responsible for that."

That statement seemed to get through the blasé act he had perfected. "That is enough," he said shortly.

"Finally. Is this the true you I'm speaking with?" she asked with interest.

"I want to stay here. I'm happy here with my family."

"You agreed to leave."

"You pushed me into it."

She didn't say anything but felt his hand tightening on her arm. As the trolly increased in speed, he started to pull her toward the side, near the exit.

At the speed they were going, she could survive a fall, but watching the carriages and wagons go by, she realized she'd be trampled to death. Pulling back, she found that he was stronger than he looked. His expression showed no strain as he moved her closer and closer to the exit.

He's planning a quick movement, she thought. *Otherwise, people would interfere.*

He leaned into her. "Had you not been flawed, I would have picked you to be my wife."

She felt him readying himself. It was going to be him or her. She worked her feet through his and when he went to push her into the traffic, she braced herself for a fall.

Instead of her being pushed off, an arm came up behind him and pushed Joseph into traffic. He fell with a scream. The milk truck coming up had no time to stop and avoid him. The trolley driver stopped, almost dislodging several other passengers.

Emma caught a glimpse of the person who had pushed Joseph. It was John's new guard from Sing Sing. *Looks like my favor has been taken care of,* she thought. The guard nodded to her and jumped off the trolley.

"What happened? Why have we stopped?" the people grumbled around her.

"Someone fell off," another person responded.

The passengers exited the now-stopped trolley slowly. The local police officer was checking what was left of Joseph. Emma saw him shake his head. She didn't feel anything. Someone had died, a family member of someone she was close to. Mark and his mom would be heartbroken, but if they knew that he was a murderer, they would have been destroyed.

She accompanied the officer to the police station. There were questions, but it was determined to be an accident. Jeremy and Cole were notified she wouldn't be at the station. McGee offered to escort her home.

The hardest part was going to the boarding house where Mark's family lived. It was just her and the officer. For once, she knocked on the door, choosing to have additional time while it was answered. Steps ran to the door and Emma knew it was Mark.

"Emma! Why'd you knock? Come in. We're in the sitting room." It was Saturday and the family was at home.

"Mark, I have someone with me," she said gently. "Can you bring your mother and father to the dining room?"

He looked at Emma and the police officer and said, "Okay. Right away."

Emma nodded toward the dining room and she and McGee went in to sit and wait.

"I don't understand why she's here with a policeman and why she needs to see us," Elizabeth said as they walked out of the sitting room.

"Let's go find out," George replied.

They entered, and Mark's mom was frowning. Her husband's face was curiously devoid of any emotion.

"What is going on?" Elizabeth asked.

"Let's sit," McGee urged.

She nodded and took a seat, not taking her eyes off the officer.

Emma started. "We have some news to share with you."

Elizabeth stood abruptly. "No! No, I don't want to hear it."

"Elizabeth, we have to hear. Please, go on," George said. But he didn't try to make his wife sit back down.

"As we were going to the train station, Joseph fell from the trolley and was trampled by a milk truck," Emma stated.

"What does that mean?" Elizabeth asked faintly.

"That means," McGee said, taking over from Emma, "that Joseph Black has passed away."

Mark began crying and Elizabeth came out of her daze and started crying also.

George walked over and took his wife in his arms. "Where can we pick him up?" he asked.

"That won't be necessary. If you'll let us know the funeral home you would like to use, we'll have him taken there," McGee stated.

"I'll take care of it and get that information to you."

"Let me know if you need any help," McGee offered.

"I think we need time alone now," George said, taking his wife and Mark out of the room.

"Yes, of course," Emma said.

"Thank you for accompanying me. These types of things can be hard," Emma said to McGee.

"Of course."

They parted, and Emma went home.

"Emma, did Joseph get on the train okay?" called Dora from the dining room.

"Oh, Dora!" she cried and ran over to her sister.

"What happened?" Dora asked, taking her into her arms.

Emma explained what had happened on the trolley. Dora

didn't say much during the story. "Let's go into the sitting room. There's more to this story," she said, making Emma look her in the eyes.

"You knew?" she asked, sniffling.

"I had a feeling he was a bad guy, especially after the morality speech he made last night."

"Yes, that was pretty horrible," Emma acknowledged.

"It all seemed to be aimed at you and Jeremy."

"It was. He considered Jeremy my greatest flaw—being together without marriage. He had plans for me to marry him."

"Marry!"

"Yes, but my flaw put me on the same list that his other engagements suffered."

"Other engagements?"

"Yes. Jeremy and Cole looked into several cases where he had been located."

"The newspapers?" Dora guessed.

"Yes. He couldn't control that. There were too many bodies and debts piling up. Once the press picked it up, it would be everywhere."

"How will you identify him and link him to all of it?"

"I have an idea on that," Emma murmured.

"Poor Elizabeth," Dora murmured. "She was so proud of him. This must be hitting her hard."

"Yes," Emma said and laid her head back on Dora's shoulder.

CHAPTER 39

The funeral was small, with only Mark's family and a few other people from both boarding houses. Mark and his mom talked about Joseph and told stories of happier times. They slowly got back to normal with the grief still heavy in their hearts.

Dora had sketched Joseph from memory. Cole and Jeremy circulated it through the different police precincts. Stories started to come back about other marriages, ones that had ended in the bride's death.

Mr. Pennington grew more fearful by the day that Mrs. Mercer was one of his victims. They had confirmed with the creditors that Joseph was the man they were searching for. He sat in his office, reading over briefs when he heard Ethan say, "One moment, please."

"Sir," Ethan said and opened the door to show him who was there. It was Eloise.

He stood and stared at her.

"James, how could I be so wrong?" she asked and held out her arms to him.

He went over to her and took her into his arms. "It's all over now."

"It's taken care of?" John Harden asked his second-in-command and son-in-law, Dan Piper.

"Yes, the man has been removed," Dan confirmed.

"Is it enough?" asked John.

"Enough?"

"Is the favor enough to close my debt to her?"

Dan stayed silent, not sure what he should say.

"I have one more thing for you to do," John said, "and then we will sever our ties with Emma Evans."

"Yes, boss."

CHAPTER 41

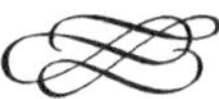

Tim called to Jeremy and Emma, "A package came for you. It's on the table."

Emma frowned and went over to pick it up. "Who is it from?" asked Jeremy.

"I don't know," she said, turning it over. There were no markings, just their names on the front. She opened it, slid out the document, and read it through. "It's the deed to the beach house!"

"What?" Jeremy exclaimed. He took the paperwork and saw the same thing she had.

Emma looked at Jeremy. "I think this is a final favor from you know who. Should we take it?"

He knew who she referenced and nodded slowly. "Yes. Yes, I think we should."

Notebook Mysteries

Books
1 - 2 - 3

KIMBERLY
MULLINS

ABOUT THE AUTHOR

Kimberly Mullins is the author of series of books titled "Notebook Mysteries". Her stories are based on historical events occurring in 1871-1890's Chicago. She holds a BS in Biology and a MBA in Business. She lives in Texas with her husband and son. When she is not writing she is working as a Process Safety Engineer at a large chemical company. You can connect with her on her website www.kimberlymullinsauthor.com.

Photo Credit: Blessings of Faith Photography

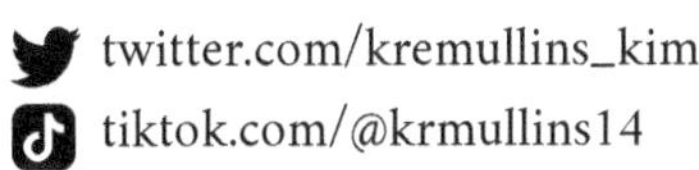

twitter.com/kremullins_kim

tiktok.com/@krmullins14